I Can't Make You Love Me, but I Can Make You Leave

Also by Dixie Cash

Our Red Hot Romance Is Leaving Me Blue
Curing the Blues with a New Pair of Shoes
Don't Make Me Choose Between You and My Shoes
I Gave You My Heart, but You Sold It Online
My Heart May Be Broken, but My Hair Still Looks Great
Since You're Leaving Anyway, Take Out the Trash

I Can't Make You Love Me, but I Can Make You Leave

Dixie Cash

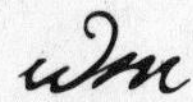

WILLIAM MORROW
An Imprint of HarperCollins*Publishers*

This book is a work of fiction. The characters, incidents, and dialogue are drawn from the author's imagination and are not to be construed as real. Any resemblance to actual events or persons, living or dead, is entirely coincidental.

HarperCollins books may be purchased for educational, business, or sales promotional use. For information please write: Special Markets Department, HarperCollins Publishers, 10 East 53rd Street, New York, NY 10022.

FIRST EDITION

Designed by Diahann Sturge

Library of Congress Cataloging-in-Publication Data

Cash, Dixie.
I can't make you love me, but I can make you leave / by Dixie Cash. — 1st ed.
p. cm. — (Domestic equalizers ; 7)
ISBN 978-0-06-191014-2 (pbk.)
1. Beauty operators—Fiction. 2. Women country musicians—Fiction. 3. Texas—Fiction. I. Title.
PS3603.A864I14 2011
813'.6—dc22

2010029070

11 12 13 14 15 OV/RRD 10 9 8 7 6 5 4 3 2 1

I Can't Make You Love Me, but I Can Make You Leave

prologue

Midland, Texas
Sunday, September 4

Roxie Denman, opening act for the old has-been, Darla Denman, sat in front of a square mirror in a tiny room that had been pointed out to her as her "dressing room." Who were they kidding? The fact was, she was in a janitor's room. It had been converted for the weekend to accommodate performers in Midland's annual telethon, raising money for Alzheimer's disease.

Someone had done a decent-enough job clearing out the space and had tried to make it attractive by adding the mirror and a vanity, even a vase of fall flowers. But the lingering, pungent scent of Pine-Sol and other disinfectants gave away the room's true purpose.

The smell offended Roxie more than anyone could ever imagine. It wasn't her olfactory senses that were bothered. What was utterly odious to Roxie Jo Jennings Denman were the memories those smells evoked—memories of being a small child and accompanying her mother to various cleaning jobs in the evenings—offices, churches or whatever she could find that someone would pay her to clean.

While her mother worked, Roxie had usually kept herself occupied with books and/or puzzles. The churches had been her favorites. Most of them had had stages. During those times, Roxie played make-believe. She would walk down the aisles, nodding to imaginary fans and autograph seekers, posing for cameras that weren't there, and then she would slowly walk up the steps to the stage. There, she would face her audience, the admirers, those who wanted to be like her.

She had been gracious to her make-believe fans, had reminded herself to be humble. Even at a young age, she had noticed that people seemed to like when you behaved as though you didn't deserve what you had been given. God knew she had watched her mother act that way each time she was paid for the work she had done. Her mother's obsequiousness had irked Roxie. Her mother had worked her fingers raw and red. Why did she have to show gratitude for what she had earned? Those hypocrite bastards were obligated to pay her and they should have paid her more. Instead, they had taken advantage of her almost apologetic acceptance of her pay and expected her to do extra.

Her mother had been spineless. And Roxie had learned at the woman's knee that the last thing she herself would ever be was spineless. She would never go "hat-in-hand" to anyone and her eyes would never be cast to the floor in humility. No-siree. If she had to, she would lie and steal, cajole and connive, do anything short of murder. When *anyone* dealt with Roxie Jo Jennings they would have their hands full.

Roxie stared at herself in the mirror. *Roxie Jo Jennings. There was a name she hadn't thought of in a long time.* And thinking of it now reminded her she needed to decide what her new stage name would be. She didn't want to use her current name, Denman. Fans might confuse her with being more than an acquaintance of Darla Denman. And one thing was for certain—being married to Darla's ex-husband was as close to a family tie to the washed-up singer as Roxie wanted.

She was mulling over a list of names when the door opened and a visitor came in. The visitor was familiar, but unwelcome at the moment. Roxie scowled. "Don't you know to knock before coming through a closed door? I could've been naked."

The visitor smiled. "I don't mind. I've seen you naked before."

"You've seen me that way only because it was *my* choice. Don't fool yourself into thinking you've got a pass to my dressing room."

The visitor looked around the room and chuckled. "But this is a closet. And a janitor's closet at that."

The mockery ignited a flame in Roxie's soul. "Get out of here! I've got to get ready."

The visitor leaned close to her ear and whispered, "What do you have to do? You can't possibly be more beautiful than you already are. We've got a little time. We could make good use of it. Like we did back in Nashville. Remember?"

What they had done in Nashville was the last thing Roxie

wanted to remember. "You ass." She picked up a long metal nail file and stabbed the hand that was making its way down the front of her robe.

The visitor yelped in pain as blood welled from an ugly puncture wound. "God almighty! How am I supposed to do my job with my hand punctured?"

The visitor appeared to be in pain, but Roxie was unaffected by the sight of blood now smeared on the vanity. "Don't you ever touch me again," she spat. "And don't you *ever* say anything about Nashville to anyone."

"Or what?"

"Or I'll *kill* you. Get out of here. Now."

The visitor walked to the door and pushed the button, locking the two of them together in the small space.

"You maniac. You stalking loser," Roxie yelled, out of patience and angry. "Open that fucking door and get out of here!"

The visitor grabbed the nail file and yanked Roxie's robe open, exposing two exquisite man-made breasts. "Suppose we take this stiletto you call a nail file and stab one of these high-priced tits you're so proud of. See how good you look on stage with a deflated balloon where a tit used to be."

Roxie picked up her hot curling iron and swiped at the visitor's cheek.

The visitor ducked, then made a lunge that took them both to the floor.

A mad scramble. A cry of pain. Then silence.

They lay entangled. Neither moved.

Then the visitor pushed away from Roxie's limp body. "Roxie?"

No response. The visitor gasped at the metal file protruding form Roxie's neck and the pool of red spreading on the floor. "Roxie? Say something." Shaken, the visitor stood, covered with blood.

A knock on the door broke the eerie quiet. "Ten minutes, Miz Denman."

The visitor looked around the room.

Run! a voice said.

A terrycloth robe was draped over a fire extinguisher mounted on the wall near the door. The intruder grabbed it and shrugged into it, wrapped it tightly, covering blood-stained clothing, then carefully opened the door and glanced outside in all directions. Seeing no one, the visitor eased out, pulled the door shut and quickstepped away.

The corpse of beautiful Roxie Denman lay on the floor of the janitor's closet, her big debut ending where her life had started—in a tiny room that smelled of Pine-Sol.

chapter one

Two days earlier
Friday, September 2

Grrrrowl . . . scre-e-e-ech . . . rumba-rumba-rumba . . .
POOF!

Unusual noises brought Darla Denman, former Queen of Country Music, out of a sound sleep. Blinking herself awake, she realized she was not moving and she should be. Her bus had come to a dead stop. She swung her feet to the floor, bent forward and searched for her shoes, a pair of strappy high-heeled sandals that were supposed to make her look sexy and feel young.

By the time she stumbled to the front of the bus and the door, a cloud of gray smoke was roiling against a pristine sky of brilliant blue and an odor that smelled like burning oil choked her. She pushed the door open and lurched out, turning her ankle when she stepped on a rock. Cussing through clenched teeth, she grabbed the door's edge for support.

That was when she saw her entourage, such as it was, huddled at the bus's rear bumper, murmuring in low tones.

Tenting her hand over her eyes to block out the glaring sun, she looked past the smoke. Noon. It had to be noon.

She shoved a sheaf of her newly dyed red hair—"Ginger Violet" the bottle it came in had called it—out of her eyes and turned in a tight circle, scanning her surroundings. Her *barren* surroundings. In any direction, all she saw was tan dirt and a gray, straight-as-a-ribbon highway disappearing into the horizon. And a pale green yucca plant in the far distance.

Her current manager and former husband, Big Bob Denman, stood a few feet away, a road map unfurled between his hammy hands. Darla limped to his side. "My God. Where are we, the friggin' moon?"

"We're a couple miles outside of Salt Lick, Texas," he answered.

"Salt Lick?"

"On this map, it looks like a small town. Surely they have someone who can tow us in and do some repair work."

Not believing what she had heard, Darla yanked the map from him and snapped it wide between her own hands. "Salt Lick, Texas? Never heard of it." She quickly perused the map, but didn't see the name. She had to admit that without glasses she had difficulty seeing anything, especially small print. "How in God's name did we get here? We had to have driven straight through Midland."

"Judy wanted to stop in and see her dad, so we made a little detour." Bob removed his sunglasses and held them up for a lens inspection. "You were asleep. I didn't see the harm."

He walked back to the bus's door and reached inside, dragged a small sledge hammer from under the first seat. For a fleeting moment, Darla wondered why a sledge hammer was riding under the seat of a tour bus full of musicians, but when Bob started for the front of the bus, she abandoned the question and followed him, still limping. "Judy who?"

He stopped and gave her an arch look. "Darla. Judy? One of the backup singers?" He started walking again.

"Yeah, yeah." Darla waved his sarcasm off as she hobbled after him. Hell, nobody had to tell her Judy was a backup singer. "You didn't see the harm in making a little detour in Texas? Bob, I was born and raised in Texas. There's no such thing as a *little* detour in Texas. Where does her dad live?"

He mumbled something that sounded like "Santonya" as he lifted the hatch on the engine housing. He craned his neck and looked inside, then started pounding something with the hammer. She planted herself beside him, but the clash of steel against steel made conversation impossible. "Where? . . . What? . . . What did you say?"

Bob stopped with a deep sigh, straightened and looked directly at her. "San. Antonio. Ever hear of it?"

"Are you kidding me? That's not in West Texas. That's three hundred miles out of the way."

"No, it's not," Bob said, a lazy, crooked smile tipping the corners of his too-attractive mouth. "It's two hundred and seventy seven miles."

Darla thought her brain might explode and completely shatter her skull. She thrust her chin and roasted him with a glare. "We're low on cash. This piece-of-shit bus is held together by a prayer and baling wire. And you take us three hundred miles out of the way?"

"Two hundred and seventy seven," Bob corrected.

"I swear to God, Bob Denman. You say that one more time and I'll kill you where you stand. After I scratch your eyes out with my new acrylic nails."

"We're ahead of schedule," he replied, then leaned in to her and whispered, "I felt sorry for her. The last time she saw him she was only nine years old."

"When was that? Last year?"

"Don't snap, darlin'. It's unbecoming. She's not that young. I told you, she's twenty."

Darla rolled her eyes. "Uh-huh. Tell me again where you found both of them. Julie, Judy, whoever."

"Their names are Judy and Kay. Like I said, sweetiekins, it was a local talent show." He returned to tinkering with the engine.

He was still acting like a damn mechanic, which was a damn joke.

The only thing he knew about motorized vehicles was the location of the gas tank cap. Darla sighed, allowing him that macho crap of looking like he knew what he was doing. Besides, staying irritated with him was too hard. He was the best man she knew. He would give a stranger his last dollar. And indeed, if it was within his power, he would make a 277-mile detour to give a young woman an opportunity to see her long lost daddy.

Darla crossed her arms under her breasts. "I'd better not find out that *local talent show* was karaoke night at Chuck E. Cheese," she grumbled.

"Sweetheart, anyone you've ever worked with has retired, quit, died or we couldn't afford them. Everyone I told we were putting a show together took on a look of panic. And when I mentioned going on the road with Darla Denman, they practically jumped out of their skins."

That remark stung so painfully, Darla almost couldn't bear it.

After a deafening thud he straightened again and made a half turn toward her. "Well, that oughtta do it."

"It's fixed? Really?" Incredulous, she couldn't keep her eyes from widening, an idiot grin from forming. "Hell, Bob, I didn't think you knew anything about motors."

"I don't." He held up a black grease-covered object shaped like a human heart. "This just fell off and I don't have a clue what it is. Like I said, that oughtta do it." He dropped the hammer and the unidentified object on the ground, yanked a handkerchief from his pocket and started wiping grease from his hands. "Guess we can start walking."

"Are you crazy?" Darla raised her sandal-shod foot. "I can't walk *anywhere* in these shoes. Hell, I can't even *stand* in these shoes."

Bob glanced at her foot. "That begs the question, shugie-pie, why wear 'em? But you're right about the walking. None of this crowd could walk a block." He plucked his cell phone from his back pocket. "I'm calling nine-one-one."

"Salt Lick's a fly speck on the map. You really think it's got nine-one-one?"

"How big does the map say it is?"

Darla found the map's legend. "I can't see a damn thing without my glasses," she mumbled. "I think it says less than two thousand people," she said louder. "*I'm* saying a *lot* less."

"Hmm." Bob rubbed his chin, leaving a smear of black grease.

Darla grinned. She couldn't help it. The smudge detracted not one iota from his square jaw and his ruggedly handsome face. In fact, he looked indescribably cute.

Whoa, girl, the voice of common sense warned. *Time to rethink your thinking.*

"I could hitch a ride into town," he offered. "Y'all get back in the bus and get comfortable."

But Darla detected no enthusiasm for that venture in the heat of the West Texas sun. "You'll never get a ride," she said. "Look at this road. There's no cars. No traffic whatsoever." She raised a finger skyward. "But I know what you can do. The map says Salt Lick's a county seat. That means they have to have a sheriff's office. Give them a ring. See if they'll send out some help."

Bob turned to walk away, calling over his shoulder, "Yep, that's a great idea. That's why I called them before I worked on the engine. They should be here in about ten minutes."

Darla stamped her foot, and sand and caliche dust covered her bare toes. *Shit!* "Well, asshole, why didn't you tell me?" she yelled.

"I just did," he shot back.

"Too bad this didn't happen when we were in San Antonio *three hundred miles back,*" she shouted, her notorious redheaded temper no longer in check. "We could've forgotten about the concert and strolled the friggin' Riverwalk instead!"

She watched as he joined the group at the other end of the bus and draped his muscular arm with familiar ease over his wife, Roxie's, shoulder, his hand resting near her oversized silicone implants. Damn him. Age hadn't changed him that much. If anything. he looked better. He had lost some weight. Yep. Trim and tanned. Probably working out, trying to keep up with his young wife. Asshole.

Regret pinched Darla. She had been in Roxie Denman's shoes once, married to Bob. Back in the day, he was not only charming and good-looking, but was one of the most successful music producers around. He'd had a small stable of talented up-and-coming entertainers and was on his way to making it big in the music business. When the two of them met, the heavens opened and angels sang. Darla had been a naïve nobody, but she'd had stars in her eyes and talent. She had also been head-strong, unfortunately, and as determined as Roxie to be the best female recording star ever.

One by one, Bob had dropped clients to have more time to concentrate on the rising Darla Denman's career alone, which hadn't been a bad move for either of them. Under his guidance, her talent had blossomed and her career had zoomed beyond anything she had ever realistically expected. As husband and wife, she and Bob had rolled in money and good times that should have given them all anyone could ever dream of, including a future together.

Then she had ruined everything. Her ego, her love of partying hardy and a weakness for sweet-talking men had destroyed her and Bob's marriage and ultimately Bob's livelihood. For her, several husbands had followed. And several more divorce settlements. Time had marched over her voice, her face and body and through her bank account like Santa Anna at the Alamo.

She made a mental sigh. Fifteen years had passed since all of that misery. Bob still had a few clients, mostly second-tier musicians just looking for a short gig here or there. Most people in the music industry still knew and liked him, but he had never recovered the reputation he had once had. These days, Darla blamed herself for that more than anyone would ever know. Thank God hard feelings had softened. Now, ironically, she and Bob were back where they started, with him managing her career again. But a few things were different. Darla Denman was thirty years older and an equal number of pounds heavier. And Bob had a new wife—a talented, headstrong, determined kid named Roxie Jo, a Darla Denman wannabe.

Darla tamped down those bitter emotions. She had no time for the luxury of self-flagellation. Her concern had to be for the musicians on her payroll. The Darla Denman self-financed comeback tour kitty had just enough funds for the trip to Midland and a swing through Abilene for the next booking, and not one penny more. Certainly no extra funds for engine repair. The crack she had made earlier about her rattle-trap old bus being held together by a prayer and baling wire was no joke.

Lighten the payroll, instinct told her as she looked at her group again. Someone had to go. Too bad Roxie was providing an opening number for free. Darla would like nothing more than telling that peroxide-bad-bleach-job-had-to-get-fake-tits-bitch to take a hike.

Then Darla's ornery streak raised its head and she thought of something. At the very least maybe she could convince her nemesis to stop spending tour money on food. Inwardly, she grinned as she walked toward the group. "Hey Roxie," she said, keeping her voice pleasant and friendly. "Since I lost some weight, I've got some clothes that are too big for me. I mean they literally fall off. But they'd fit you just fine. Would you like to have them?"

"Get real," Roxie said. "I wouldn't touch your sixties-era hand-me-downs wearing rubber gloves."

None of the troupe held high esteem for Roxie Denman. The group leveled a collective glare in Roxie's direction.

Hah! The day wasn't a total loss. Buoyed by a feeling of their support, Darla added, "Well, darlin', if they don't fit there's plenty of room to let out the seams."

"I think some of her clothes are cool."

That remark came from Valetta Rose Somebody, the makeup artist Roxie had insisted on bringing along. Bob had said Roxie hired her away from some funeral home in Nashville, but Darla was unsure if that was the truth or a wisecrack. She still hadn't figured out the relationship between the two women. Valetta Rose was even younger than Roxie. She wore no makeup usually, which seemed odd for a makeup artist. And most of the time, she was a timid little thing with not much to say. Did Roxie see herself as a mother figure, a sister to the younger woman? Or did she simply enjoy playing the big VIP star with her own makeup artist following her around?

Valetta Rose was met by Roxie's icy stare. "What would you know about clothes from the sixties?"

Before Valetta Rose could defend herself, a siren pierced the air. Glancing in the direction from which it came, Darla saw lights flashing on the horizon and an official-looking vehicle moving at high speed. Instinctively, she moved closer to the side of the tour bus. The group took the cue and stepped out of the way also.

The red and white car slowed and came to a screeching stop in the middle of the road. A man, tall and skinny beyond description, hopped out of the car and stamped straight to Darla. "Oh, my gosh! It's Darla Denman's bus. Miz Denman, I can't believe I'm meeting you."

Darla flashed her camera-worthy smile and tossed her hair over her shoulder for effect. "Guess you don't get a chance to see many celebrities stranded on the side of the road, do you, Deputy?"

"I'm the sheriff, ma'am." He lifted off his white straw

cowboy hat and blushed a deep crimson. "Sheriff Billy Don Roberts, ma'am. At your service."

"Oh, pardon me," Darla gushed. "For a minute, I didn't see that big star on your chest."

He set his hat back on his head. "I thought you were dead, Miz Denman. I sure as heck remember somebody telling me that. Man, oh man. When I was a little boy my mama used to sing your songs. She even dyed her hair to look like yours. She'll pop a gasket when I tell her I met you."

Darla's smile froze. *Christ.* If she had a dollar for every time a fan had said she looked good for a dead person, she could side-step this bus tour and fly to her shows in a private jet. "Well, isn't that nice? . . . Listen, Sheriff, I'm afraid the eight of us aren't going to fit in your car."

"My deputy's behind me. He's got a pickup truck. I figure I can take four of you. He can haul two in front with him and two can ride in the bed."

The group exchanged looks and scowls.

"I'll ride up front with you, Sheriff," Darla purred, slipping her arm around his. "Bob, why don't you and your bride ride in the deputy's pickup bed? That windblown look might be attractive on you, Rox. I figure it can't hurt."

Roxie propped a hand at her waist, her mouth flattened into a reptilian grin. "This coming from a person everyone thinks is dead?"

"Ladies, ladies," Bob interjected. "Let's not start something we can't finish. Look, Sheriff, Darla, me and Roxie will ride with you. Judy, why don't you join us?"

"I want Valetta Rose to ride with us," Roxie said.

Bob sighed. "Okay, Valetta Rose, *you* ride with us. Judy, you ride with the deputy." He motioned to Mike and Eddie, the drummer and keyboard man respectively. "Guys, how about y'all ride in the bed of the deputy's pickup? Everyone else can sit in the front with the deputy."

"Sounds like a plan," the sheriff said enthusiastically. "Man, oh man, this is the coolest thing I've ever done."

When the deputy's pickup arrived and came to a stop, the group began to file to their assigned seating.

In a move that was surely made to irritate, Roxie darted ahead of Darla to the passenger door of the sheriff's car and grabbed the passenger seat for herself. As soon as she was seated, she twisted the rearview mirror toward herself, checked her lipstick and fluffed her long hair.

Darla held her tongue and scooted into the back, leaning away from Valetta Rose and snuggling against Bob's side. "Bobby," she said sweetly, "this reminds me of the times we had limos taking us everywhere we wanted to go. Sheriff, let's pretend you're our limo driver and Roxie, you be the go-ahead person."

Roxie returned the mirror to its original position and glared over her shoulder into the backseat. "The what?"

"The go-ahead person, sweetie. You know, you go ahead of us and make sure everything is set up properly."

"Oh, you mean the person who tells everyone who you are and confirms that you're not dead."

On a growl, Darla reached for the back of the seat to pull herself forward. She intended to slap that little bitch silly.

"Cut it out!" Bob roared. "I am sick and tired of this sniping between you two. You're making the rest of us miserable and there's no need for it. Darla, if you don't want us here, and yes, I said *us*, we'll leave. But make no mistake about it. If I'm here,

Roxie will be with me. She's my wife and I expect her to be treated with respect. You don't have to like each other, but you do have to get along. Behave like adults, forgodsake."

Silence filled the car. Sheriff Roberts sat with his spine straight as a board, his hand frozen on the ignition, his eyes aimed straight ahead.

An evil little smile played with the corner of Roxie's mouth.

"Don't look too smug, Roxie," Bob added. "The same damn thing goes for you. Opening for Darla is giving you a break in the business and you should be grateful."

A longer silence.

Finally the sheriff said, "Is it okay if I drive now?"

Darla gave Bob a drop-dead glare, then said sweetly to the sheriff, "Of course, darlin'. We're sorry to involve you in our little family problems, aren't we, Robert?"

Bob blew a great breath from puffed jaws. "Yeah, sorry, Sheriff. Let's get on into town. Sheriff, do you know someone who can work on our bus?"

The sheriff gave a snorting laugh. "Only about half the population in Salt Lick. We all drive old cars or trucks that need fixin' up. If they can't fix it, they can't drive it. Know what I mean?"

Bob nodded. "Certainly do, Sheriff, certainly do."

"Where y'all headed?" the sheriff asked. "Bet you got a show in Vegas or Reno. Am I right?"

"Sugar, we're going to Midland," Darla answered. "We've paused our schedule and volunteered our time to be on the telethon for Alzheimer's this weekend."

"No kidding? Man that's big. Last year they had those folks that starred in *The Brady Bunch*, that TV show with all them kids? And the year before that, it was Mr. T. Remember him?

The one that says, 'I pity the fool?'" The sheriff chortled. "Man, he was great. Do you know him?"

"No, sir," Bob said. "I don't believe any of us do. But you're right. He's great."

They rode a few more minutes in uncomfortable silence, until they drove into a town—a one-street, one-traffic light town with aged and dilapidated buildings flanking the highway.

The sheriff announced brightly, "Well, this is it. Our little town of Salt Lick. Not much to look at, but there's real good people live here."

Darla stared out the window. The town looked the same as dozens of other small towns she had seen all through her childhood. Her dad had worked as an oil field hand and they had moved from place to place. The oil business and the West Texas economy hadn't gone bust until after Darla had left home.

And so far, it hadn't really recovered. Nowadays, the whole vast area was filled with what had once been thriving small towns but now looked like ghost towns holding aging populations. The young people always left for greener pastures, but back when Darla had been a kid, every teenage boy's plan was to go to college and become a "petroleum engineer." And every teenage girl's plan was to either become a schoolteacher or to marry one of those well-paid "petroleum engineers." Only Darla had set her sights on a music career.

"Is this the whole town?" Roxie asked, interrupting Darla's stroll down memory lane.

"Yes, ma'am, it shore is," the sheriff answered, beaming. "Best little place between Odessa and El Paso."

Even from the backseat, Darla saw Roxie roll her eyes, which added a new layer of resentment. The citizens of Salt Lick, whoever they were, were Darla's people. She was unwilling to tolerate their being criticized by anyone as vapid as Roxie. Then a new thought direction intruded. Would the citizens of Salt Lick remember Darla Denman and her music? Would they come to see her show or watch her on the telethon? Would they be happy to learn she was touring again? Or would they just be surprised she wasn't dead?

The public was a fickle lover—happy in your presence but seeking a replacement the second you left the stage. And if anyone knew that from experience, Darla did. And if anyone knew that time and that friggin' mirror couldn't be fooled, Darla knew that, too.

She spotted what looked like a gas station. Or something. Someone had put skirts and sweaters with college letters on the antique gas pumps that stood out front.

"Wow," Valetta Rose said. "That's what I call making the best of a bad situation."

A large white sign with hand-painted red letters was mounted on the roof ridge. THE STYLING STATION.

An easel sign stood beside the front door.

THE DOMESTIC EQUALIZERS
Don't Get Even! Get evidence!

"The Domestic Equalizers," Darla mumbled against her window. "I wonder what that is."

"Who cares?" Roxie snapped.

Then it dawned on Darla that the Styling Station was a beauty salon. She could well imagine a beauty salon's struggles in a town like this one. She looked around at the tumbledown surroundings. *Bless their hearts*, she thought.

chapter two

With no warning, Sheriff Roberts made a sudden right turn, jerking Darla from her thoughts. Bodies zoomed across slick vinyl seats, crashed against doors and rib cages. Darla couldn't hold back from sputtering a string of cuss words. Before she, or anyone in the backseat, could right himself, the car came to a screeching halt, throwing all of them forward.

"Good God almighty," she shouted. "Did we hit something or did something hit us?"

The sheriff tilted his rearview mirror downward, allowing eye contact between him and Darla. He was grinning like a fool. "Sorry, ma'am. Guess I'm used to driving in high-speed pursuits of fugitives."

Pursuits of fugitives, my ass, Darla thought. She opened her mouth to blast him, but Bob's *don't-do-it* look silenced her.

She didn't always heed her ex's warnings, but without fail she always wished later that she had. Few people knew her softer side, the one she hid beneath her tough act. But Bob did, and he also knew it took only one look from him to stop her cold.

But that wasn't true of his current wife. "You backwoods ignoramus," Roxie yelled. "I just about broke my nose on the windshield." She pointed at the windshield. "Look! Those lip prints are mine!" She flipped her visor down and studied her reflection in the mirror.

Darla noted that Roxie wasn't in a position to see Bob's scowl, not that it would have mattered. She was young enough to think her own opinion was the only valid one in the room.

Refusing to look in Bob's direction, Darla purred to Roxie, "Well honey, if proof of your presence is in lipstick smears, that's going to cover a lot of territory, including beast as well as man."

Just then, the dimwit sheriff announced loudly, "This here's Hogg's Drive-In. I thought you folks might like to rest or get a bite to eat or a cool drink while your bus is being towed. Y'all know about Hogg's, don't you? It used to be Mr. Elvis Presley's favorite place to get a hamburger."

Darla looked out the back window and spotted a sign she had missed earlier. "Elvis Presley ate here," she read aloud. "Hmm . . . seems like I remember reading something about this place last year in *The Nashville Scene.* Wasn't something that had belonged to Elvis stolen from here?"

"Yes, ma'am. His danged ol' blue suede shoes," the sheriff answered. "My deputy and I solved that one PDQ, though." A smirk of pride played across his thin lips.

"I think I read that two women who have a detective agency solved that," Bob said.

"Uh, well, some people might look at it thataway," the sheriff said. "But without the go-ahead from the sheriff's office it wouldn't have happened. Ya see, we only got me and a deputy. If we need extra help, we call on them two women. They call themselves the Domestic Equalizers."

Darla thought of the other sign she had seen in front of the beauty salon. At least now she knew what or who the Domestic Equalizers were.

"This shithole town has a detective agency?" Roxie said, looking around. "What does it do, look for something to do?"

"No, ma'am," the sheriff said indignantly. "The Domestic Equalizers have solved lots of crimes. Them two girls are smart."

"The Domestic Equalizers?" Roxie said, her eyes big with incredulity stacked on top of indignation. She turned toward the backseat and her heated gaze landed on her husband. "You know something, Bob? This whole fuckin' trip is right out of the twilight zone."

Darla waited for him to say something back, but before he could utter a word, Darla felt Roxie's venom turn on her. "You should feel proud, Darla. Your comeback tour is a big success. We're stuck in a one-horse town with no decent places to eat or shop, but it's got a detective agency. Maybe you can hire them to find your lost career."

Darla was concocting a stream of blistering insults when the sheriff spoke up. "Miss, I don't know what's going on, but I don't think you're talkin' very nice to Miz Denman. And I'll have you know we got more than one horse in this town. Lots more."

Roxie blurted a loud laugh, opened her door and stumbled out of the car, still laughing uproariously.

The sheriff looked across his shoulder into the backseat at Darla. "She shouldn't oughta talk to you that way, Miz Denman. You're a living legend, 'specially since you're not really dead. She should show you more respect."

Darla was touched by the sheriff's defending her, a sudden reminder of why this tour was important to her. It was more than the money or the satisfaction of being worshipped again. It was the people like the sheriff and his mother who still saw her as a star and not a washed-up has-been trying to reconnect with her youth. "Come inside the café with us, Sheriff," she said. "Let me buy you a cup of coffee."

The sheriff leaped from the driver's seat, yanked open her door and reached inside for her hand. "Oh, no, ma'am, y'all go on in and get comfortable. I gotta go find Little Earl and send him out to tow the bus in."

"Is he the mechanic you spoke to me about?" Bob asked, sliding out of the backseat behind Darla.

"Yessir. Little Earl Elkins. I swear he could make a dead mule get up and run again."

"Funny you should say that. I think that's just what it's going to take. We'll go into the café and wait to hear from you."

The rest of the group was now assembled near Hogg's front door. Bob walked over to them. "Come on," he told them. "Let's go on inside. We can sit in the air-conditioning and have a bite to eat."

Eddie pulled open the door. "Sounds good to me. I'm 'bout starved to death and I'm pretty near parboiled in this sun."

Darla looked at the ground. Her guitar player and keyboard man ate non-stop. If he was awake, he was eating. Eddie had been in the music business more years than she had. His waist-long ponytail—once black as the coal his daddy had mined from the ground—was now a silver gray. He was a great guitarist, but he had once been a heavy drug user, which had ruined his chances to get into the bands of the big stars. She had always considered him a friend and now they had something else in common: They were both trying to make a comeback.

Darla hung back and stood with him as he held the door for the group. The aroma of hamburgers assailed them.

As Roxie passed behind Bob, she said, "Jesus, Eddie, when was the last time you took a shower?"

Darla gasped.

Fuck you, the guitarist mouthed silently and raised his middle finger at Roxie's back.

"Don't worry about it, Eddie," Darla said, placing a supportive hand on his shoulder. "She's just mean."

"I ain't worried. She keeps pissin' people off and she'll get hers one of these days."

"Let's get inside out of this heat."

They joined the group in a large corner booth and picked up laminated menus that were greasy and worn from use.

"Looks like the choice is a hamburger with all the fixin's or a cheeseburger with all the fixin's," Bob said, smiling. "Wonder why they bothered printing menus?"

"Humph," Roxie said, too loudly. "I'm wondering why anyone would bother doing anything but leaving a shithole town like this."

"Roxie," Bob said quietly, "lower your voice. This town might not look like much to you, but people are loyal to their hometowns. They don't appreciate strangers coming in and running things down."

"Yeah, hot stuff, where're you from?" the backup singer named Kay drawled. "Any place anybody ever heard of?"

Roxie gave her a phony smile. "Oh, maybe. How about Los Angeles? Ever heard of *L.A.*?"

"Sure, but I don't own up to it. That explains why you ain't fittin' in as part of this group."

Darla let out a sigh of exhaustion. Scanning the room, she spotted an arrow that pointed to the rear of the café for restrooms. She picked up her purse. "I'm going to the ladies' room. I'm bored with this whole conversation." Winking at Bob, she slid across the cracked vinyl booth seat. "Y'all try to settle this before I get back."

A few minutes later she was standing before the mirror examining her artfully applied eye shadow when she heard the sound of two male voices just outside the door. She opened the door only to be startled by Bob leaning against the wall.

"Dammit, Bob, you scared me. Are you waiting for the john? 'Cause if you are, the men's room is farther on up the hallway."

"No, I'm waiting for you," Bob said in a hushed tone. Taking her by the arm, he led her a few steps away from the restroom door. "Honey, we're in real trouble."

"What kind of trouble?"

"The green kind you fold and put in your wallet."

"Oh, *that* kind," she said with a flip of her hand. She started to walk past him, only to be spun around and jerked back to face him. "Bob," she said testily, "a shortage of green has been our problem from the beginning. Why are you acting like this is some late-breaking news moment?" She lifted her arm from his grip. "I want to go order a burger, if you don't mind."

Bob stepped in front of her and blocked her path. "You can't afford a burger."

Darla stared at him for several seconds, studying his serious expression. "Okay, I'm listening."

He explained that minutes earlier, he had been talking to Little Earl Elkins, who had driven out to the bus, completed an inspection and worked up an estimate on the repairs. "Getting the bus fixed will wipe us out until we finish the next paying gig," Bob said in conclusion.

"What about our reserve? We had some put back."

"I'm including the reserve." He thrust his fingers through his neatly combed salt-and-pepper-gray hair, a gesture that told of his worry. Darla had always loved his hair. It was just as thick now as it had been when they were kids. No balding for Bob.

"I'm sorry," he said. "It's my fault. I should've never let you talk me into this. And unfortunately, Darla, I can't foot the bill for this myself."

Darla knew hard times had befallen her former husband. Once he had lived large, but now she suspected his only clients were herself and Roxie. And neither of them was making him rich. "It isn't like you to jump to conclusions. Let's wait and see what the real cost is. It could be less than the estimate."

"Or it'll most likely be more. Besides, it can't be less. Little Earl said he was charging us for parts only. Apparently he's a big fan of yours. I don't know anything about repairing engines, but Mike does—"

"Wait. Tell me again. Who's Mike?"

Bob sighed. "Mike's the drummer."

"Oh, yeah. Okay, what did Mike say?"

"His brother is a mechanic for Greyhound. They've talked before about the cost of maintaining those bus fleets. He said Little Earl has given us a helluva good price."

Darla's mind whirled, trying to formulate a plan. "We can cover the repair, right, then scrimp on everything else?"

"It's not just the repair, honey," Bob said softly. He began ticking off reasons on his fingers. "We're talking days to get the parts in. We all have to sleep somewhere. We won't be able to use the bus as planned." He went to finger number two. "We've got to eat, so there's the cost of food for all of us." Finger number three. "There's transportation, now that we don't have a bus. It's going to take a miracle to get us out of this one, Darla."

Darla's mind was too busy wrapping itself around the situation to comment.

Bob ran his fingers through his hair again. Now his usually neat hair looked as if it had never been combed. "We might as well go tell the others."

"Tell them what?

Bob's shoulders sagged, his arms hung limp. "Are you even listening to me? We can't pay them until at least two weeks from now. We can't even get them back to Nashville. After I pay for these burgers, I might have two hundred dollars left on my credit card, but I doubt it."

"You don't think they can wait two weeks for payday? Big companies only pay every two weeks all the time."

"That's true, sweetheart, but these people were all broke when I hired them. I promised them a paycheck now. Just this morning, even before we got on the bus, three of them approached me for an advance."

"I know how they feel," Darla said. "I'm tapped out myself. I couldn't get a dime if I swallowed one and had to wait for it to pass. I maxed out my own credit cards at that Fort Worth beauty salon."

"Why, when we've got Valetta—"

"No way am I letting that Valetta Rose touch my face," she snapped.

And Darla meant it. Before the bus ever left Nashville, Roxie had demanded that Valetta Rose be hired despite Darla's protests that a makeup artist wasn't needed. But wherever Roxie was, Valetta Rose was stuck to her like Velcro.

"You should use her," Bob said. "She's one of the few things around here that's paid for." He glanced toward the dining area. "We'll have to talk to them. Try to make them understand."

"We didn't plan on this. They have to understand. What other choice do they have?"

Shouting erupted from the dining room. Darla and he exchanged glances. "Hell. That's them, isn't it? It sounds like we need to go referee something."

"I don't know what they're arguing about," Bob said, "but this news isn't going to make them any happier. Let me do the talking. I'm better than you are at talking to musicians and singers about money."

"I'm not so sure of that," Darla grumbled as he brushed past her. "You just talked to me about the subject and now I feel like shit."

She followed Bob back to the dining room. They found their corner booth empty except for Roxie and Valetta Rose. Roxie was pounding the bottom of a ketchup bottle above a mound of French fries.

"What the hell happened here?" Bob demanded. "We heard shouting. Where did everyone go?"

Before answering, Roxie set the plastic ketchup bottle on the table with a thud, then gingerly picked up a fry with her fingertips and popped it into her mouth. "I told them we didn't have the money to pay them. There was a trucker in here getting coffee. He told the girls he was headed east. He said he'd take them to the bus to get their things, then they could ride with him to Nashville."

Darla's jaw dropped. "What about the band? Did the guys leave too?"

"Naw, they've got nowhere to go, but the trucker offered to take them to the bus to make sure no one made off with their instruments."

Darla looked to Bob, bug-eyed, waiting for a response. His face had turned a bright scarlet and his eyes were watering. She had seen this gentle man really angry few times. She chose to remain silent.

"You . . . did . . . what?"

Darla knew he was close to sputtering, but Roxie was unfazed—or unconscious. She continued stuffing French fries into her mouth. "That's what you told me, *Robert.* And you didn't tell me it was a secret that I needed to keep to myself."

"But you had to know how they would react. Why in the hell didn't you let *me* break the news?"

"I would've been happy to let you tell them," Roxie sassed, "but you were in the back with country music's only living fossil. I was left to handle the situation and I did it the best I knew how. Let's just say it was a judgment call."

Darla bent forward, her chin jutted. "Here's another *judgment* call, dimwit! You're a damned idiot!"

Roxie sprang from the booth, her fists knotted at her sides. "Let's do it, Darla! Right here, right now!"

"Damn right!" Darla began tugging off her rings and throwing them into her purse.

Bob placed himself between them. "No one is going to do anything. Not now or any other time." He looked from one woman to the other. "We are up a shit river with no paddle and the tide is coming in. Do either of you have an idea to get us out of this? If so, I'd really like to hear it."

Roxie glared at her husband. "Don't you dare offer to pick up a dime of her expenses, Bob Denman. If you do, you'll never climb into my bed again." She turned to Darla and gave a syrupy smile. "It's your comeback show, Mizzz Denman. I guess that makes this whole fiasco *your* problem."

"Hell, this isn't a problem," Darla drawled with bravado. "Having five hungry kids and no money to buy groceries or pay the rent is a problem. We've still got a band and I've still got a voice."

"Darla, we need the backup singers," Bob said. "They're a big part of the show."

"Perhaps. But I'll tell you who isn't part of the show. And that's Valetta Rose. Why didn't she go back to Nashville with the backup singers? I think I've already said if there's anything we don't need, it's a makeup artist."

"Valetta Rose is none of your business," Roxie said. "I hired her myself. She stays."

Valetta Rose sat silently in the booth, nibbling on Roxie's French fries.

"Roxie's paying for her," Bob said.

"No, she isn't," Darla countered. "*You're* paying for her, Bob."

"Darla, Roxie's my wife and this is her debut. If she thinks she needs a makeup artist, that's fine with me."

Darla stared into his eyes for long seconds trying to read his thoughts, but finally told herself how utterly silly it was for her to argue with him over something Roxie wanted. Of course he would side with Roxie. She was, as he said, his wife.

Darla didn't want to use her energy to argue anyway. A possible solution was forming in her mind. "Look," she said. "I've got an idea. A chance of a lifetime for someone. A chance to become a part of music history. Y'all wait here for the guys to come back. I'm going to the beauty salon. I'll be back in a little while."

chapter three

Debbie Sue Overstreet, lifelong resident of Salt Lick, Texas, and co-owner of the Styling Station and the Domestic Equalizers detective agency, hung up the phone. When she had first seen Sheriff Billy Don Roberts's name on caller ID, she had dreaded answering, but now she was glad she had.

His call brought some excitement she could never have foreseen when the day started. She wouldn't have believed she would have the chance to see, or possibly meet, the Queen of Country Music, alive. She thought Darla Denman was dead.

Now, after her partner, Edwina Perkins-Martin, had gone home for the day, Debbie Sue had to get her back to the salon. Edwina was a true, diehard Darla Denman fan. Many times she had said, "Next to Patsy Cline, nobody sings country better than Darla Denman." Edwina's vintage Mustang was littered with the singer's CDs. She had seen her perform in venues from honky-tonks to concert halls. And when given the opportunity to drop her coins in a juke box, Edwina always picked Darla Denman's old songs. Without a doubt, she would flat-out die if she missed this opportunity to see her idol in person.

Five *burrs* later, Debbie Sue had Edwina on the line. Bypassing "hello," she said urgently, "Ed, what are you doing? I mean, are you doing anything you can't stop?" Not allowing an answer, Debbie Sue rushed on. "Listen, whatever you're doing, get back to the salon quick. Have I got a surprise for you."

"What in the hell have you done?" Edwina asked in her twangy Texas drawl. "Tell me now. Don't make me come back to the shop."

"No, I'm not telling you. I want to see the look on your face. Now hurry up and come back."

"Can't you bring the surprise to me?"

"Not possible. Stop arguing, Ed. Trust me. If you miss this, you'll never get over it."

"Well, my stars. Okay, then. But it's gonna take a while. I'm in my robe. I came home, washed my makeup off and put an egg-white mask on my face. And I've got a rinse on my hair. That new color we got in, Java Mist. It's got thirty minutes to go."

"Ed, why didn't you let me put color on your hair here at the shop?"

"Me? Take a chance on the public seeing me with my beehive hairdo combed out and a rinse on my head? Puleeze. I'd rather be shot."

Debbie Sue chewed on her thumbnail. Billy Don hadn't said how long Darla Denman and her band would be at Hogg's.

They could be leaving any minute, which meant that not only would Edwina miss getting a glimpse of her idol, she wouldn't get a once-in-a-lifetime chance to meet her in person either. "Dammit, Ed, I don't know how long she'll be here."

"Who? Listen, hon, I don't care who it is. I wouldn't let *anybody* see me in my current state. Whoever it is, take a picture."

Debbie Sue, with the phone still pressed to her ear, stamped to the window. Two women and three men were walking out of Hogg's. They were too far away for her to identify them, but if she didn't spill the secret to Edwina soon, she herself wouldn't get close enough to Darla Denman for a handshake, much less a picture. Panic overtook her. She shook her free hand frantically. "Darla Denman, Ed! Darla-fuckin'-Denman is at Hogg's Drive-In! Alive and well! Her bus broke down outside of town and I don't know how long she'll be here."

A high-pitched squeal pierced Debbie Sue's eardrum.

Bang . . . clatter . . . crash . . . Then silence.

Oh, hell. "Ed? . . . Ed, you still there?"

Debbie Sue couldn't waste any more time on the call. Her job was complete, her duty done. She had to get to Hogg's. But first—Edwina had been right about the picture—she had to find her camera. Damned thing was never where it should be when she needed it. Scurrying from one styling station to the other, she opened all drawers and pawed through the contents.

Frustration building, she thought of the camera on her phone, even though she had yet to make a picture with it that had turned out well. She strode toward the storeroom, shoved back the floral curtain that covered the doorway and grabbed her purse off a shelf. Digging inside it and finding nothing, she had to acknowledge she was getting nowhere at an alarming rate. And to make matters worse, the Christmas bells tied to the front door jangled, signaling the arrival of a walk-in needing a hairdo or something.

"Dammit, not now," Debbie Sue mumbled under her breath, throwing a hairbrush out of the purse. "I'll be there in a sec," she yelled at the doorway.

"Where in the hell is that fuckin' camera," she whispered through clenched teeth, finding three tubes of lipstick she thought she had lost.

"Hey," she shouted at the doorway again, "you wouldn't happen to have a camera on ya, would you? You know, one of those disposable things?"

Now she had a wad of old receipts in hand that had probably been in the bottom of her purse for months. "Shit," she stage-whispered, then yelled at the doorway, "I need to get to Hogg's and prove a living legend isn't dead."

She threw her purse back on the shelf and started back into the salon. Yanking open the floral curtain, she halted in her tracks. Her eyes had to be playing tricks on her. Either Darla Denman or a damn good double was sitting in Edwina's styling chair. Her right leg was crossed over her left knee. Silver high-heeled sandals were strapped onto her feet and she was wearing a pair of jeans that could only have come from BrazilRoxx. Debbie Sue was sure she had seen them in *Cowboys and Indians* magazine boasting a stratospheric price tag.

The visitor removed her dark sunglasses and showered Debbie Sue with one of the most photographed smiles in the music industry. "I don't have a camera. Would an autograph suffice? That is, if *I'm* the living legend you thought was dead."

Debbie Sue jumped as if zapped by a cattle prod and stepped into the salon. "Oh, no, Miz Denman. You *are* Darla Denman, right? I was talking about . . . uh, I meant that . . . well, you see—"

"You aren't trying to convince me there was more than one living legend at that little café this morning, are you?"

The woman's crimson smile and the fact she was trying to stifle laughter made Debbie Sue relax and release her own nervous titter. "I'm so sorry. I've been a fan of yours for as long as I can remember. It's just that it's been so long since we've heard anything new from you. We just assumed—"

"That I was dead? Yeah, I get that a lot. Too bad my creditors didn't make that assumption. Those bastards will dig you up for a late charge."

"God, don't I know it," Debbie Sue said.

With the discovery of something in common and Darla Denman's friendliness, Debbie Sue plopped into her own styling chair and fell into a chat with her new visitor. Darla explained that she was on her way to Midland for an appearance at the annual telethon raising money for Alzheimer's disease. "You haven't heard I'm going to be there?" she asked, a troubled expression on her face. "We were told there would be publicity for the event."

"Oh, I'm sure there was—er, is," Debbie Sue said quickly. "But I never read the papers. And since I got my iPod I don't listen to the radio like I used to. I don't have time for TV. My husband and I rarely turn the set on."

The corners of Darla's lips tilted into another smile. "Yeah? You've got a good marriage?"

"Lord, yes. Buddy Overstreet and I have been in love with each other since before we knew what it was. He's a Texas Ranger."

"A professional baseball player?" Darla pointed a French-manicured finger at the floor. "And he lives here? In this little town?"

Debbie Sue's brow tugged into a frown. "No, ma'am. He's a law-enforcement officer. Salt Lick's part of the territory he's responsible for. You've never heard of the Texas Rangers?"

Darla Denman straightened, sat back in her chair, then laughed. "Oh. *Those* Texas Rangers. I thought you meant the baseball team. Why, as I live and breathe. Honey, I was born and raised in Texas, but I don't recall that I've ever met a real Texas Ranger."

"They're kind of rare," Debbie Sue said. "Texas is a big place, you know, and there just aren't that many of them. Come to think of it, I guess we don't need many of them. You've probably heard that corny old joke, 'one riot, one Ranger?'" Debbie Sue chortled at the well-worn joke, then grew serious. "Besides being my husband and my lover, he's my best friend."

Darla leaned forward and patted her hand. "Keep it that way, darlin'. Don't let anything, and I mean *anything*—career, money or your damned ego—change it, either. Best friends are hard to find and one that's also your lover is a blessing straight from heaven."

All at once, the singer paused and her expression changed, as if she became lost in a memory. Then she seemed to snap out of it and went on to talk about the importance of the telethon gig and her ensuing concerts. "I guess this is my grand finale, my swan song."

"But you're too young to quit," Debbie Sue protested. "You've got years to go on singing. Just look at my mom."

"Your mom's a singer?"

"She's a songwriter. Lord, she didn't even start until she was sixty. Now she's moved to Nashville and she's famous. She's even won some awards."

"Your mom is a songwriter? Who is she?"

"Virginia Pratt," Debbie Sue answered proudly. "One of the songs she wrote is 'Since You're Leaving Anyway, Take Out the Trash.'"

Darla Denman gasped. "Oh, my God!"

"And she wrote 'She's Left Lipstick Traces in Too Many Places,'" Debbie Sue added. "And Gretchen Wilson recorded it."

"I would've killed for that song," the singer said solemnly. "Absolutely *killed*."

"She'll write another one for you," Debbie Sue said. "Just ask her."

Darla Denman's lips curved down in a wry grin. "You think an award-winning songwriter wants to write something for a singer everyone thinks is dead? Songwriters have to think of their careers too, you know."

"Oh, uh, listen, Darla, I'm sorry I said anything about that dead thing. It's just that—"

"Don't apologize," Darla said, and laughed with a trace of bitterness. "I've been out of the public eye for too long. For the record and according to Wikipedia, I'm fifty-one. In the music business, that's ancient for a singer. But I'm prepared physically, if not mentally. I've been plucked, tucked, and sucked. I'm prepared to go out in style."

"Attagirl," Debbie Sue said as the sound of screeching tires and pea gravel striking the window broke up their conversation. They both shot looks toward the front door. Then Debbie Sue heard the thud of the back door's doorknob hitting the wall. Edwina made her entrance with the finesse of a marching band.

Her hair was plastered to her head like a shiny, wet black cap and her face was snow white. She didn't look in Debbie Sue's or Darla Denman's direction but strode straight to the back room and disappeared behind the doorway's floral curtain.

Horrified, Debbie Sue said to Darla, "Excuse me," and followed Edwina.

In the back room, Edwina was standing beside the teal green shampoo bowl. She had the spray nozzle in her hand and was testing the water temperature.

"Ed, what in the hell—"

"Is she still over there? Did you see her? Bless her heart, I bet she looked like death warmed over." She dropped the spray nozzle in the sink, sank onto the shampoo chair and placed her neck in the shampoo bowl's *U*. "Hurry up, dammit. Wash this shit off my hair. Use the spray nozzle on my face, too, so I can get rid of this mask in a hurry. While my hair's drying, I'll put on some makeup."

Debbie Sue hadn't moved from her frozen stance in the doorway.

"Don't just stand there, Debbie Sue. Help me!"

Debbie Sue turned back to the salon and patted her pursed lips with her finger. She motioned for Darla to come to the shampoo room. Then she picked up the spray nozzle and began washing the inky color rinse from Edwina's hair.

"I've been doing the math in my head," Edwina said, her eyes squeezed tightly shut. "Darla Denman has got to be seventy years old. I mean, she was at the top of her game when I was in my teens and we both know how long that's been. Don't forget my face, Dippity-do. Just squirt a little bit of water, not much. Just enough to get this mask damp."

Debbie Sue was reluctant to spray Edwina's face with water

from the spray nozzle. "I don't know about that, Ed. This thing's got enough water pressure to sting bare skin. Aside from that, I could end up dousing this whole damn back room."

"Debbie Sue," Edwina whined. "Just do it."

"Okay, okay. But keep your eyes closed."

Debbie Sue motioned Darla Denman over and handed the nozzle to her, indicating with her hand what she wanted her to do.

Getting the joke, Darla hid a giggle behind her hand and nodded.

She moved to a spot beside the shampoo bowl, took the nozzle in hand and began to carefully release a small stream of water across Edwina's forehead.

"Here, hit me here." Edwina raised her hand to indicate a spot on her face. Her hand struck the spray nozzle Darla held. Darla lost control and drenched the wall behind the shampoo bowl and the two shelves above it.

"Oh, my God!" She dropped the nozzle into the sink and clapped both hands against her cheeks. The nozzle danced in the bottom of the sink like a hyped-up cobra, erratically squirting everything and everyone within four feet.

Debbie Sue's eyes flew wide. She leaped to grab the nozzle before more damage was done. Water dripped off the shelves, even the ceiling, onto the floor and onto the back of the sink.

And worst of all, off Darla Denman's chin.

"Shit," Debbie Sue said, grabbed a damp shop towel off the shelf and handed it to Darla.

Darla sniffed and began to blot her face.

Edwina's eyes remained tightly closed. "What? What the hell happened?"

Debbie Sue's heart was pounding, but she managed to control the water pressure with her thumb. "Nothing, Ed." She finished rinsing the white mask off Edwina's face.

"That feels about right," Edwina said. "That oughtta do it. Hand me a towel."

With her adrenaline ebbing, Debbie Sue reached overhead for another towel, only to find the remaining ones soaked. She handed one to Edwina, who applied it to her face, appearing not to even notice that it was wet. Her eyes still closed, Edwina jutted out her chin. "Check out my face real close. Go ahead and study it. It's supposed to look smooth as a baby's butt. Does it?"

Darla retrieved a pair of glasses from her jacket pocket, perched them on her nose, bent forward and studied Edwina's face. As Debbie Sue bent to look too, Darla stroked Edwina's cheek with her index finger. "I don't know about a baby's butt, but it looks pretty good. But then I'm seventy years old and look like death warmed over, so what do I know?"

Edwina's eyes sprang open. She looked into the singer's hazel eyes just inches from her own. She said nothing, only stared.

"Ed, can't you say something?" Debbie Sue asked.

"Sweet Jesus and all that's holy. Woman, you look just like Darla Denman."

Darla straightened. "I am Darla Denman."

"Shit," Edwina said, sitting up. "I thought you were dead."

Darla sighed. "Yeah, I get that a lot." She continued to dab at her face with the damp towel. "But ladies, I didn't come in here to discuss my obituary. I need help."

Meanwhile, in Hogg's Drive-In, Roxie Denman admired her reflection in her gold compact mirror before snapping it shut and returning it to her purse. Several men had come into the shithole cafe and cast shy but admiring looks in her direction.

She had smiled back boldly, giving them a show. She knew the effect her appearance had on men and used it to the max. Why not? What were her good looks for, if not to make her life easier and more exciting?

Contemplating the journey that had brought her to this point, she cast a disdainful look across the table at music producer Bob Denman, the man to whom she had been married for two long years, four endless months and twelve boring days. She had met him in a Nashville nightclub known for discovering new talent, where she used to sing three nights a week. He had been single then and came in often with various beautiful women. His reputation in the music business was widely known.

Roxie had waged an all-out campaign to win his attention, used every trick in the femme fatale handbook. Once she had maneuvered an actual date with him, she let him have a taste of mind-blowing sex, then rationed it. She professed her affection for him, then stepped out with another man. Through the whole process, she had navigated a slippery slope that could have become an avalanche if not properly managed, but she knew what she was doing. Soon she had reeled him in like a big fish. She had his promise of promoting her career and a big diamond ring on her finger and a marriage license, which oddly enough had turned into a pain in her ass.

Indeed she had won, but lately she wondered what the prize was. The past year the only client Bob spent time with was his ex-wife. He seemed to be obsessed with making her happy and helping her make a comeback.

Roxie knew better than anyone what her husband denied the loudest—that he still loved Darla Denman. Roxie wasn't jealous, hell, no. She hadn't married a man old enough to be her father because he was the last great love of her life. She had married him for what he could *do* for her life, here and now. She didn't give a shit who he loved, but she did care that his sappy affection for his ex-wife interfered with Roxie Denman's grand plan.

"Where in the hell is she?" she demanded of Bob.

"Roxie, you know as much as I do. She said she'd be right back and she will. It's not like we've got somewhere to go."

"That's the first thing you've said today that was accurate. We've got absolutely no fucking place to go."

"Please keep your voice down," Bob said, reaching across the table and covering her hand with his. "Making a scene can only make things worse."

Roxie yanked her hand away with enough force to knock the plastic ketchup bottle from the table to the floor, where the lid popped off and splattered ketchup in a four-foot radius.

"Great," Bob said, grabbing a handful of napkins. "Look at the mess you made." He bent and began wiping up the floor.

Roxie slid from the booth, jammed her fists against her hips and fixed him with a look of pure disgust. "That's right, Bob. Clean it up. Cleaning up messes is what you do best."

With that parting shot, she flounced out of the café.

chapter four

Debbie Sue was blown away by the proposal Darla Denman had just made, but before she had a chance to react, Edwina sprang to her feet, wrapped her long skinny arms around Darla and pressed her wet cheek to the visiting celebrity's, whose makeup was slightly smeared and uneven after being dampened by the aberrant spray nozzle and wiped with a wet towel. Hugging the superstar was no easy feat for Edwina. The singer couldn't be over five-three and was a little on the chunky side, and Edwina, wearing her trademark four-inch platform shoes, towered over her.

Debbie Sue pried Edwina away. "Miz Denman, I could not have heard you right. Would you mind repeating what you just said?"

"Please don't call me Miz Denman, doll. It's Darla, okay?"

"Okay, Darla. Please say what you just said again."

"Wait a minute." Wet black hair plastered against her head, Edwina strode out of the shampoo room. Debbie Sue and Darla followed and found her straddling the rolling desk chair behind the payout counter, prowling the interior of her monstrous black-and-white cowhide hobo bag. "Let me get Vic on the phone so he can hear you say it." Edwina pulled out a tube of mascara and threw it aside, then looked up and flashed an idiot grin that, without the aura of a beehive hairdo, made her face look like a smiley face. "Vic's my husband. He's a retired navy SEAL. He liberated Kuwait."

Darla smiled wanly. "Well, that's real nice."

"Ed," Debbie Sue said. "Cool it with the phone and let Miz Den—I'm sorry—let *Darla* talk." She turned to Darla, gesturing toward Edwina's salon chair. "Sit down, Miz Denman. Sorry beauty shop furniture is all we've got."

Darla reclaimed her former seat in Edwina's styling chair and Debbie Sue sank to the seat of her own styling chair.

"What do we have to sign?" Edwina asked. "And where? When do we perform?"

"Just hold on, Ed," Debbie Sue said. "You're getting way ahead of things. You might be on board with this, but I'm not. I'm thinking there's probably one of our customers who'd like to do it."

Edwina's grin turned to a scowl as she tucked back her chin. "You're gonna sacrifice this opportunity to one of our *customers*? Who? Just *who* do you think would be better at this than we would?"

"I don't know. But—"

"Fine." Edwina slapped her phone on the counter with a pronounced *clack* and turned to Darla. "Say it again. I want to be sure I heard you right."

Debbie Sue wanted to scream. Darla probably thought she and Edwina were insane. Or at the very least, just plain stupid. And to prove it, she was looking at them as if they were monkeys in a cage.

"Okay, here it is again," Darla said slowly. "I need two backup singers"—she held up two fingers—"when I perform at the telethon in Midland on Sunday. Would you two like to give it a try?"

Edwina squealed, sprang to her feet and did a little jig. She grabbed a can of hair spray and, as if it were a microphone, broke into singing the opening lyrics from one of Darla's biggest hits from years back. "She may have initials after her name, but I turn you on PDQ."

While Darla stared drop-jawed at Edwina's performance, Debbie Sue reached for her hand. "Try to understand, Miz Den—er, Darla. Ed's overexcited. With all due respect, is this some kind of publicity stunt? I mean, as you see"—she nodded in Edwina's direction—"she's taking your request really serious."

"And you aren't?" Darla asked.

Flustered, Debbie Sue struggled for the right words. "Yes, I mean, no, I mean . . . surely you have your own. Backup singers, that is. I saw some women coming out of Hogg's earlier. They weren't Salt Lick-ites. I know everyone from here and near and I didn't recognize any of them. So they had to be part of your crowd."

"You're right, darlin'. They *were* with me, and I do mean *were*. A small problem has raised its ugly head. It seems the situation we've found ourselves in caused them to be a little less than loyal."

Debbie Sue didn't want to bluntly declare that the people she had seen leaving Hogg's were the most pissed-off people she had observed in a while, so she tried for tact. "From the way they were stalking out the door, I'd say it's more than just a *little* less. What made them bail on you?"

Edwina halted her performance. "They bailed? Well, my stars and pass the biscuits."

"My, my," Darla said, giving Debbie Sue a pointed look. "Such perceptive questions. You really are a detective, aren't you?"

"I never heard of such disloyalty," Edwina said. "I can't imagine anything that would make *me* run out on you, Miz Denman."

Darla cleared her throat. "Well, you see, it seems this little mechanical problem we've had with the bus is going to take the last of our funds. We can't pay anyone until we get back to Nashville."

Oops, Debbie Sue thought.

Edwina's brow tented into a look of sympathy. "That seems reasonable to me. What I mean is, payday is payday, no matter where it takes place, right?"

"Well, er . . . it's a little more complicated than that, you see. Bottom line, ladies, the Darla Denman comeback tour is busted. We couldn't even afford to get those people back to Nashville. That's why they hitched a ride with a trucker."

"Yikes," Debbie Sue said.

"Hell's bells," Edwina drawled. "I take back what I just said."

"So you're on the level," Debbie Sue asked, cocking her head and narrowing her eyes. "You want *us*? You haven't even asked if we can sing, which we can't."

Edwina smirked. "Speak for yourself."

"Like I said," Debbie Sue countered. "We can't sing."

Edwina fixed a fist on her hip and seemed about to say something when Darla cut her off. "Not a problem. All my backup music is prerecorded. The only live singing is done by me. We hired the backup singers at the last minute back in Nashville. They don't even know the words to the songs. I can't risk that one of them might sing off-key or mumble the words at the wrong time, so we're using old tapes. All you have to do is move around a little. Keep time with the music and mouth the words. You know, lip-sync."

"I know every single word of every single song you ever sang," Edwina said. "And baby, I can move it." She began snapping her fingers, stepping in a circle and gyrating her hips. "I'm miles ahead of those disloyal bums already. And I work for free." She did a little salsa step. "Cha-cha-cha."

Darla laughed. "That's good, because I can't pay you. What I can do is mention your business and introduce you individually. You can even say something on the air if you want. I know it's asking a lot, but gosh, ladies, don't you think it sounds like fun?"

"We sure do!" Edwina said, snapping her fingers and thrusting a hip to one side. "Oom-pah!"

Debbie Sue shook her head. "*We?* . . . Ed, when I look in a mirror I don't see *we*. Best to speak for yourself. You go ahead. I'm not in. Sorry, I'm just not." She turned her attention to Darla. "But there's a couple of other local women who might do it and be pretty good at it."

Edwina stopped dancing. "What is wrong with you, Debbie Sue? Just who do you think would be better at this than us?"

"I was thinking of Avery Carter. Or Paige Atwater. They're both younger than we are and a lot better-looking."

"And they've got husbands and kids. They're busy." Edwina dropped to one knee in front of Debbie Sue. "It's the stage fright, isn't it? You're afraid you'll freeze."

Darla turned her attention to Debbie Sue, a puzzled expression on her face. "You freeze up onstage?"

"Like a popsicle," Edwina answered for her.

"I used to barrel race in ProRodeo," Debbie Sue said. "Almost made it to the national finals in Vegas. So I've been in front of crowds before. That never bothered me because I had my horse with me. He was more important than I was. But standing alone in front of a crowd without Rocket Man terrifies me."

"But, hon, you wouldn't be alone," Edwina said soothingly, taking one of Debbie Sue's hands in both of hers. "I'd be there with you. And if you need a horse, we could haul Rocket Man with us. Just look at that pretty trailer you've got for him to ride in. Or if you don't want to do that, we could probably find you a horse up there in Midland."

"Forgodsake, Ed." Debbie Sue freed her hand. "I don't need a horse."

"Hmm," Darla said, staring at the floor. She tapped a knuckle against her upper lip. "Bringing a horse onstage is out of the question anyway. How about a disguise instead? Fixing yourself up to where no one would recognize you? I've known plenty of big names who had stage fright, but they've told me that in costume or some fancy getup they feel like a different person, and they don't care what people think of *that* person. They not only don't have stage fright, they crave getting up in front of people."

"Oh, hell, yes," Edwina exclaimed, getting to her feet. "You know I can fix you up to where no one, not even Buddy, will recognize you, Debbie Sue. Think how proud your mama would be if you were singing backup to one of her songs."

"Let me think about it, okay?" Debbie Sue said with little

show of confidence. "This is something I've never, ever, planned on doing. I'm afraid I'll embarrass you, Darla. Worse yet, I'm afraid I'll embarrass my husband."

Darla tilted back her head and laughed. "Dear girl, your embarrassing me is the least of my worries. It isn't humanly possible to embarrass me at this point in my life. And we can just tell your husband to cowboy up."

"Ma'am," Debbie Sue said, "my husband is the last man anyone who knew him would ever tell to cowboy up. He spends every waking, breathing moment totally cowboyed up."

"Oh. Well, I . . . whatever," Darla said.

Debbie Sue looked at a beaming Edwina. Excitement and enthusiasm oozed from the woman's pores. Debbie Sue smiled weakly, knowing full well that when it came to something Edwina Perkins-Martin wanted, she would stop at nothing.

"Well, I'd best get back to the café," Darla said, standing and reaching for her bag. "Bob will be wondering what happened to me. You ladies think about it." She flashed that huge trademark smile. "But don't take too long."

"Bob?" Debbie Sue asked.

"That's her manager," Edwina said. "Used to be her husband, if memory serves me right."

Darla gave Edwina a look. "You know that much about my life?"

"I read it a long time ago. Back when I was quitting smoking. I read everything, including big books."

"Yeah, Ed knows what's in all the books in all the world," Debbie Sue said.

"Really," Darla said, obviously amazed. Then, "Well, it's no big secret. Bob was my first husband. Should've been my last, too. But life's not worth living if you don't screw it up every now and then, is it?" She tossed her hair nonchalantly, but Debbie Sue thought the display of audacity was false.

"Didn't I read that he's remarried?" Edwina asked.

"Sure did. Roxie Jennings is her name. Roxie Denman now, I should say. She's a singer. She's also my opening act. Yep, she's the new Mrs. Bob Denman, and would desperately like to be the new *Darla* Denman."

"Y'all are all traveling together?" Debbie Sue asked, an incredulous tone lacing her question. "How's that working out?"

"We've had our moments. Bob and I've been divorced a long time and I've been married three times since. I'm past the jealous stage, but Roxie doesn't make it easy to be liked. In fact, she makes it pretty damned easy to be despised. I don't think there's anyone on the bus who would miss her if she fell *under* the bus, so to speak."

A pregnant pause followed, then Darla hoisted her purse to her shoulder.

"I think I've said too much. I'll get back to you ladies as soon as I talk to Bob. And Debbie Sue, I hope you decide to join us."

"Hold on," Edwina said. "What are y'all gonna do for transportation 'til your bus is fixed? It could take days before it's running again."

"I haven't thought much about it. That's Bob's department." Darla's brow furrowed. "But now that you mention it—"

"Problem solved," Edwina said, returning to her hobo bag and pawing through it again. She pulled out a set of keys. "Y'all can use Vic's pickup. It's a crew cab, so it'll seat all of you and you can put your equipment and stuff in the bed."

"But won't he need it?" Darla asked, reaching for the keys. Almost too eagerly, Debbie Sue thought.

"Nah. He's on the road all week. Drives big rigs now. Can't stand to be shut in. He'd be proud for y'all to use it."

"Are you sure? That's just too generous of you. I mean—"

"He won't mind. It's parked in the back. I'll get a ride home with—" Edwina stopped, then exclaimed, "Oh, my God. Sleeping. Where are y'all gonna sleep?"

"Like I said, that's Bob responsibility and—"

"Debbie Sue, isn't your rental vacant?" Edwina asked. "They could stay there, couldn't they?" She turned to Darla. "It's fully furnished."

"Yeah, my renters just moved out just last week," Debbie Sue said. "It's got three bedrooms and a bath. It's in good shape. I just had it cleaned and the utilities are still on. You're welcome to use it."

"Beats the hell out of the Starlite Motel," Edwina said. "And it's free. Right, Debbie Sue?"

"A camping tent's better than the Starlite Motel, Ed," Debbie Sue replied.

Darla's eyes rimmed with tears. She looked away, made a swipe at her face and cleared her throat. "I don't know when I've ever met better folks."

"Nonsense," Debbie Sue said, feeling her cheeks heat up with embarrassment. "We're happy to help out."

"Yeah, we're tickled to death," Edwina said, looping an arm around Debbie Sue's shoulder in a one-armed hug.

Darla laughed self-consciously. "All I wanted was a couple of backup singers and I'm walking out with that, a vehicle and a place to sleep. I feel like I just won the lottery."

"Don't be too happy," Edwina said. "You haven't seen any of those things yet."

"True, all too true," Darla said, laughing as she turned

toward the doorway. "If it's okay, I'll send Bob over for the pickup."

"Great," Debbie Sue said. She stood arm in arm with Edwina and watched as their new acquaintance picked her way across the gravel parking lot in her high-heeled sandals and on up the street toward Hogg's. She looked back and waved before disappearing from sight around the corner. Debbie Sue couldn't keep from wondering what she and Edwina had gotten themselves into.

"You didn't give her the address," Edwina said.

"Oops. Well, I will when they come to get the pickup."

"Ain't life a hoot?" Edwina said.

"Like you're reading my mind, Ed. Like you're reading my mind."

Keys to a vehicle lying on his open palm, Bob stood and looked at Darla, obviously stunned. "A vehicle *and* a house?"

Eddie hovered at his elbow. "Wow," he said.

"Great," Mike said. "I was getting tired of flea-bitten motels."

Darla winced inside. She couldn't blame Mike for his sarcasm. Through the tour, Bob, Roxie, and Valetta Rose slept, along with her, on the bus, but she had paid for motel rooms for Mike and Eddie and the two backup singers. She couldn't deny that the rooms she had rented for them hadn't been the most luxurious, but they were all she could afford.

"No questions asked? No security deposits?" Bob said.

"Nope. Just my good name." Darla glanced smugly in Roxie's direction.

Bob sighed. "Man, I feel like the weight of the world has been lifted off my shoulders."

"But honey, you haven't even heard the best part," Darla said enthusiastically.

"You're finally going to give up and return to Nashville?" Roxie asked. "Feel free to go. I won't have any trouble keeping the show going."

Darla shot an icy stare at the younger woman. "Nooo. I went into that salon to ask the owners, Debbie Sue and Edwina, to help me find some backup singers. And they volunteered. For free."

"Uh-oh," Eddie muttered.

"Crap," Mike said.

Mike and Eddie's remarks Darla could ignore, but she was dismayed to see the look of excitement on Bob's face fade from happy to quizzical and horrified. She deliberately didn't look at Roxie or the makeup artist, Valetta Rose. What she did with her show was no business of either one of those empty-headed girls.

"Darla," Bob started, speaking slowly as if picking his words carefully, "you've been drilling into my head how important this telethon is. Why would you approach a couple of women you've never met and ask them to be backup singers? Don't you think that's a bit of a gamble?"

"You take the cake," Roxie accused, standing up from her slouched position in the corner booth, planting both hands on her hips and thrusting her chin forward. "This isn't just *your* big-ass fucking career that's on the line. What about mine?"

Darla had had enough of Roxie's venomous criticism of everything that happened. It was time for all of them to pull together as a team and deal with this crisis the best they could. She faced her ex-husband's young wife squarely, nailing her with a piercing squint. "*Your* career? Up to now, including this very moment here and now, you've had a *job*. When in the hell did it become a career?"

"Enough of that," Bob said, stepping between them. "God almighty. Both of you wear me out. I'd go back to Nashville myself, but I'm afraid to leave you two alone. Roxie, zip it. Let me finish this conversation. Darla, tell me more about these women. I wish you had discussed this with me before doing it."

"I wasn't sure myself what I was going to do. I went into the beauty salon to ask them if they knew of someone we could hire. But after I met them, I thought they were precious. One is older than the other but they're both younger than me and very attractive. I told them we're using recorded backup so they don't have to sing."

"Fine, but can they mime the words and move to the music?" Bob asked.

"A better question is do they have all their teeth and can they stand erect?" Roxie sniped. "From what I've seen of this town, I'll be surprised if they're not using canes or pushing those damned walkers around."

Bob glared at her.

Darla ignored her and focused on Bob. "Let me finish. Here's how I plan on playing it to the audience. I'll announce that two of their very own friends and neighbors have been selected to be on stage with me as my backup. The crowd will love it. They won't care if the ladies do good or bad. They'll be so proud it simply won't matter."

"Hmm, I like that," Bob said, frowning and nodding. "Hometown pride. You might be onto something."

"I know I am, Bob. We could even make this a contest for

the entire tour. Select two women from each town to be on-stage with me. We can use the Internet for fan club sites. Think of the money we'd save."

Bob paced back and forth, rubbing his chin. Darla watched anxiously, hoping he would buy into this great idea that had just jumped into her head.

Finally he stopped and a big grin spread across his face. "It's brilliant."

"Sounds like a good idea to me," Mike put in.

"I'm okay with it," Eddie added.

"It's bullshit," Roxie spat, obviously barely able to control her rage, much less keep her mouth shut. "And if there's anyone who does *not* have a say in this, it's you, Mike."

"It's the way it's going to be," Darla snapped at her. "And you can take it or leave it."

Roxie huffed. "I think I'll leave it."

She grabbed Valetta Rose's arm, dragged her out of the booth and pulled her across the dining room to the front door. She hit the plate glass door with the heels of both palms, making a loud thump, then sailed through the open doorway with Valetta Rose scrambling behind her.

Bob turned to Darla, his mouth set in a grim line. "You can't say she doesn't know how to make an exit."

"No kidding," Darla said numbly. She was exhausted. Confrontations with Roxie left her drained, but pride and her sense of justice wouldn't allow a spoiled twit to hurl random insults at will and run roughshod over everyone with whom she came in contact. "I'm just glad they've got good glass in that door."

chapter five

Debbie Sue waited impatiently for Edwina to finish her second phone call. She had tried to remain quiet, but her anxiety had intensified with each passing second. Edwina hung up and immediately keyed in a number for a third call. Debbie Sue's patience expired. "Good grief, Ed. Would you just give it a rest long enough for me to talk to you?"

Edwina snapped the phone shut and shoved it into her pocket. "You've got my full attention, Dippity-do. What's up besides your dander?"

"My dander is not up. I'm just not as thrilled as you about being a backup singer. I haven't even checked with Buddy about it."

"You don't check with Buddy about anything, or maybe I should say you never have before."

"That's not true and you know it. Buddy and I have one

hundred percent open communication. I run everything past him and then—"

"And then you go ahead and do whatever you want. Baby girl, who do you think you're talking to here?"

"Okay, okay. I'll be the first to admit I'm hardheaded, opinionated and an altogether pain in the ass, but I do discuss things with my husband, especially things that are going to put me in the public eye. Publicity doesn't help him in his job, you know. Especially since he got promoted to sergeant. I don't want to embarrass him."

"Come again? Who do you not want to embarrass?"

"Him."

"Who?"

"Okay, dammit, I don't want to embarrass myself, either. We didn't even ask what we'll be wearing, Ed. What if it's an itty-bitty, next-to-nothin' thing?"

"Well, first off, this is Darla Denman, not Lady Gaga. Personally, I'm more worried we'll be in Dale Evans costumes with cowboy hats and boots. That's what scares the shit out of *me*."

"Now that I would love. I'd feel right at home."

Edwina looked toward the clock above the payout desk. "We're running out of time." She combed her fingers through her flattened hair and picked at it with her fingertips. "My hair's dry now. Let me get my wig from the back. I'll throw it on and we'll just go over to Hogg's and ask Darla. Hell, they aren't going anywhere for a while and Maudeen won't be in for half an hour—"

"Maudeen canceled," Debbie Sue said.

A worry crease furrowed Edwina's brow. Maudeen Wiley was their favorite octogenarian. Her advanced age and declining health were cause for concern. She lived at Salt Lick's only retirement residence. "Is something wrong with her?"

"Don't worry. She's all right," Debbie Sue answered. "She's hungover is all. She bought a beer-making kit off the Internet and whatever she concocted didn't agree with her. In fact, it made a bunch of those old ladies at the retirement home sick."

"Sweet Jesus," Edwina said. "How'd I miss hearing about that? All I can say is please let me go out like Maudeen. She's the only person I ever met who really understands we only go around once."

"I know. We can agree on that much."

"Well, then what's your problem with the telethon, girlfriend? You've got a chance to strut on stage and definitely have something to someday tell your kids about and you're pulling up on the reins. I don't see a single reason for hesitation. I say bring it on and let's do it."

"Hell, you're probably right, Ed. God, I'm glad you're around to set me straight every now and then." Debbie Sue picked up a tube of lipstick and leaned nearer the mirror. "Go shake the dust off that damned old wig and let's get over to Hogg's before Darla changes her mind."

Edwina pumped a fist. "Yes!" She disappeared into the storeroom.

As Debbie Sue swiped on a fresh coat of lipstick, a video of mishaps she and Edwina had found themselves in played in her mind. "But being on the telethon is harmless," she mumbled to the image in the mirror. "We'll stand there, mouth the words and move a little. What could go wrong?"

As encouraging as those words sounded, a part of Debbie Sue's psyche shuddered.

Fifteen minutes and a full makeup application later, Debbie

Sue and Edwina stepped out of the salon, locked the door and headed for Hogg's. Looking in Edwina's direction, Debbie Sue studied her. "I don't know why you don't wear that wig more often."

Edwina touched the ends of the spikey, coal-black synthetic hair. "You don't think it's a little over the top?"

"That's exactly what I think, but it's you. It works."

"Good. That's what I was going for when I bought it. Maybe I will wear it more often. I've got lots of wigs, you know. You should see the ones I keep at home for Vic."

"For Vic?"

"Well, you know, *I* wear them, but they're *for* Vic. It spices things up in the bedroom, you know? I swear, one evening he put one on and . . ."

As Edwina's voice trailed off, an image formed in Debbie Sue's mind. Vic was six-feet-five, weighed close to three hundred and was bald as an egg. Visualizing him wearing Edwina's black wig made Debbie Sue chuckle.

At Hogg's entrance, before opening the door, Debbie Sue drew a deep breath and looked across her shoulder at her friend and partner. "Here we go, partner. Off on another crazy adventure. In a way, I feel silly for being reluctant. These are professional people who know what they're doing, right? What's the worst that could happen?"

Pulling open the door and stepping inside, Debbie Sue halted mid-step. "Whoa!"

Standing on a chair, slightly off balance on her high heels, Darla Denman, former Queen of Country Music, fired a saltshaker at the head of a younger blond woman who was shielding herself with a laminated menu. An arsenal of the café's tabletop articles—a napkin holder, a plastic squeeze bottle of ketchup and one of mustard—was stuffed under one of Darla's arms.

Debbie Sue's eyes darted everywhere, making a quick perusal of the scene. Hogg's small dining area was in disarray—two chairs overturned, the floor littered with items that usually sat on tables.

The wide order and pickup window between the dining area and kitchen was shut off by its metal shade rolled down. Apparently the cooks had closed it in self-defense. Julie Rogers, the teenager who worked as order taker and cashier, was nowhere to be seen.

"Holy shit," Edwina mumbled, halting beside Debbie Sue. "Where's Julie?"

"Good God," Debbie Sue replied. "She must be hiding out in the kitchen with the cooks."

A tall, good-looking man was ducking and dodging, attempting to referee and at the same time, trying to shield the younger woman. Just then a plastic mustard bottle bounced off his forehead.

"Ouch!" He straightened and slapped his palm against his forehead. "Dammit, Darla, you hit me!"

Still frozen in place, Edwina winced. "Oh, shit."

Darla climbed down from the chair, looking genuinely contrite. She placed a napkin holder and a ketchup bottle on the table. "Oh, Bob, I'm so sorry." She reached up and touched a goose egg that had popped up on his forehead. "You've got a knot. Let me get some ice for that."

Edwina leaned toward Debbie Sue and whispered, "That's her ex-husband and manager, Big Bob Denman. The good-looking blonde's his child bride."

"How do you know?"

"'Cuz I read it in the *National Enquirer* and saw their pictures."

The battling trio turned its attention on Debbie Sue and Edwina.

"Gosh, did we come in at a bad time?" Edwina gushed.

"No, no, not at all," Darla answered with too much enthusiasm. "We're just having some fun, aren't we, Bob?"

Debbie Sue noted that the child bride had not lowered her shield.

"Yes, that's right. Please pardon us." Bob scooped a handful of crushed ice from a drinking cup and plastered it against his forehead. "We were just, uh . . . we were just negotiating a new agreement. Yep, just run-of-the-mill contract negotiations."

"Holy cow," Edwina said. "I'm not sure there was this much negotiation during the last L.A. riot."

"I'm just blowing off steam," Darla said, laughing too loudly. "Isn't that right, Bob? . . . Roxie? . . . Just blowing off steam. An artistic difference is all it is."

"Call the cops!" Roxie cried to Debbie Sue and Edwina and pointing at Darla. "This woman's insane! I want to press charges!"

"No! No cops!" Bob's voice boomed loud enough to rattle the window panes. "It'll be over my dead body, or yours, before that happens."

"Bastard!" The younger woman plopped onto a booth seat beside an even younger blond woman, grabbed a purse and began digging inside it. The other blonde petted her and stroked her hair.

Debbie Sue could hear frantic but undecipherable voices speaking in both English and Spanish from the shuttered kitchen. She knew Hogg's kitchen help was Hispanic. She only hoped the English-speaking voice belonged to Julie Rogers.

Darla walked over, took Debbie Sue and Edwina by the arm and urged them toward her ex-husband/manager. "Bob, these are the two women I was telling you about. They're going to help us out onstage." She gave a breathless little laugh. "That is, if we haven't scared them off with our little family feud."

Bob dumped his handful of ice back into a cup, grabbed several paper napkins from a holder and dabbed at his forehead.

"Hmm," Edwina said, looking closer at his swollen forehead. "Good aim. Good thing she only hit you with a mustard bottle."

"Call the cops, Bob," Roxie said from the booth. Near tears, she dabbed at her eyes. "Besides being old, that bitch is nuts. Be a man. You're my husband. You're supposed to take care of me."

Ignoring his wife, Bob extended his right hand to Debbie Sue. "I'm so glad to meet you." He gestured toward the corner booth where two of the men Debbie Sue had seen go into Hogg's with Darla's group earlier cowered. One of them needed a shave and wore big black sunglasses and the other had longer hair than most of the Styling Station's customers. It was mouse gray and he wore it in a two-foot-long pony tail.

"This is Mike, our drummer," Bob said, "and Eddie, our guitarist and keyboard man." He moved his hand toward the two blond women. "And my wife and her makeup artist."

The two men, still cowering, gave slight nods.

"I can't thank you enough for what you're doing for us," Bob said. He turned toward the two men in the booth again. "We're grateful, aren't we, guys?"

The two men straightened slightly and nodded again.

"We're in a real bind here," Bob went on. "But don't worry. I'll reimburse you for your trouble as soon as we return to Nashville."

"Uh, that's okay," Debbie Sue said, peeking past his shoulder at the child bride, who was throwing objects back into her purse. "We're happy to help. We didn't mean to intrude. We only came over to get more details about the show. You know, the rehearsal times, the costumes. We will be wearing costumes, won't we?"

"Well, not exactly," Darla said quickly. "We had asked the young ladies who left earlier to wear simple black dresses and red high heels. Those are my signature colors, red and black." Her gaze swerved from Debbie Sue to Edwina and back. "You've got a plain black dress and red heels, don't you?"

"Oh, hell, yes," Edwina said. "I've got a killer black dress. Debbie Sue, you can wear the one you bought for the governor's ball when you went to Austin with Buddy that time."

"But do I have to wear the heels?"

"Well . . . yes," Darla said, looking to Bob for support.

"What she means is," Bob said, "what you wear should be similar in color and style. Preferably black and red."

"Right," Darla added. "It'll just look better if you match. And if you match me."

"Listen, I've got a pair of red Jimmy Choos I bought in New York City," Edwina said. "Those babies will steal the show. I hardly ever get to wear them in Salt Lick." Her mouth spread into a huge grin and she rapidly clapped her palms. "Oh, this is so exciting!"

"How about you, Debbie Sue?" Bob asked. "Are the high heels a deal breaker?"

"No, no. Believe it or not, I've actually got some red high heels. I'll wear them. But there's just one thing."

"What's that?" Bob and Darla chorused.

"I pretty much live in my Tony Lama boots. I've never been very good in high heels."

"Oh, a little wobbling won't be noticeable," Darla said with a little too much reassurance. "You won't be doing much walking."

"It's not the wobbling that worries me. It's the falling on my face I'm nervous about."

Now the child bride was on her feet and standing beside Bob, staring at Debbie Sue and Edwina. "This show is a friggin' joke." Her glare swerved to Darla. "This is just perfect, Darla. Only you could find us a punked-out old scarecrow and a nervous Nellie who can only *stand* in high heels and might fall on her ass if she has to take a step. It'll go down—"

"Roxie! Shut up," Darla said.

At a loss for words, Debbie Sue gasped.

"Rox, you should apologize to these—"

"Punked-out old scarecrow!" Edwina shouted.

Splat!

A glob of ketchup landed between Roxie's eyes.

"*Aargh!*"

Everyone turned and stared drop-jawed at the source of the ketchup.

Only Debbie Sue wasn't surprised. She had known trouble was coming the minute she heard Roxie utter those words, *punked-out old scarecrow.* Hell. Hadn't Edwina started a riot in a New York City hotel for less cause?

Roxie stood in place, hopping from one foot to the other as if she were jumping rope. "Oh, my God! Oh, my God! Look what she did! Bob! Look what she did!"

Debbie Sue saw Edwina, her teeth clamped down on her

lower lip, shaking the ketchup bottle with both hands and readying another squirt. She leaped to Edwina's side to grab the bottle, but before she could, Edwina squeezed off another blast of ketchup with perfect aim.

Splat!

Debbie Sue snatched the ketchup bottle away before Edwina could do more damage.

Now the child bride was bawling and cussing and swiping ketchup from her eyes. Bob picked up a metal napkin holder from the floor, yanked out a handful of napkins and rushed to his wife's side.

"Will you just get us out of here!" Roxie screeched. "They're all insane!"

Bob looped an arm around her shoulder and offered her the napkins.

"Rox, I'm sorry. Rox—"

"Oh, get the fuck away from me!" Roxie batted away the napkins and shrugged off his arm. "You impotent fool."

The quiet blond makeup artist had come to her feet. She began to soothe Roxie, dabbing at the ketchup on her chin with paper napkins.

Bob looked bewildered, his gaze swerving from Roxie to Darla and back to Debbie Sue and Edwina. "Er . . . uh . . . now, now, ladies . . . ladies, please." He patted the air with his palms. "Let all calm down. Before this gets out of hand."

"Yeah, Bob, don't let anything get out of hand," Roxie yelled, bent at the waist, her hands fisted, her face contorted into a red mask of rage. "You get everything calmed down! Kiss everyone's ass! That's all you're good for!" She grabbed her purse and stamped toward the restroom, still wiping away ketchup, her high heels clicking on the tile floor. The no-name blond woman followed her.

Debbie Sue's insides were shaking. She set the plastic ketchup bottle on a nearby table with a thud. "I think I'd better check on the kitchen help." She quickstepped to the kitchen's doorway, eased the door open and stuck her head through the crack. The three people inside began talking all at once, but she calmed them and assured them it was safe to reopen the metal sliding shade.

She returned to the dining room just in time to hear Edwina say, "God, I'm sorry, Bob, Darla. I don't know what came over me. Rude behavior just does something to me. I've been trying to learn to control myself, but I don't react well to insults. I don't like it when some asshole insults my friend, either."

"Ed, Ed, it's okay," Debbie Sue said, grasping her arm. "Let's just get back to the shop. No real harm done, right Bob?"

The last thing Debbie Sue wanted was for the Salt Lick grapevine to report that she and Edwina had been involved in a brawl in Hogg's. Buddy would have a cow. Debbie Sue began wiping ketchup off her own hands with a napkin as Edwina explained to Bob that the truck on loan was parked behind the beauty salon.

"Right," Bob and Darla chorused, and Bob thanked her again.

Bob's repeated gratitude rang with enough sincerity that Debbie Sue felt her own anger abating. Now, all the wanted to do was escape. "Listen, Bob," she said hurriedly, "the house is one block east of Main Street on Scenic View. It's 210 Scenic View. Small white frame house on the corner. Red awnings on the front windows. You can't miss it. The key's under a pot of geraniums on the porch. Y'all make yourselves at home. The only thing that isn't working is the phone."

Bob raised his cell phone. "That's okay. We've all got these."

"Ah, yes," Edwina put in. "How did we all get along before we all had cell phones?"

"It's been a long day," Bob said with a phony chuckle. He touched his forehead. "We should all land somewhere and get settled."

"Right," Debbie Sue said. "We've got a no-appointment-needed policy at the shop. We'll catch hell if someone shows up and we're not there."

Bob again put out his right hand to Debbie Sue and she again took it. "Thanks," he said. "All this commotion doesn't change anything. I'll see you two bright and early at rehearsals."

"We'll be there with bells on," Edwina said.

"Sounds good. Seven A.M. at Midland Civic Center. Any problems getting there?"

"Nah. We know where it is." Debbie Sue took Edwina's arm.

Bob stepped forward and opened the door for them. "Once again. I—"

"Please, there's no need to thank us," Debbie Sue said, absently returning the hug that Darla offered. "Everyone finds himself in a bind from time to time. What kind of people would we be if we didn't help those in need?"

She and Edwina left the café and hotfooted it across the parking lot. Debbie Sue was still rattled. "Fuck! What a mess. My God, Edwina. I can't believe you did that."

"Punked-out old scarecrow," Edwina grumbled. "Screw her and the horse she rode in on. I wish I'd slapped her."

"I'm sure a blob of ketchup in the face equals a slap," Debbie Sue said.

"That was worse than one of my family reunions."

Debbie Sue had never attended one of Edwina's family reunions, but she had heard plenty of stories.

"God, Ed, what have we got ourselves into?"

"Nothing. It's no big deal. We're just gonna stand onstage for a few minutes and pretend we're singing, then it's over. Fini. Done."

"But still—"

"Don't get your panties in a wad," Edwina said. "We don't have to worry about them and their problems. We didn't take them to raise, you know."

"I'm not so sure of that. Hell, they're driving Vic's pickup and sleeping in my house. I just hope they don't wreck either one. Do you suppose they fight like that all the time?"

"If they do, it's a wonder somebody hasn't killed somebody."

Debbie Sue shook her head. "God, what have we got ourselves into?"

They soon reached the Styling Station. "The day's over and I'm too shook up to work anyway. We might as well clean up, wipe up the shampoo room, and go home. I've got to figure out how to tell Buddy about this backup singer deal. And that I've lent them our house rent free."

Leaving the ladies' room, Roxie had had it. Ketchup in the face, then having to wash it off with public restroom soap and paper towels that felt like corn husks, was the last straw. She picked up her purse.

"Where you going, Rox?" her fool of a husband said.

"For a walk. I'm losing my mind. If you need me I'll be

headed north. You can't miss me. There's nothing to block the view." She stormed out of the diner, cussing and mumbling.

Ten feet from the café she fished her cell phone out and keyed in a number, pressed it to her ear and listened to the ring, cussing the notion that her call might go to voice mail. Suddenly a man's voice broke the irritating ringing sound: "Hey, what's up? Where are you?"

"Where in the hell do you think I am? I can't even have a conversation in private. I have to make up a lame excuse like going for a walk to have a moment's peace and privacy with you. I don't think I can stand much more of this."

"But you have to. . . . We both agreed—"

"You don't have to remind me of our agreement," she said on a sigh of exasperation. "I'm all too aware of what I agreed to. I'm just so fed up with this whole charade."

The voice laughed softly and she pressed the phone tighter to her ear. "Think of this as just another stage in your career," the voice said. "One that will pay off in dividends far exceeding what you could ever imagine. I'm going to see to it."

"I know, but . . ."

"Babe, I've seen six-figure contracts given to people who didn't have half the talent you do. Some got it for their looks alone. Their voices were secondary. Sound engineers in the studio can fix the vocals. But you've got the pipes *and* the looks. You could be the next Nashville millionaire. Can you see yourself living in the suburbs of Belle Mead?"

"I'd rather live downtown," she replied, brushing hair from her eyes. "I need stimulation you can't get in the suburbs."

"I know the kind of stimulation you need," the voice said, growing deep and husky.

"I know you do," Roxie purred, "and that's another area you've neglected of late."

"I promise to make it all up to you soon as you get back."

"You'd better," she snapped. "Because if I have the looks and talent like you said, there'll be someone besides you who'll take notice. And don't think for a minute I won't move on another offer if you don't come through."

Roxie snapped the phone shut and tossed her long hair over her shoulder. She had stood in the wings for as long as she intended to. Her time was coming and she would *arrive.*

The window of opportunity was open for only a short time and she had no problem slamming it shut on fingers that tried to stop her. If the dude in Nashville with all of his big-shot claims couldn't do it for her, someone else could. She didn't care how many bodies she had to walk over to get there. She was tough enough, talented enough and good-looking enough to get what she wanted.

Belle Meade. Bull shit. She was going for the world.

chapter six

As the day waned, Debbie Sue and Edwina finished their chores at the Styling Station. They had been cleaning and mopping and straightening in silence, as if each of them had found her purpose in life and was going for it. Debbie Sue was worried. She couldn't believe she had allowed crazy people the use of her and Buddy's little house rent free. Or at all. "I was just thinking," she said to Edwina. "With Koweba Sanders living right across the street from our little house, I could call her and ask her to keep an eye on things."

"Why? Koweba's blind and deaf. If that whole bunch stripped naked and had a brawl in the front yard, she most likely wouldn't see them. And if they fired up a band with electric guitars she couldn't hear them."

"But I think I'll call her anyway." Debbie Sue set her broom aside and made the call. Of course Koweba was happy to help out a former neighbor. She even mentioned that she might have a frozen casserole she could deliver to the temporary occupants.

After Debbie Sue hung up and picked up her broom again, Edwina said, "I was just thinking too. Wanna know what?"

"Tell me, Old School. What's on your mind?"

"I'm thinking Darla and Bob have still got the hots for each other. That's one reason why there's so much friction in that bunch. Lord, you could cut the tension with a knife. Their marriage was cut short by her fame and it wouldn't take a helluva lot to get them back in the sack again."

Debbie Sue stopped sweeping, grabbed Edwina's elbow and turned her to face her. "Jeez Louise, Ed. Don't you ever get tired of matchmaking? Bob is a married man. You dare interfere with that and the next time you have an encounter with that little banty-rooster bitch of a wife of his, she might claw your eyes out before you can get to a ketchup bottle. Then *I'll* have to whip her ass." As the thought jelled in Debbie Sue's mind, a devilish grin played at her lips. "Second thought, I might like a good excuse to teach her some manners."

"My eyes and I both thank you," Edwina said. "But I'm serious, Dippity-do. Darla and Bob even look like they belong together. They're probably too stubborn to admit it to themselves and certainly not to each other."

"I know a little about that," Debbie Sue said wistfully. "When I think of the five years of pure-dee, hardheaded pride that kept Buddy and me apart I could cry. Thank God I didn't go off with Quint. Where would I be today if I had?"

Edwina let out a cackle. "I can tell you *exactly* where you'd be and it isn't better off."

Edwina couldn't be more right and Debbie Sue had no trouble giving her kudos for that. Leaving Salt Lick to work for her old boyfriend, Quint Matthews, would have been a disaster, even if he was sexier than all get-out. Unfortunately, he was as ornery as a sack of mad cats. "It would be fun to fix Roxie up with Quint. That might be the worse thing we could do to her."

"Or him."

"I think that does it with the cleaning. Let's just call it a day and go on home."

"Good idea," Edwina said. "I'm ready."

Before trekking to the storeroom to put away the broom, Debbie Sue dug in her pocket, pulled out her set of keys and offered them to Edwina. "Here, go start my pickup and turn the air conditioner on high. I'll lock up and be right behind you. You want to ride to Midland with me tomorrow morning? No point in us taking two rigs."

"You bet. Wish Vic was going to be here for this. We should ask the TV station if they can provide us a tape so he can see it. He'd get a kick out of the whole thing."

"I'm sure he would," Debbie Sue agreed, "but I'm a long way from being sure about Buddy Overstreet's reaction."

"Are you gonna tell him about what happened in Hogg's?"

"I probably should. Hell, he'll hear it eventually."

"He might not. Nobody knows about it but us and the cooks and Julie Rogers."

"You think Julie won't tell her folks and everyone else she knows? Shit. A free-for-all in Hogg's is probably the most exciting thing that's happened in Salt Lick this month."

Edwina giggled wickedly. "Well, it's only the second day of the month."

"Are you going to tell Vic?"

"Oh, hell, yes. He'll think it's funny, but he's not as tight-assed as Buddy."

"I'll think about it," Debbie Sue said. "First things first. I'm going to tell him about the telethon first and see how that goes down."

As soon as Edwina was out the door, Debbie Sue walked to the front door, thinking of the acrimonious altercation she and Edwina had walked in on in Hogg's. Those people hadn't been kidding; they didn't like each other.

As she pushed the lock and pulled down the shade, she wished she could ignore the nagging feeling that something wasn't right. Buddy teased her about her hunches, calling them more a matter of luck than extrasensory. But she was a true believer in female intuition and something about this whole situation wasn't right. It went beyond her stage fright, beyond anything she could put her finger on.

Oh, well, she accepted in her mind. She had made a commitment, bought a ticket for the ride, so to speak. She might as well sit back and enjoy it.

After Roxie stormed out of the café, Bob had gone looking for her. He found her in the parking lot, just as she was putting away her cell phone. "What do you want?" she said quickly, a deer-in-the-headlights look in her eyes.

Guilt, was his first thought. "Are you okay?" he asked.

"Of course I'm okay. A bunch of rubes in some hick town don't affect me. They are dirt under my feet."

"I meant the ketchup," Bob said.

"Hah. I'll tell you this. That scrawny old sow just better not let me catch her alone on a dark night."

Bob sighed. "Okay, Roxie, I get it. I'm going to walk over

to the beauty shop and pick up our ride. I'll be right back. Tell the others."

The beauty shop was dark when he arrived, so he climbed into the only pickup parked behind it. He drove the black behemoth back to the café to pick up everyone. Before all of them had a chance to even get organized, Roxie claimed the shotgun seat. Darla, along with Eddie, Mike and Valetta Rose, scooted into the backseat, and they set out for 210 Scenic View.

The group was quiet. Even Roxie was subdued. It was possible that the altercation in the café had quelled her meanness, but Bob doubted the change was permanent. A rattlesnake with no venom was only a temporary situation. The poison always came back. Nature was like that. And to his great dismay, he had learned the hard way that Roxie was like that, too.

"Them's good people," Eddie said of the two women who had become not only their backup singers, but also their temporary benefactors. "Salt o' the earth. It's hard to find people that'll give you the shirt off their back, more or less."

Typical country people, Bob thought. He knew Darla had grown up among them, knew she loved them to their bones. They had made her singing career what it had once been. He hadn't grown up in a rural area himself, but he knew many in country music who had.

"I hope we can repay them one day," Darla said from the backseat.

"That'll be my number-one priority when we get back to Nashville," Bob replied, catching her gaze in the rearview mirror. "I plan on sending both of those ladies payment for the use of this truck and the lodging. I know they said they don't expect it, but I'm doing it all the same."

"Good," Darla said.

"Oh, Jesus Christ," Roxie snapped. "How can you be so damn dumb? If you think they did it without expecting something in return you'd better think again. *Anyone* who makes an offer like this expects something in return and they got it. My God, Darla promised them a fuckin' part in her great comeback show."

A few beats of silence passed while Bob wondered how long Darla would be able to control her temper. He didn't have long to wonder.

"Who in the hell raised you, Roxie?" she said. "You act like you've had to scratch and scrape for everything you've got."

A tight knot formed in Bob's stomach. To his relief, Darla refrained from calling his wife profane names.

"You damned sure didn't get *here* by scratching and scraping," she went on. "You got here by—"

"Darla—" Bob stopped her. He didn't want to hear her say, *You got here by screwing Bob Denman.*

"I know your past, little girl," Darla said. "You might've hoed a tough row, but it wasn't any harder than what the rest of us had to do. Lord, when I was little, we didn't even have running water."

"I grew up that way too," Eddie said. "My mama raised six kids and hauled buckets of water out of the creek every day to do the cooking and the washing. If I hadn't been able to pick a little guitar and play the piano, I guess I'd still be living like that. Or working in a coal mine."

Bob knew some of Eddie's history as well as his ability and reputation as a musician. Indeed he had come from an impoverished coal-mining family, but he could pick more than a *little* guitar and was unequaled on the keyboard. Bob saw him as an inspiring, self-taught musical phenomenon.

Just then, the white frame house they would be calling home for a couple of days came into view. Bob was sure it was the right one. By following Debbie Sue's directions, he had been able to drive straight to it. "I still can't believe anyone would be this generous," he said, slowing and steering into the driveway. He shoved the gear shift into park. Eddie and Mike and Valetta Rose scrambled out of the backseat as if they couldn't wait to escape the company inside the truck.

"Assuming this country villa has running water," Roxie said, pulling on the door latch, "*I* am going inside where *I* am going to take a shower and wash the fuckin' ketchup out of my hair. Then I'm going straight to bed."

"Fine," Bob said.

She leveled a drop-dead look at him. "I've got a headache and I do not want to be disturbed."

He restrained himself from saying, *Don't worry.* He saw no point in making the situation worse.

She slid out and slammed the door so hard the glass rattled.

Mike and Eddie had found the door key under the flowerpot on the porch and unlocked the front door. Roxie pushed past them, causing Eddie to have to step off the porch. Without so much as an "excuse me," she disappeared into the house. Valetta Rose followed her, then Mike and Eddie.

In the silence left behind, Darla looked at him in the rear-view mirror. "I'm sorry, Bob," she said softly. "Looks like I ruined any plans you might have had for tonight with the little woman."

If only she knew, his plans of a sexual nature with Roxie had been ruined many months back. They might have been married only a couple of years, but it felt like a hundred.

"Honestly, Bob, I'd love to get along with her. But everything she says ruffles my feathers. On top of that she's flitting around like some damn diva. I'm trying to understand what you see in her, but I just don't get it."

His memory spun backward, to when Darla had been one of the hottest young talents in Nashville. She had been a diva herself. And she had mesmerized him. "You don't? Good Lord, Darla, she's so much like you were when you were . . . uh—"

"When I was younger? Go ahead and say it. I know I was stubborn and ambitious. But Bob, I was never mean."

"I know, I know. Look, I'm not asking that the two of you be best friends. Just try to peaceably share a little space on this ol' planet for a short time is all I ask. I'll tell you like I've already told her. You've got to learn to live together for the next few days. She's my wife, Darla. And as your manager and friend, I'm asking you to show her some respect. Can't you do that for me? . . . For just a little while?"

He knew he was asking a lot.

From the backseat, Darla held her ex-husband's gaze in the rearview mirror for long seconds. How could she refuse to make the effort? She knew there wasn't an unchivalrous bone in Bob Denman's body. When they were married, he had always come to her defense, just as he was doing now for Roxie. He had been unwavering in his support of her career, just as he now supported Roxie's.

Beyond that, when they were married, as far as Darla knew, he had never failed to honor their wedding vows. She only wished she could say the same. A great surge of sentimentality rose from somewhere. She was torn between what she wanted, what she expected and what he expected of her. She looked down and studied her hand as she rubbed one finger of her left against the lacquered talon nail on the right, fearing that if she looked directly at him again she would do or say something very foolish. And today had already been full of enough foolishness. *Hell.* She had thought age brought wisdom. All it had brought her was conflict and indecision, both of which she could live without.

"So how about it?" he said, and she glanced up. He was still looking at her through the rearview mirror. "Can we agree?"

He was waiting for her answer, but she hesitated. Finally, with a flip of her hand, she said, "Yes, yes. Of course, I agree. Let's go inside. It's hotter 'n hell sitting out here. What's left of my spackling, otherwise known as makeup, is starting to melt." She opened the door and slid to the ground, hanging onto the edge of the door to keep from twisting her ankle. *Damn these spike heels.*

She rounded the back of the pickup and almost ran into Bob, who was waiting for her on the other side. Together they started for the front door. "This looks like a cute little place," she said. "Let's hope it has a good air conditioner."

She had tried to make that comment sound upbeat, but all she could think about was that she and her ex-husband were walking into a house that looked like the honeymoon home they had shared decades ago, a place that had been heaven on earth for them. She had blown that, and at this moment, that fact hurt more than the thought of losing her career.

Bob walked ahead of her, stepped up on the porch, reached for the screen door and pulled it open for her. Darla stepped up onto the porch too, to his level. "This reminds me of our first house after we married." She laughed softly and looked into his face. "Remember when we moved in? When we sat the sofa down and it fell through the floor?"

Bob smiled down at her. "I was just thinking of that very

thing. When we called the landlord, he blamed us for buying furniture that was too heavy."

Darla laughed as the memory came to her. "That's right. He did. I forgot that part."

Now Bob chuckled, a look in his eyes she hadn't seen in a long, long time. "As I recall, we stayed in bed for an entire week, afraid to get out."

Darla laughed more. "And when we did, we walked around tiptoeing so we didn't end up like that sofa."

"Man, I haven't thought of that in years," he said.

Darla's laugh faded to a weak smile. What the hell was she laughing about? That remark was like a spike driven into her heart. She didn't know what pained the most—the memory of that week in bed that was gone forever or the fact that he hadn't thought of it in years. She brushed past him abruptly and entered the cottage.

They found everyone except Roxie in the small kitchen. Bob came up behind her and looked around. "Hey, not bad," he said. "I think we'll all get along just fine here." This would be the first time they had all slept in one place.

"I ain't so sure about that," Eddie mumbled.

Bob, Mike and Eddie went outside to bring back everyone's suitcases and duffels.

"Well," Darla said to Valetta Rose. "Come on, let's see what we've got here." She walked up the hallway. One door was closed, so Darla assumed that was a bedroom that had already been claimed by Roxie. She peeked inside another bedroom, saw a neat, clean room with a sofa that probably made into a bed. The third room was a small bedroom with a double bed. A bathroom was located between the two bedrooms and she peeked inside that, too. Valetta Rose walked with her. Just then, Roxie opened her bedroom door, strode from behind them and passed them as if they weren't there.

"Small place," Darla said to Valetta Rose. "Looks like it's you and me sharing a room."

"That's okay, Miz Denman," the girl said shyly. "But you don't have to. I don't mind sleeping on the couch . . . or wherever. Or I can sleep on the floor or with the guys. It doesn't matter."

Darla gave Valetta Rose a look, wondering what the strange girl's life in Nashville might have been like and observing that she looked young enough to be her granddaughter. Just then, to her relief, voices from the kitchen distracted her. "Well, looks like they're back. Let's go back in there and see what's going on."

They entered the kitchen again to see Roxie rummaging through the empty cupboards and grousing. "Wish to hell Dale Evans had left some food behind. If she's going to give us a house, she ought to feed us too."

"Oh, shut up, Roxie," Mike said. "Stop being such a pain in everybody's ass. We're damn lucky Darla found them and made friends with them or we wouldn't even have a place to sleep."

"Eat shit, Mike. You too, Eddie."

"What the hell did I do?" Eddie said. "Keep your fuckin' hateful mouth to youself, little lady. Or you might find yourself without a keyboard for your big debut."

Roxie turned around and gave him the finger. "That's what I think of you and your keyboard, you old doper."

Just then Bob walked in rolling a huge suitcase. "Roxie! Can't I leave you alone for a minute? Can't you get along with anyone?"

"I thought you were going to take a shower and go to bed," Darla said.

"I would have, but my wonderful husband just now got around to bringing me my suitcase." She walked over and snatched the handle from him. "You know, Bobby Boy, you'd better be careful. I just might not favor you with a tip, if you know what I mean." She gave him an evil smile. "Those BJs don't come cheap."

"Rox—"

"Jesus Christ, Roxie," Mike said before Bob could get his wife's name out. Darla threw a look Bob's way. His face had turned a color she had never seen.

"There's just no end to it with you, is there?" Mike said to Roxie. "We'd all be better off if you weren't even on this tour. We wouldn't even miss you." He turned to Darla. "Which bedroom are you and Valetta Rose taking?"

"Uh, the first one," Darla answered. "I assume Bob and Roxie will take the master bedroom."

"Which is nothing but a stupid joke," Roxie said. "That bathroom doesn't even have a walk-in shower."

Eddie picked up his canvas duffel. "Come on, Mike, let's put our stuff at the end of the sofa in that other room. We ought to get out of this kitchen in case a big-ass lightning bolt decides to come down and give that bitch what she deserves."

"I hear you," Mike said and picked up his own suitcase.

"I need to go outside for a smoke," Eddie added.

The two of them walked out of the kitchen.

"Good riddance," Roxie said, and left the kitchen dragging her suitcase.

Darla heaved a sigh and looked at Bob.

"Don't say anything," he said to her, then turned to Valetta Rose. "Honey, if you want to share the bedroom with Roxie, I'll sleep on the sofa. There's a king-size bed in the master. The two of you should be comfortable."

"Are you sure?" Valetta Rose asked.

"Never been more sure of anything in my life," Bob answered.

Darla gave him another long look as a thousand questions swirled like smoke in her mind.

chapter seven

The drive from downtown Salt Lick to Edwina's double-wide was short, but it seemed like it had lasted forever. Debbie Sue usually enjoyed Edwina's company, but this evening the skinny brunette was talking like a magpie and hadn't stopped for a breath once. When she got out of the pickup, Debbie Sue let out a whoosh of air.

The drive to her own home, on the other hand, was silent. She didn't even turn on the radio, which usually blared out a tune as she drove. Sometimes she sang along, but thinking about getting up on that stage had left her mute. Singing with the radio was one thing, but anticipating a performance in front of a real audience was sobering, even if she and Edwina wouldn't really be singing.

She crossed the cattle guard at the entrance to her and Buddy's twenty-five acres and headed up the long driveway for home. In the distance, one of her loyal old friends grazed—her horse, Rocket Man. She tooted the horn and he raised his handsome head. She buzzed down the window and called out to him, "Hey, Rocket Man. How you doing today?" He answered with a toss of his head and a whinny.

She hoped Buddy would be at the house. He had been away two days on a case. She had gotten accustomed to his job pulling him away for days at a time, but she would never adjust to the loneliness she felt in his absence. As she drew nearer, she saw his car parked in the carport. Her spirits lifted.

She had no sooner parked her sexy red pickup beside his ugly white state SUV before he greeted her at the door with a big grin. "Hey, Flash." He was the only one who called her by the nickname her father had given her when she was a small girl, when circling three barrels on a fast horse had been the most important thing in her life. "Man, you're a sight for sore eyes," he said.

She rushed into the strong arms of the one individual who consistently provided love and security to her life. She didn't know how she had ever lived outside this comfort zone. The conversation with Edwina and Darla Denman crossed her mind and reminded her how his disapproval could threaten her well-being and she trembled.

"You okay, sugar? I just felt your whole body shake." He tightened his embrace. "I hate to say it, but it felt kind of good, if you know what I mean."

"I know exactly what you mean." Debbie Sue rose to her tiptoes and planted a long, lingering kiss on his lips. "How was your trip?" she asked when they parted.

"Typical."

"You caught the bad guys, huh?"

"Nope. But we gathered a lot of evidence."

"Did they do something really bad?"

"Murder."

Debbie Sue frowned. "Oh, shit. Really?"

"I don't want to talk about it."

She knew that. And she knew that even if he did want to, he couldn't and wouldn't. The crime he dealt with every day went beyond serious. "Let's go in the house," she said. "I've got something to tell you that you are flat-out not gonna believe."

They walked into the kitchen to an antique Formica dining table that sat on one end of the room. It had belonged to her mother and had sat in this spot in this kitchen for as long as Debbie Sue could remember. When her mother had remarried and moved to Nashville, she had sold the house, everything in it and the twenty-five acres it sat on to Debbie Sue and Buddy.

He eased his big frame into a chair, looking amused and perplexed at the same time. "You're making me nervous. Is something wrong? Is it my mom? Yours? Edwina? Did something happen to Ed?"

Instantly Debbie Sue decided definitely not to tell him tonight about the incident in Hogg's. Maybe she would *never* tell him. She leaned forward and took his hand. "Nothing is wrong with anyone. I got an offer today I want you to hear about."

"An offer?"

"Promise me you'll keep an open mind and give it some thought before we have a big argument."

Buddy's jaw flexed and he pulled his hand away. "This offer isn't from that no-good sonofabitch Quint Matthews, is it? Because I haven't forgotten the last time he made you an *offer.*"

"Don't say that. How many times do I have to tell you that Quint's no threat to you and me? Don't you know there's not a living, breathing human being who could take me from you?"

He seemed to relax and the pink color that had risen on his face faded. She took a deep breath and explained the day's events, omitting the ketchup fiasco in Hogg's, adding that she had offered the use of the house she and Buddy owned in town and not pausing long enough to let him get a word in. When she had finished the story she said, "So that's it. That's the whole thing. I told Ed you wouldn't go for it and I don't blame you. I'll call her and tell—"

"Wait a minute. Why would you think I wouldn't go for it? I think it's great. It's a good thing to help people out when they need it. And this singing thing is something you and Ed will always look back on as fun."

"Well, remember we're not really singing."

"Whatever. I gotta say, sugar, I'm relieved. After some of the hare-brained stuff you and Ed have gotten into, this is mild."

Hare-brained? Debbie Sue felt a frown tug at her brow. Buddy could be such a chauvinist sometimes. She tried to be annoyed over his trivializing the Domestic Equalizers' activities, but how could she when he had just said it was great that she had donated the free use of their house and it was great for her to be on stage with Darla Denman?

"Hare-brained?"

Ignoring her comment, he came around to her side of the table and squatted by her chair, bringing himself eye to eye with her. "I can't wait to see you onstage, Flash. When is it?"

"Sunday. We're supposed to go to Midland to rehearse tomorrow morning. It sure worries me that we'll have only one rehearsal."

Buddy's face took on a worried look. "Flash, I won't be here Sunday. I haven't had a chance to tell you, but I have to leave for Austin tomorrow morning for a refresher course in forensic mapping."

"But you just got home."

"I know, I know, but—"

"How long will that take, that mapping thing?"

"Couple of days. Maybe three."

"Aww, Buddy—"

"I know, I know. I just found out about it today or we could've planned for it better. But I'll watch every minute of the telethon when I get the chance. It'll give me something to brag about, you performing backup singing for Darla Denman."

Debbie Sue couldn't keep from grinning at the idea that he bragged on her. "Really, Buddy?"

"And something new to get teased about," he added with a chuckle. "I'm tired of being teased about being married to a private detective."

Debbie Sue felt her hackles rise. This was the way conversations always went with Buddy. First he would say something that would make her spirits soar, then he would follow with a reality statement that left her confused as to how he really felt. She was the first to admit she was touchy when it came to what she and Edwina did in their roles as the Domestic Equalizers. In her mind, they had been very successful. She didn't want to have to point that out, but she could not, would not, allow anyone, even Buddy, to make fun of the Domestic Equalizers.

"C'mon. Who teases you? And why do they think Ed and I are so damned funny?"

"Calm down now. They tease me because you and Ed have

solved as many mysteries as I have. It's no secret you do more than spy on cheating husbands and wives."

"I've never put Ed and me in the same league with the Texas Rangers, Buddy. Not once have I ever done that. And I wouldn't. Ed and I don't have to build a case that will stand up in court like the Rangers do. But if they think we're some kind of joke—"

"Flash," Buddy said, speaking softly, running his hand down her arm, "you know that's not true. Forget I said anything. I didn't mean to hurt your feelings. It's just guy stuff. We tease each other about lots of things."

"Like what? Tell me something else y'all tease each other about."

Debbie Sue could see he was deliberately thinking with a measure of difficulty. "Well . . . we tease Carlton Wilcox because his wife sells Mary Kay and drives one of those titty-pink Cadillacs."

Debbie Sue giggled.

"We tease John Davis because he and his wife met in the reception room of a marriage counselor's office while they were married to other people."

Debbie Sue laughed. "They didn't."

"They did. And next to us, they're probably the happiest couple around."

"A distant second to us?"

"Very distant. Not even in the same zip code."

They kissed and this time the kiss was hungry and more demanding. Buddy stopped abruptly. "Just promise me one thing. Promise me you won't get into any kind of trouble."

"Trouble?" Debbie Sue echoed with a show of wide-eyed innocence, while annoyance oozed from every pore. "What kind of trouble could we get into, standing on a stage and moving to music?"

"I don't know, Flash. And that's what bothers me the most. When it comes to you and Ed, I seem to *never* know."

Midnight. Debbie Sue lay by her husband's side staring into the darkness thinking about shoes. Those damned, ever-lovin', ankle-breaking, red high-heeled shoes, to be precise. They were stashed away in her closet awaiting the next time she would bring them out, which was usually for a wedding or a funeral. She was capable of getting to and from the church wearing them, but she would never risk anything as daring as dancing, or even swaying.

She had often marveled at women who could dance in high heels, turning and moving with catlike grace as if they were wearing flat shoes. Hell, even Edwina was a wonder to behold. That woman's gravity-defying heels and platforms would have put Debbie Sue Overstreet's face in the dirt before she knew what had happened.

Buddy's breathing sounded deep and rhythmic, which meant he was sleeping soundly. After they had properly celebrated his homecoming, he had gone right to sleep and hadn't moved since. She carefully folded the covers back from her body and eased from her warm cocoon. She tiptoed to the walk-in closet and opened the door, cringing as its old hinges whined. Stepping inside, she closed the door behind her, reached overhead and pulled the tassel attached to the beaded chain extending from the overhead light fixture. The sudden bright light made her shield her eyes for a moment, then she reached for the shoe box. She could have found it in the dark. Hell, she had only two boxes of shoes—the red high heels and a pair of black flats.

The rest of her footwear was an assortment of western boots. She and Buddy both spent most of their lives in boots.

She lifted the shoes from their box, slipped her feet into them and instantly became three inches taller. Confined to one spot, she swayed to and fro and tried to grind her hips, but the narrow closet was too restrictive. She clenched her jaw and eased the door open, praying the hinges' prolonged whine didn't wake Buddy. She stopped and listened, could still hear his relaxed breathing.

Hanging on to the wall for balance, she tiptoed to the bathroom. The bathroom not only gave her more room, it was dimly lit by a bright full moon. She could see her full naked image in the mirror that hung over the vanity. She picked up a hairbrush in the way she had done as a kid and brought it to her mouth, making it her microphone. She began grinding her hips, her gyrations growing bolder. Her ankles didn't buckle and the longer she danced the more confident she became. *Hot damn!* She was going to do this and she even began to believe she was going to enjoy it. Finishing her number, she held the microphone/hairbrush by her side and began to take bows in front of her imaginary audience. She was cut short by the clapping of a sole occupant attending her private show. Looking over her shoulder with dread, she saw Buddy's partially raised torso resting on one elbow.

"Encore," he said, laughing, and she could feel her face go beet red.

"Dammit, Buddy, that isn't funny. You should have told me you were awake."

"And miss the greatest show I've ever seen? I wasn't about to stop you. Besides, I'm not making fun, sweetheart. I'm just happy."

Debbie Sue stamped her foot. "No, you're not. You're laughing at me. I'm gonna sleep in the other room."

Buddy plumped her pillow and smoothed her place beside him. "Come back to bed, I've got some moves of my own I'll show you."

Debbie Sue grinned. "You're the devil." She bent to remove one of the red high heels.

"Hold on," Buddy said. "Who said anything about you taking off those shoes?"

chapter eight

The next morning, Debbie Sue sat in her pickup in front of Edwina's double-wide, drumming the steering wheel with her fingertips. Sometimes it seemed as though her life was just one long episode of waiting for Edwina. She checked the dash clock. 6:45 A.M. She had been up since five. She wanted to be sure they had time to get to Midland by eight o'clock. Buddy had left at six and Debbie Sue had followed immediately after feeding the three dogs and Rocket Man.

Releasing a sigh she shifted in her seat and pressed the horn. More than just a tap this time, in an attempt to send a nerves-on-edge, get-your-ass-out-here message.

Seconds later, Edwina emerged, carrying the ever-present oversize Styrofoam cup that was most assuredly filled with Dr Pepper. To navigate the few narrow steps that descended from her wooden deck, she had to turn her size-ten feet slightly outward. Most noticeable today was that Edwina wore a straw hat with a huge floppy brim that Debbie Sue had never seen before. This was a startling development, since Edwina never allowed *anything* to muss her beehive hairdo. Oversize sunglasses with dark lenses hid most of her face, preventing Debbie Sue's seeing her eyes and reading her current state of mind, but a jaunty walk gave her away. Yep, she was jazzed.

Opening the door, she threw her arms wide and proclaimed, "Good morning, Dew Drop! Isn't this a glorious day? Isn't this exciting?"

Debbie Sue giggled. She had to admit this performing thing was beginning to feel like fun, especially now that Buddy had shown some enthusiasm for it. "What's with the hat? I've never seen you willing to mess up your hair before. That thing has to date back to Woodstock. You trying to shield yourself from the paparazzi?"

Edwina climbed onto the passenger seat. "For your information, I was a mere infant when Woodstock happened."

"Just a wisecrack, Ed. Not a comment on your age." Debbie Sue yanked the Silverado into gear and pulled onto the road.

"You ain't gonna friggin' believe what I did," Edwina said.

"Yes, I will. I always believe what you do. I might not understand it, but I always believe it."

"I melted that damn wig."

"The black spikey one? The one I liked?"

"The very one. And I looked like a fox in it too."

"How in the hell did you melt—"

"Vic was in the shower and hollered out and asked me to check his casserole in the oven. He was packing a lunch for the road, you know. No sandwiches or fast food for him. Any-hoo, that's how my wig got roasted."

"You left a big part of this story out, Ed. How did checking his food—"

"Dammit, I guess I stuck my head too far inside the oven."

"Ed, you kill me. Why would you stick your head into a hot oven?"

"Well, du-uh. How else was I gonna see what was going on in there?"

"Why didn't you use a pot holder and pull the rack out?"

Edwina seemed to chew on that question for a few beats. "I guess I could've done that, but I don't know where Vic keeps those potholders these days. It's his kitchen, you know. I gave it to him a long time ago, when we got married. Nowadays, when I go in there, I'm just a visitor. My passport doesn't authorize the use of any appliance but the microwave."

"Oh, hell, Ed. There's only so many places you can put potholders in a kitchen."

Edwina made a little huff of indignation. "Like you'd know a lot about cooking and kitchens."

"Were you hurt? Is your scalp burned?"

"Naw, I'm fine. But that wig will never see light of day again, unless you need a reverse Mohawk next Halloween. Girlfriend, I tell you, there's a stripe about three inches wide down the middle of that thing, front to back, that's just plain bald."

Lord, a simple conversation with Edwina was entertaining. Debbie Sue laughed, imagining the destroyed wig. "So we're back to the beehive hairdo?"

"Well, not quite. Today, it's a hat. But I'll go back to the beehive later. My public demands that of me anyway."

"You're probably right, Ed. Why alter a classic?"

"Exactly. I ask you, would you inject the haunting lips of

the Mona Lisa with collagen or put prosthetic limbs on Venus de Milo?"

"So what're you gonna do if you have to take the hat off today?"

"Oh, hell, I'll just say the damn thing messed up my hair."

"Well, I'm just glad you weren't hurt. You have to take care of yourself, Ed. I need you."

"I do take care of myself, hon. I do." Ed reached across and patted Debbie Sue's forearm. "You don't think I want to miss out on any of this fun we're having, do you?"

They reached the Salt Lick city limits and turned northeast on the highway. "What did Vic say about us being on the telethon?"

"He hates to miss it. I knew he would. He didn't even mind that I lent them his pickup. Of course I didn't tell him that they're all crazy. Did you tell Wyatt about the ketchup fight?"

Edwina was referring to Buddy. Debbie Sue often affectionately called Buddy "Wyatt Earp," so in private, Edwina did, too.

"Of course not. I'm taking a chance he won't hear about it until it's so far behind us it won't matter."

"But you did tell him about the telethon."

"Yep. He was okay with it."

"I suppose you persuaded him in the usual fashion."

"How I persuaded him is none of your business, Edwina Perkins-Martin. Actually, he didn't need persuading. He thought it was a great idea. But he won't be able to come to Midland and watch us. He's got to be in Austin for some kind of damn class. So like you said yesterday, we need to get a tape." Debbie Sue pulled a silver disc from above her visor. "And speaking of the telethon, I found this in my pile of CDs.

Let's practice our vocals to *The Best of Darla Denman* while we ride to Midland."

"Oh, hell, yes! Slide that baby in."

The enticing aroma of frying bacon woke Darla from her slumber. Morning had come too quickly. She would have sworn she hadn't slept at all, but the fact was, the last thing she remembered was looking at the alarm clock on the bedside table, and it had registered one in the morning. Now it was seven, meaning she'd had at least six hours of sleep.

She saw no sign of Valetta Rose or that the girl had slept in the bed beside her overnight. Maybe she really did bed down on the floor in the guys' room. She pulled on the robe she had left at the foot of the bed and padded up the hall. In the kitchen she saw her drummer frying bacon in a large black skillet and with his free hand, beating out a rhythm with a spatula. She walked in, stretched and said hoarsely, "Mike, you look like you know your way around a kitchen."

Stopping to remove a device from his ear, which Darla assumed was some sort of music gadget, he smiled and presented her with a plate piled high with strips of crisp bacon. "Between gigs I work as a short order cook wherever anybody's hiring. I hate being broke."

"I know what you mean," Darla said sarcastically. "I can cook. That's an option for me to consider."

Taking a slice of bacon, she chewed slowly, savoring the taste. Still trying to lose a few pounds to get in shape for her great comeback, she didn't usually eat bacon. "Where did we get food? Was it in the fridge?"

He shook his head. "I had a few coins in my pocket. I had

Bob drop me off at the corner store before he left for Midland earlier. It's only three blocks away. I walked back."

Darla was touched that he would spend his own money on breakfast for all of them. She watched as he broke eggs into a bowl. "You know we'll reimburse you when we get back to Nashville, right?"

"I know."

She was suddenly keenly aware that she was in her nightshirt, alone with a man she scarcely knew. She cursed her decision to not dress before appearing in the kitchen. *Dammit, Bob, why would you leave me alone with a stranger?* "Bob's already gone, huh? Did Roxie and Eddie go with him?"

"Eddie went, but Roxie's still here. Bob said he was going to talk to the show manager." He poured the eggs he had stirred up into the skillet and began to scramble them. "They're going to set up the equipment and do a sound check."

Darla was comforted knowing another female was in the house. Not that she could depend on Roxie to come to her aid if she were in trouble. Roxie would be more apt to grab a camera and put a video on the Internet. Beyond that, Darla felt guilty for thinking evil thoughts about Mike. "Roxie's sleeping in?"

"Haven't heard a peep out of that pig."

"Mike, you shouldn't—"

"What, call her names? Don't worry. I'd never let Bob hear me. But she is what she is. She's left footprints across everybody's back, including mine. I'll get even with her one of these days though, when she doesn't see it coming. Want some coffee?"

Darla didn't disagree with Mike's conclusion about Bob's current wife, but hearing him threaten her made her uncomfortable. "Lord, yes. Coffee sounds great." She picked a mug from the mug tree that sat on the kitchen counter and extended it to Mike, who poured it full.

"What time did Bob say he'll come back for us?"

"By eight o'clock. They say it takes an hour to drive from here to Midland."

"Oh, then we'd better hurry." She scooped a helping of scrambled eggs on her plate, laid slices of bacon on each side and topped it off with a couple of slices of toast. "I'm hungry as a bear. Thanks again."

As she turned away, she had a vision of Bob's face the evening before when he had begged her to try to get along with his young wife. Contrary to what Roxie and the new band members might think of Darla Denman, she was actually a very nice person and making peace with Roxie wasn't beyond her. Sighing heavily, she set down her plate, plucked a second mug and extended it toward the cook. "Hit me with some more coffee. I'll take a cup to Roxie."

She carried the hot coffee across the living room, turned left at a narrow hallway and made her way to the door at the end of the hall. She rapped softly with her knuckle and waited for a response. She heard a giggle and a muffled voice. Opening the door slightly, she called, "Roxie? You up? I've got coffee if you want some."

She saw Roxie on her cell phone. The woman reacted to Darla's appearance as if she were a teenage girl caught whispering forbidden words to a secret boyfriend.

"Oops, sorry," Darla said. "I didn't know you were on the phone. I thought you'd like some—"

"Can't you see I'm busy?" Roxie snapped.

"I only wanted—"

"What do you want that would make you ignore a closed door? Why are you snooping around where you aren't welcome?"

Darla felt the small hairs at the nape of her neck stand up, her pulse quickened and her heart pounded. She supposed this reaction was part of the survival system built in by nature, whether you were in need of fleeing an attacking T. rex, escaping a fate at the hands of the Grim Reaper or slapping the shit out of a prima donna with no manners. She was gathering just the right words to yell when a soft-spoken male voice behind her stopped her.

"Let it go," Mike said. She turned and saw him standing in the entrance to the hallway. "Come on back to the kitchen and have breakfast before it gets cold."

His invitation was so unexpected, his delivery so calm it had a hypnotic effect on Darla. Pulling the bedroom door closed, she turned and looked at him, really looked at him for the first time since they left Nashville. He was actually quite handsome in a scruffy kind of way. He was much younger than she would have guessed earlier, had blondish hair, had to be over six feet tall and she could see from his muscular neck that his body was most likely firm and toned. And he had the bluest eyes. "Are you wearing contacts?" she asked him. "I've haven't seen eyes that blue since Paul Newman, God rest his soul. I've tried colored contacts but never found any that looked that good."

Mike laughed. "These baby blues are all mine." He took her by the arm and led her up the hallway, across the living room and to the dining area attached to the kitchen. He pulled back a chair and she dutifully sat. He put her plate in front of her and asked, "More coffee?"

She was about to decline when the front door opened and Bob and Eddie entered.

"Man, I could smell that food all the way out in the driveway," Bob said cheerfully, "and I was praying it was coming from here."

"We got any coffee?" Eddie mumbled. Darla hadn't seen him eat anything, and the fact that coffee was his first choice surprised her.

"How'd it go in Midland?" Darla asked, seasoning her eggs. "Any problems we need to take care of?"

"Nope," Bob said, grinning at the plate Mike had set before him. "Everything's great. The acoustics are surprisingly good for an auditorium. Tickets for your portion of the show are sold out. You'll be pleased with all of it. The stage manager is a big fan and can't wait to meet you."

"Dammit, Bob, it's bad luck to say everything is great and nothing's gone wrong. Tell me something bad. Say it's hopeless, but don't say all is wonderful."

"Sorry," he said, laughing, "I forgot that old saw in entertainment. Uh, let's see, the lighting in the dressing room could be better."

"You're on the right track. Tell me more," Darla prompted him.

"I'll have to think of more later on. Hurry now and get dressed. We need to get back for rehearsal. Is Roxie up and around yet?"

"When you were sweet talkin' her on the phone a few minutes ago, didn't you hear me barge in and . . . ?"

The expression on Bob's face stopped her short, told her more than she wanted to know. Darla was positive Roxie had been talking to a man on her cell phone and from the look on

Bob's face, it wasn't him. Darla had seen that pained expression on Bob's face years before and it was one memory she would just as soon not revisit. She felt uneasy and embarrassed at her blunder.

"I'll, uh, I'll just go make sure she's up," Bob said. "Y'all enjoy your breakfast." He rose and disappeared up the hall.

Shit. Darla might not want her ex married to a mean bitch, but she didn't want the job as the messenger of Roxie's philandering ways, either.

chapter nine

The drive to Midland barely allowed Debbie Sue and Edwina to complete every song before they reached the civic center, located on the outskirts of the city.

"It's a damn good thing we'll be mouthing these words," Debbie Sue complained, pulling into the civic center's parking lot. "After that practice session, I can see we'd be hard-pressed to carry a tune in a bucket."

"Not me," Edwina said. "I sing like a nightingale." She warbled a verse of the last song they had been listening to.

"Humph. What I lack in talent I make up for in complete inability to remember the words."

Making a wide circle, Debbie Sue parked and killed the engine. She grabbed her purse and they were on their way across the paved parking lot. The early September sun beat on their backs, but the air hinted of upcoming balmy days.

Inside the large complex they were met with an array of signs giving directions to various meeting rooms bearing the names of legendary Texas ranches—PITCHFORK, 6666, XIT, WAGGONER and KING. But the greatest confusion and noise seemed to be coming from an area marked, simply, AUDITORIUM.

Debbie Sue and Edwina walked into the cavernous, dimly lit auditorium, looking around for Darla, Bob or the face of anyone who appeared to be in charge. Their gazes landed on a small, wiry man wearing huge glasses. He was shouting orders through a bullhorn—which everyone seemed to be ignoring.

"Dammit, Gary," he yelled. "I know you and Jimmy can hear me. Everyone in the county can hear me. Put the buckboard wagon to stage left like I directed. . . . What do you mean 'which left?' There's only one left."

As the two teenagers started pushing the object to the right, the man with the horn screamed, "Stop it, stop it, stop it! You're going right!"

The teenagers halted and straightened, looking bewildered. "Well if we're going right, why'd you make us stop?" one of them said.

The man let his bullhorn sag limply by his side, closed his eyes and shook his head.

" 'Scuse me," Debbie Sue said, touching his arm lightly. "Are you in charge here?"

The man's shoulders slumped with dejection. He looked at her through glasses that were as thick as they were huge. "Do I look like I'm in charge here?"

"No, hon, you really don't," Edwina said gently.

"Shut up, Ed." Debbie Sue redirected her attention to the man with the bullhorn. "Yes, yes, you do look like the man in charge. I'm Debbie Sue Overstreet and this is Edwina Perkins-Martin. We're backup singers for Darla Denman."

The man's expression brightened and he became animated again. "Oh, my goodness, is Miz Denman here? I'm a huge fan of hers."

"I'm not sure where she is. We just got here and we're looking for her. What did you say your name is?"

"Oh, how rude of me." He offered his hand. "I'm Matt Rash. My mother volunteers me to direct this telethon every year and I hate it. I had one semester of theater arts at Sul Ross and she thinks that makes me qualified to do this job."

"What's your regular job?" Debbie Sue asked.

"I'm a tattoo artist. I own Tatts by Matt off Interstate Twenty. Corny, huh? But I was going for a play on words. When you speak to me, please don't call me Matt. Call me Tatts by Matt. Having people call me by the name of my business is my own little way of advertising. You see, someone will invariably ask me what that means and that gives me the opportunity to give a business card and the address of my tattoo parlor."

"Ah," Edwina said, lifting her chin knowingly.

Debbie Sue frowned. "Guess that's better than Rash Tatts."

"Is that next to Love's Travel Stop?" Edwina asked with more interest than Debbie Sue thought necessary.

"Yes!" Matt answered. "Do you know it?"

"Y'all stay open on Saturdays 'til midnight?"

"We sure do, although I'm closed today. Sounds like you do know my business. Love the hat, by the way."

"Thanks," Edwina said, preening and placing her hand on the back of the hat.

Wondering what circumstances had taken Edwina to Tatts

by Matt's business, Debbie Sue turned her full attention to her partner.

"It's Vic," Edwina stage-whispered close to Debbie Sue's ear. "I'll explain later."

"Now I remember," Matt exclaimed. "I thought I recognized you. I did a yellow-and-black ruler on your husband. How'd he like that tatt after he wore it for a while? One of the better ones I've done, I must say. I was extremely proud of that work. I wanted to get pictures, but well . . ." He shrugged his shoulders and opened his palms.

Debbie Sue thought she saw a hint of color on his cheeks. She switched her gaze to Edwina again. "A yellow-and-black ruler?"

"It's kind of personal. It was one of his Navy buddy's ideas. He and Vic had a bet and wanted to see—"

"Eeew! Yuck!" Debbie Sue contorted her mouth. "Do not say another word, Ed. I mean not another word. There are some things best left unknown and I wish I didn't know all the other personal stuff I already do about Vic."

"I'm not the one who brought it up," Edwina said defensively. She broke into a cackling laugh and slapped Matt's shoulder. "Brought it up. Get it?"

"Matt," Debbie Sue said loudly. "Could you please tell us where we need to go?"

Tatts by Matt raised his index finger and gave a phony smile. "That's Tatts by Matt, remember? Advertising?"

"We got it," Debbie Sue said.

"I'll take you to the hospitality room," Tatts by Matt said. "You should be able to catch up with the other performers there. My notes say one of you is twirling a flaming baton. We want to make sure that person stands near a fire extinguisher."

Debbie Sue stared at Edwina, who stared back. They both swerved their eyes to Tatts by Matt. He broke into a belly laugh. "I'm kidding. I'm kidding. You should see your faces. What a hoot. Come on, girls. We're gonna have a ball the next couple of days."

"Good Lord, Ed, I thought he was serious," Debbie Sue whispered as they trailed behind Tatts by Matt. "All of these show-business people must be crazy."

"I know," Edwina said. "I've always heard that about them."

As their borrowed crew cab pickup, filled shoulder to shoulder with passengers, pulled into the Midland Civic Center's parking lot, no one spoke. Darla was content to keep it that way. A whole flock of butterflies fluttered in her stomach and she didn't want to reveal to anyone that she had a case of nerves. After all, she was the star as well as the one in charge. She was the glue between the mosaic pieces, the musicians that were part of her performance, so to speak.

If she had felt this insecure when she performed years ago, she couldn't recall it. Back in those days, a free midnight performance in a West Texas town would have been laughable to her, but now, even a rehearsal was pressing on every hot spot in her body. *It's just pre-performance jitters*, she told herself, but the fact that she had never, ever, not once, been nervous about singing in front of an audience made those emotions difficult to handle.

They exited the pickup and started toward the large auditorium. Mike trotted ahead of them, pulling his cell phone from his pocket as he went. Valetta Rose ran ahead, too, a cell phone glued to her ear as well. What in the hell was going on? Darla wondered. Couldn't anyone get along without a cell phone?

No matter where you were nowadays, a majority of people were talking, texting or punching in numbers. It was a major nuisance and an invasion of privacy, but Darla had to admit she didn't know what she would do without a cell phone herself.

Just then, the musical notes of Jennifer Nettles's heartfelt plea to "*Stay*" warbled from someone's phone. Roxie fished hers from her jeans pocket and veered off at a right angle, distancing herself from everyone else. Seeing her comb through her thick blond hair with her fingers and release it over her shoulder, Darla thought of those shampoo commercials on TV where a woman tossed her glossy, luxurious mane, teasing the viewers with its gleam and softness.

"That girl gets more phone calls than the Psychic Hotline," Darla said to Bob. "Do you suppose she's running a sex-talk service?"

Bob's face took on that look again and Darla wished immediately she could take that remark back. His expression showed a mix of puzzlement, embarrassment and anger. All subtle, but there nonetheless. She had never noticed just how obvious it was that Roxie cheated. And that Bob knew it.

Darla clamped her mouth shut and enviously watched Roxie's youthful, confident stride, the chin uptilted as if she was ready to take on anything. Darla tried to mimic the younger woman's walk, hoping the new posture and gait would somehow help her overcome her fears, but she found herself thinking of something she had heard her sassy country grandmother say long ago: *You can call piss perfume, darlin', but it's still piss.*

A familiar voice, close to her ear, caught her off guard, "Nervous?"

Bob. Darla looked to her right and gave him her best smile, "When was I ever nervous?"

He gave a good-natured laugh. "I'm teasing. Never did I ever see you wired like most performers. I never could understand that either. I'd be *behind* the curtains, for chrissake, sweating bullets and you'd be applying a fresh coat of Rooster Red gloss to your nails. Cool as a cucumber."

"How do you think those two gals from Salt Lick are going to work out? I sure have taken to them. I almost wish they could join us permanently."

"Don't be too quick extending offers, Darla. They haven't shown us anything, yet. But I'm not too worried about it. The hometown folks will love them, good or bad."

"Hmm. Maybe having them around will help lighten up some of the tension."

Bob gave her a sideways glance and hooked his arm around her shoulder, giving her a brotherly squeeze. "I thought you weren't nervous."

Darla slid her arm around his waist. "Oh, hell, Bobby, you know how it is. If my lips are moving, there's a fifty-fifty chance I'm lying."

Just inside the vast civic auditorium, Roxie rejoined them. Darla stopped to gather her bearings. Immediately she heard her name called. "Miz Denman. Miz Denman. Darla, over here!"

She looked in the direction of the frantic voice and saw a tall, skinny woman wearing an outrageous straw hat and waving her arms over her head. She recognized Edwina Perkins-Martin.

Roxie snorted a sound of disgust. "Shit. That John Deere calendar pinup and her *Hee Haw* buddy give me the creeps. I'm going onstage."

As she strode away, Darla called after her, "Don't forget she and her partner also are giving you a place to lay your head at night and wheels to haul your ass around while we're stranded."

Without turning around, Roxie flipped her middle finger.

Darla gasped. "Robert Thomas Denman! If that woman makes it back to Nashville with all of her bleached hair it'll be a miracle. I might list profanity as a second language, but giving someone the finger in a public place is as unladylike as standing up to pee. I wouldn't dream of doing that."

"Let's go see what Edwina's excited about," Bob said.

Before they could reach the brunette, she had rushed up to them.

"Y'all, this is just about the coolest thing I've ever done," she gushed. "Do you know they're treating us like celebrities? They're bringing us drinks and food, asking if there's anything they can do for us, taking our picture for the newspaper. Why, I even had someone ask me for an autograph." She rapidly patted her chest. "Me! The last thing I was asked to sign was a traffic ticket."

Darla released a throaty chuckle. "It's fun, isn't it? Hard to believe all this attention can eventually become a pain in the ass."

"What, this? Never. I love it. I'm thinking of becoming famous at something so I can be treated like this all the time. Do you know that friend of Roxie's even offered to do my hair *and* my makeup? Of course nobody touches my hair and makeup but me, but still . . . Lord, listen to me babble on. Of course you know these things. You're Darla Denman, forchristsake."

Just then Debbie Sue walked up. Darla noticed she was wearing red high heels.

"Mornin' everyone." Holding onto Edwina, Debbie Sue lifted a foot. "See? I've got 'em on." She turned to Edwina. "Ed, Tatts by Matt wants us in the audience, then we have to see someone named Valetta Rose in makeup. Roxie will run through her number first, then we'll do our part, God help us."

"Valetta Rose is with us," Darla said. "She was in the café yesterday, but you probably didn't get a chance to meet her during the food fight." Glancing down at Debbie Sue's feet, Darla laughed. "How are you getting along with the high heels?"

"This is a rehearsal, right?" Debbie Sue said. "If there's anything I need to rehearse, it's wearing these shoes."

Darla laughed. She liked these two women so much. Hooking an arm around the crook of each of their elbows, she turned them toward the auditorium seating. "Let's go get a seat and listen to Roxie sing. And while we're waiting for her to start, you can tell me the story behind, what was it, Tatts by Matt?"

"Oh, honey, *he* is your biggest fan," Edwina confided.

"Well, my goodness, that's one thing in his favor already." Darla winked at Bob, who merely smiled.

"Ed," Debbie Sue whispered, "you can get rid of the hat."

"Oh, hell, no. My hair would be flat as a fritter. Besides that, I'd rather wear it than carry it."

Debbie Sue heaved a sigh.

"Follow me, ladies," Bob said. He led the way through the darkened hall. Debbie Sue followed Darla and Edwina, feeling as if she were hobbled. Dimmed stage lights provided the only illumination. Spotting an empty seat was impossible. Everyone stopped, bumping into the person in front.

"Just find a place anywhere and sit," Darla whispered.

As everyone's eyes became accustomed to the low light, titters broke out. Each of them was sitting in a different row, not even in an arm's reach or a whisper of each other.

This struck Debbie Sue as funny, but she worked feverishly to control her laughter. The attempts were contagious as Edwina tried muffling herself, snorting in her failed effort.

Even Bob got caught up in the moment and lowered his head below the seat in front of him.

Roxie was onstage with her back turned. She was saying something to a man wearing a set of headphones around his neck. As the noises from the audience grew, she turned around, shielded her eyes and looked out from the stage, her face clouded with anger.

The glaring disapproval only heightened Debbie Sue's amusement. She rose from her seat and as best she could, quickstepped and stumbled up the aisle to the lobby area. She was soon met by Edwina and together they broke into guffaws.

"I don't know why that hit me so damn funny," Debbie Sue said, wiping tears of mirth from her eyes. "I guess I've got a case of nerves and it doesn't take much to jump-start them."

"I'm not even nervous," Edwina said, "but you know you can't laugh around me without me losing it too." She dabbed a glisten of moisture from the corner of her eye.

"Okay," Debbie Sue said, squaring her shoulders and shaking them to relax herself. "I'm ready to go back in. How about you? You okay?"

"Roger. Laughing's all over." Edwina pointed a crimson nail at her blank face. "See? No laughing."

Satisfied they were both past the urge to laugh, Debbie Sue pulled the auditorium door open but stopped just short of opening it wide. A voice like none she'd ever heard singing country music floated, a capella, from the stage. It was strong and pure, spanning octaves, expressing so much gut-wrenching emotion Debbie Sue was genuinely moved. It was like in church, when sometimes a member of the choir, with no musical accompaniment, would transfix the congregation with a simple religious hymn.

There was no hint of Bible stories in the song Roxie was singing. It told of heartache, of lust and yearning and eventual learning. The kind of tune only a woman who had lost the love of her life could perform with so much feeling.

"*. . . And then those funny, familiar, forgotten feelings started walking all over my mind . . .*"

She glanced over at Edwina, whose eyes were closed. She was swaying slowly, her face reflecting how she had tuned in to the singer's woes.

Debbie Sue eased the door shut, abruptly shutting off the music. "Hell, Ed. That's Roxie singing. I've never heard anyone sing like that. Even Simon Cowell wouldn't find fault with that performance. She's right. She's going to be a huge star. Damn it all to hell."

"It couldn't have been her," Edwina said sharply. "That voice I heard had a heart, and we agreed there's a dog turd where Roxie's heart should be. Let's go back in. I need to see this and hear it for myself."

Reentering the auditorium, they took the nearest seats at the back and sat quietly, listening and watching as Roxie, smiling and amicable to everyone onstage, raised the microphone to her lips again and sang, "*Last night, quietly, you walked through my mind . . .*"

Everyone in the hall gave rapt attention. No one even appeared to breathe. When the last note lingered and died, the only sound left was the soft *whoosh* of the air-conditioning system kicking in. Clapping erupted from places throughout the auditorium. Only twenty or so people were present, but they all made their appreciation of the singer's talent known.

Debbie Sue sat slack-jawed.

"Shit," Edwina griped. "Why in the hell did God give that much talent to such a shit? On top of that, she's good-looking."

"I suppose He *had* to give her something," Debbie Sue said.

"Oh, so the body of a ballroom dancer, tits that shade her toes and a face that would melt chocolate isn't enough?"

"You do have a way with words, don't you, Ed?"

"Well, it's true."

"Ed, I like to think there's something salvageable in everyone, no matter how big an SOB they might be. She could have been nervous and had the jitters all this time, same as me, and being mean was how she reacted to that."

An arch look came from Edwina. "Oh, yeah?"

"I can't help it if that's how I feel, Ed. Look, she's motioning that she's finished. Maybe she's feeling friendlier after singing. Let's go tell her how good we think she is."

"If you say so," Edwina grumbled.

Debbie Sue hobbled toward the stage with Edwina in tow. Looking up she said, "Roxie, that was wonderful. You almost—"

"Freddie Lou," Roxie said, studying her manicure.

Debbie Sue looked around, to assure herself Roxie wasn't speaking to someone else. "Are you speaking to me?" she asked. "My name's Debbie Sue."

"Whatever." Roxie dismissed her, clarifying her name with a flip of her hand, and immediately Debbie Sue's temper began to rise. "Is there anything you can do about the mattress at your house?" Roxie asked. "I suppose it's the one in the *master* bedroom, if you can actually say that about a room that small. I'd appreciate it if you could take care of it today. I hate the thought of another night on that pile of rocks."

Without waiting for a comment, Roxie turned and walked back to the group of people who milled in a corner of the stage.

Stunned, Debbie Sue looked at Edwina, who was displaying an I-told-you-so grin. "Say there, *Freddie Lou*," Edwina said. "You think there's still something salvageable in that asshole girl?"

"Yeah," Debbie Sue growled. "Her gold fillings. After I knock her teeth out."

chapter ten

Darla sat beside her ex-husband, listening to Roxie's performance. The girl had the voice of an angel, the face of a heavenly soul and the body of a temptress, making her appearance on stage almost ethereal. This must be why Bob had fallen in love with her.

Indeed Roxie had the voice Darla had always dreamed of standing before an audience and delivering. Darla's own voice was fine and it had made her a fortune, but it was country—a sweet voice that had a combination of sass and heartbreak, a necessary quality to sing "Every Beat of My Heart Breaks a Little Piece Off." Roxie, on the other hand, had that arcane combination of talent and stage presence. Charisma, even. Oh, yeah, she could crash the barriers between country and pop.

Darla stole a glance at her ex's profile. He was busily working on columns of figures in his checkbook, completely unaffected by the sound that had everyone mesmerized. Roxie might have it all, Darla thought, but at this moment she did not have Bob Denman's undivided attention.

But she was still his wife, dammit.

And that reminder took Darla to darker thoughts. She suspected Roxie would drop Bob the second she hit it big. She had seen it happen a dozen times in the ruthless music business. And seeing the edginess between Roxie and Bob and believing Roxie had other men on the side left no doubt.

But Darla knew her ex-husband wasn't totally stupid. He had to know the obvious about his current wife. He was twice Roxie's age. He might be well thought of and respected in the music community, but even his good reputation meant nothing in the larger circle of the music world. Perhaps he was holding on to a dream too. Perhaps in his private moments with Roxie, she gave him hope to go on.

After Roxie dumped him, would he return to the past and Darla Denman? With his heart aching, would Darla be who he leaned on, as she had leaned on him for years?

Darla fought the urge to reach for Bob's hand. If she were magically given the chance to have a life with him again, would she do things differently? Would she, could she, swallow her pride and not be so damned determined to win every argument? She swore if opportunity ever arose, the next time, she wouldn't make the same mistakes she had made before. She shook her head, dispelling what she was thinking. Daydreaming didn't serve purpose to anyone.

Bob turned his head and looked at her quizzically. "Everything okay? You look funny."

"I'm fine," she said softly. "Everything's just fine."

* * *

Debbie Sue jumped as "Foggy Mountain Breakdown" suddenly blasted through the sound system, followed by a thundering clatter that could only be matched by a team of Clydesdales loping across the wooden stage floor. No one, not even Tatts by Matt yelling, "Not now!" into the bullhorn, could override the clamor of the twenty-four-member West Texas High-Stepping Lone Star Cloggers.

Debbie Sue's gaze swung to Roxie, who now stood offstage watching the dancers with a scowl, arms crossed over her chest. Without a doubt, the younger singer wasn't pleased to be upstaged so soon after her stunning vocal performance.

For the briefest moment, Debbie Sue felt sorry for Roxie. She had been blessed with eye-popping beauty and an extraordinary voice. She was young enough to enjoy both for years to come, but as far as Debbie Sue could tell, the girl's heart was black as coal.

Unable to get the cloggers' attention with the bullhorn, Tatts by Matt dashed to the front of the stage and began waving his arms and making throat-slashing gestures with one hand. Gradually, the sound of clogging feet waned to a single *clack*, then halted altogether. "Not now!" Tatts by Matt yelled again through the bullhorn. As one last *clack* emanated from the stage, Tatts by Matt's shoulders sagged, his bullhorn hanging by his side.

"If we can't rehearse now, when can we?" a voice said from the group.

"Soon," Tatts by Matt said. "Soon."

Debbie Sue saw Darla with Bob. Darla waved them forward and headed for the stage with Bob accompanying her. Debbie Sue and Edwina walked down the aisle and met them.

"Edwina," Darla said, "you aren't planning on wearing the hat as part of your costume, are you?"

"Oh, no," Edwina said. "I'm just wearing it now because my hair would be a mess if I took it off."

A look of relief passed over Darla's face. "Oh. Well, good. Because it would conflict with my signature colors and you and Debbie Sue wouldn't match."

"Oh, I know that." Edwina gave a thumbs up. "You don't have to worry, Darla. I got it. Red and black. Black and red."

Tatts by Matt came over and gushed all over Darla, going into great detail about how each of her big hits had spoken to him on a personal level. Darla was being a pro, smiling appreciatively. "Matt, darlin'," she said, "these are my backup singers, Debbie Sue and Edwina. They're both from Salt Lick. We're hoping that having them as part of the act will appeal to the local fans."

"We've already met," Tatts by Matt said, "but y'all didn't tell me you were from Salt Lick. How cool is this? A couple of local gals touring with Darla Denman."

"Oh, we're not touring," Debbie Sue was quick to say. "We're doing backup for this show only."

"Now, never say never, Debbie Sue," Darla said. "You might turn out to be such a hit I *have* to take you on tour with me."

"Oh, holy night, Christmas lights and Santa Claus," Edwina said breathlessly. "Debbie Sue, wouldn't that be something? What if Darla gets the Country Music Award for Entertainer of the Year? We could go up onstage with her. I can see it now." She looked heavenward with a starry-eyed gaze. "I'll tell all my ex-husbands to kiss my butt on national TV."

"You've already told them to kiss your butt," Debbie Sue said. "Several times, I might add."

"But not on *nation . . . wide . . . T . . . V*," Edwina said with emphasis.

"Let's not put the cart before the horse, Ed," Debbie Sue said.

"Ladies, I've been out of contention for that award for years," Darla said, laughing. "The performers who win do hundreds of shows in a year. My little tour would scarcely make a ripple."

Tatts by Matt became animated. "And you starting with our little telethon is such an honor, Miz Denman. Are all of your people here?"

"Yep. Let's knock some dust off this thing."

As Mike and Eddie made their way to their instruments again, Debbie Sue and Edwina climbed the side stairs onto the stage and stood behind Darla.

"Listen," Darla said, speaking in a low voice to avoid being overheard, "you haven't explained why you're calling him Tatts by Matt. That can't be his name."

"That's the name of his business," Debbie Sue replied. "Tatts by Matt is a tattoo parlor. He asked us to call him that because it's his way of advertising."

"I see," Darla said, but the blank expression on her face said she didn't get it. She cleared her throat and said, "Matt, honey, what do you say we run through a couple of numbers now with full lighting? Let these ladies get accustomed to the bright lights."

"Perfect." Tatts by Matt agreed. "Let's get you girls in place. I'm sure I don't have to tell Miz Denman where to stand."

Taking Debbie Sue and Edwina each by an arm, he steered them to a couple of microphones just behind the single one at front center stage. "Pole mikes are kind of old school," he explained. "Most performers nowadays choose the head gear apparatus, but Mr. Denman wanted these for the nostalgic look." He stood each woman behind her individual mike and went on, "I have to admit I like the look too. Also, it gives you something to hold on to when the music gets emotional. He's got a good eye for showmanship, Mr. Denman does."

"How close do we need to stand?" Edwina asked, moving back and forth from the microphone.

"It doesn't matter. Your mike won't be on, but it'll look more authentic to the audience if you stand close."

"The mike won't be on?" Edwina asked.

"Ed, did you forget?" Debbie Sue said. "We're not singing. Only Darla is singing. All we're doing is mouthing. Mouth and move and sway. Mouth, move, sway. *Only*," Debbie Sue added with finality.

"I know that," Edwina said. "But she might appreciate me singing. I don't have that bad of a—"

"Mouth. Move. And sway. Got it? Ed, I don't want you embarrassing us."

"How could it embarrass *us* if I'm the one singing?"

"Because I'm the one who'll have to beat the shit out of *you* and that will embarrass *me*. I still haven't forgotten the result of that karaoke bit in that hotel in New York."

"Oh," Edwina said in a tiny voice. "Okay, okay already."

Turning his attention to Mike and Eddie, Tatts by Matt said, "Looks like y'all are all set up. I'm going to find a seat in the audience and enjoy."

Darla waited until he found a seat. Then she looked over her right shoulder to Eddie and Mike. "You boys ready? Let's run through *Whispers from West Texas*. That's one this crowd should appreciate." Turning back to the left, she asked, "You gals know that song well enough to lip-sync?"

"I'll say," Edwina piped up. "That was the lullaby I sang my babies to sleep with."

Darla smiled and turned back toward the audience, raising her hand in what Debbie Sue imagined was a signal for the band to begin. And they did.

The mournful sound that could only be captured by an electric guitar unfurled a tender introduction and Darla stepped to her spot and sang.

For the second time that day Debbie Sue was transfixed. She had never heard Darla Denman sing in person and was pleasantly surprised that her voice was richer and stronger than a recording could capture and that she sang perfectly on key. She sang a song so heartfelt that anyone who had ever experienced a broken heart must have felt it shatter again, and those who hadn't had to be suddenly made aware of the torture it could bring.

She stole a glance in Edwina's direction and to her horror saw that she was engaged in some sort of sign language, seemingly putting action to the words of the song like a hula dancer telling a story with her hands.

Reaching over, she grabbed Edwina's wrist, stopping her. "What in the hell are you doing?" she stage-whispered.

"I'm giving the song a face," Edwina whispered back, continuing to undulate her opposite hand. "You know, character. Something the listener can relate to. A visual image."

"Edwina Perkins-Martin, I want you to look closely at *my* face. If you continue with this bullshit I'm going home. I will not do this with you."

Suddenly the music stopped and Darla turned in their direction. "Is there a problem, ladies?" The question came at them in a stern, all-business tone. "I thought we had a clear understanding of your role."

"Absolutely clear, Darla, er, uh, Miz Denman," Debbie Sue stammered. "We won't interrupt you again. Sorry."

"And may I just say," Edwina said, "you have never sounded better."

"Well, thank you. Now, can we continue?"

"Sure," Edwina said. "Let's take it from the top." She turned to Debbie Sue. "If that's all right with you, *Freddie Lou*."

"Bite me, Ed," Debbie Sue said. Looking at Darla, she shrugged her shoulders. Darla turned back to face the auditorium.

Debbie Sue knew that in resurrecting her career, Darla had prepared for many obstacles. She only hoped it could withstand Edwina Perkins-Martin.

But perhaps her fears were unfounded. For the next three tunes Edwina behaved perfectly and Debbie Sue was able to let down her guard. Teetering on her red high heels, swaying her hips, she pressed her lips in a phony hum and watched and listened to Darla as she finished her closing number. The singer still had it, Debbie Sue thought. She could still belt out a honky-tonk tune with the best of them.

Bob called from the middle row of the auditorium, "Darla, I'd say that's a wrap."

Darla shielded her eyes as she looked toward the direction of the voice. "I think so too."

Debbie Sue whispered to Edwina, "What do you think that means?"

"I think he means we're finished. You know, wrap it up," Edwina whispered back.

"You mean we're finished?" Debbie called out to Bob. "But I hardly did a thing."

"But what you did do was spectacular." Bob said, having

made his way down the aisle and onto the stage. "You girls were terrific. There won't be a soul in the house who'll think you're lip-syncing. Debbie Sue," he said, singling her out, "when Darla hit that big long note and you grabbed the mike and stepped back, your face mirrored the pain and misery she was singing about. That was fantastic. Your instinct for stage dramatization was dead-on. Try to do that again tomorrow night."

As Bob and Darla walked away, Edwina propped a hand on her hip and leaned in to Debbie Sue. "What was all this 'don't embarrass me' bullshit you bitched at me about? You're over there being all dramatic and after what you said to me, I was afraid to move."

"Dammit, Ed, I don't even know what stage dramatization is. My ankle buckled and I fell off my shoe. I grabbed that mike stand for balance, like that skinny little thing could keep me from falling on my ass."

"Oh, hell, I'm sorry," Edwina said. "Why didn't you grab me instead?"

Debbie Sue began to giggle. "I just figured it would better if only one of us had her legs up in the air instead of both of us."

Both women broke into laughter that halted only when Darla came over. "I've never in my life seen two people have more fun together," she said.

Roxie approached, looking bored and detached. "What's keeping us from going back to whatever the name of that town is we came over here from?"

Until that moment, the three of them had been oblivious to Roxie joining them. "You don't have a very good memory, do you, Roxie?" Debbie Sue said.

"I have an excellent memory for the things that matter."

"Believe it or not, knowing where you come from is pretty damned important. And it oughtta matter."

Roxie gave Debbie Sue the head-to-toe. "Not if you know where you're going. And I have a real clear view of that."

Without looking back, she sashayed over and sidled up to Bob, who was speaking to someone on the far end of the stage.

"Oh, I just can't stand her," Debbie Sue said. "I'm sorry, Darla, but she's impossible. Does she piss off everyone, or is it just me?"

"Oh, she's not so bad once you get to know her. She's—Oh, hell, who am I kidding? Everyone in the group would like to flush her head in the toilet."

chapter eleven

Due to being able to use the stage and equipment in only bits and snatches, the rehearsal had taken all day, but it had gone without a hitch. Still, Darla was in a black mood. Memories mixed with the current state of her affairs sometimes did that to her, even though her good sense told her that thinking back on past mistakes was like trying to un-ring a bell, and walking on the splintered glass of memories didn't change anything but your attitude.

Her entourage milled around the stage, talking and joking, and she tried to mix in, but wasn't doing it very well.

"It's getting late," Bob said. "Let's gather up and go back to Salt Lick and eat and rest."

A collective agreement came from the group. Darla headed for the exit alone. Dark had descended, but she stepped outside into the well-lit parking lot. She walked toward the borrowed pickup, but the closer she got to it, the less appealing spending another evening under the same roof with the current Mr. and Mrs. Denman became. Her two new backup singers were walking a distance away. "Hey, ladies," she hollered, and waved. The two women stopped, then came toward her. "Which one of you knows how to make a good margarita?" she asked.

Edwina gave her a big grin. "I'm in negotiations this very minute with Jose Cuervo to put my picture on his bottles of tequila."

These two women were so likeable. Darla's melancholy began to fade. "I knew it. You can't come to Texas and not find someone who makes a good margarita. Do you put Grand Marnier in it?"

"Does the male animal leave the toilet seat up?" Edwina drawled.

"Then if you don't mind the intrusion, I'd like to go home with one of you tonight. I'm not up to being nice to Roxie this evening."

"Hey, both our husbands are out of town," Debbie Sue said. "We'll have a slumber party. Like kids. We can flip a coin whose house."

"No, let's not," Edwina said. "My trailer looks like somebody went through it with a leaf blower. Let's go to your house, Little Homemaker Debbie Sue." She turned to Darla. "Her house is always cleaner than a starving man's dinner plate."

"That's only because Buddy likes it that way," Debbie Sue replied.

Edwina cackled and said to Darla, "You have to overlook her. She's whipped. That man of hers—"

"I am not whipped. It isn't just Buddy who likes things tidy.

I like everything neat too. We don't have any kids running around, so we don't have any excuse for it being messy."

"You don't have kids?" Darla asked, surprised. Being childless herself, she always found a kinship with the rare woman who didn't have children. Back when she had been at an age when she might have borne children, her only interest had been her career. "I just assumed you did."

"I'll go get my pickup and drive it over here," Debbie Sue said. "No need in all of us walking all the way to it." She appeared to be fishing her keys from her jeans pocket as she walked away, but Darla had noticed that she had ignored the question and comment about children.

"Oh, Edwina," Darla said, mortified and watching Debbie Sue trek toward a red Silverado. "I said something that hurt her feelings. I wouldn't have done that for the world, I just assumed—"

"Oh, hon, don't blame yourself," Edwina said. "That's a story we'd need several drinks to get into."

Debbie Sue wished she hadn't let the comment about kids slip out of her mouth. She and Buddy might have buried their son's tiny body in the Salt Lick cemetery years ago, but the memory was as fresh as if they had lost him only yesterday. She knew she could count on the talk of kids not coming up again, because Edwina knew to steer the conversation away from that tender spot in Debbie Sue's heart.

Ten minutes later she and her two companions were headed toward Salt Lick. Like giant candles, flames showed in various distant spots against the black horizon—gas being burned off from oil wells. Cabell County had almost as many oil wells as people.

"Haven't seen that in years," Darla murmured from the backseat. "My daddy worked in the oil fields, you know."

She began to quietly hum and sing along with the radio. The soft sounds were soothing and Debbie Sue stared out the windshield as if on autopilot. The tension that had squeezed her shoulders and spine all day began to ease and the knots in her muscles began to untie.

"Hey." An all-too-familiar voice next to her broke the silence. "You trying to see how slow you can drive before the engine rolls over and dies, or what?"

Debbie Sue's eyes popped wide and she looked at the speedometer. She was driving ten miles an hour. Hell, she usually didn't even get in the pickup until it was going at least twenty. She couldn't remember the last time she'd driven up a paved road at less than seventy. "Whoa! Guess I was getting too relaxed." She laughed, punching the accelerator and kicking up the speed to what was, for her, normal.

"I don't think there's any such thing as being too relaxed," Darla said. "It seems like I'm always wound tight about something or someone."

"Then you're in for a treat," Edwina exclaimed. "Tonight we all get the full treatment. Mango masks, manicures and margaritas."

"Yum," Darla replied. "Those are some of my favorite things that start with the letter M."

"Men aren't on that list?" Edwina said.

"Nope. For me the word *men* begins with the letter E. *Eligible* men."

Debbie Sue laughed. "Spoken like a woman with a good head on her shoulders."

"I wouldn't go so far as to say that," Darla said, "but I've learned a thing or two in this ol' world."

"If you don't mind me asking, isn't there a man in your life now?" Edwina said.

"Ed, that's personal," Debbie Sue said.

"Oh, that's okay, Debbie Sue," Darla replied, "I don't mind her asking. Nope, I don't have anyone in my life. Not sure I ever will have again. I've had four husbands, you know. Some would say I've had my share."

Debbie Sue was sure she heard a hint of wistfulness in Darla's tone. "And speaking of mango masks," she said, hoping to change the subject, "that woman Valetta Rose put this crap on my face and it feels like paste. I can't wait to wash it off."

"It might feel like paste, but under stage lights, it makes your face look luminous," Darla said.

"I didn't let her touch my makeup," Edwina said. "She might be a makeup artist, but *nobody* paints my face but me."

"She's sure a quiet one," Debbie Sue said. "I haven't heard her say two words. What's her story, Darla?"

"I don't have a clue," Darla answered. "I met her for the first time when we boarded the bus back in Nashville. She was Roxie's idea. I told that overbearing girl I couldn't afford to pay a makeup artist, but Roxie said she wanted a professional and she'd take care of it out of her own pocket. Or I should say, Bob's pocket." Darla laughed. "I'm like you, Edwina. I've done my own makeup for years. Never used a pro, but with this new high def they talk about all the time, Roxie might have the right idea."

"Oh, hell, I forgot about that," Edwina said. "Remind me to add an extra layer of foundation. I might be ready for my big moment in front of the camera, but this forty-year-old face definitely ain't ready for high def."

"Is that so?" Debbie Sue said. "How come your face is five years younger than the rest of you?"

Edwina huffed indignantly. "I was speaking in general."

When they neared Salt Lick city limits, Debbie Sue slowed her speed. They turned the corner where the Styling Station was located and headed out of town toward Debbie Sue's home.

"Looks like everything's okay in the shop," Edwina remarked.

From out of the blue, Darla said, "Roxie always gets what she wants. By hook or crook, she always gets her way. Turns out that might work out in Mike's favor. He and Valetta Rose shared the bedroom last night."

"The hell," Edwina said. "I hadn't pegged them as a couple."

"I'm not saying anything happened between them," Darla said. "I don't know and don't care. All I know is they shared a bedroom. Hell, tonight she might be sharing with Eddie. Nothing would surprise me. There's just no telling. It's like the old pea under the shell game, you never know what you might find."

Darla smirked.

"The hell," Edwina said again. "Musical beds among the musicians, huh?" She chortled at her own joke. "Musical beds. Musicians. Get it?"

"Yes, Ed," Debbie Sue said. "We got it. We didn't like it, but we got it."

Darla heaved a huge sigh. "Show-business people are a little like that." She sounded almost apologetic. "Our worlds move a little faster than everyone else's, I suppose."

"Not really," Edwina said. "The way it looks to me, most of

them, present company excluded of course, are so wrapped up in themselves, they don't even know the speed the rest of the world moves. They think the world belongs to them and none of the rest of us are a part of it. Now, me, I've always—"

Debbie Sue cleared her throat, stopping Edwina's mouth. "Thank you, Obi Wan Kenobi. What say we change the subject before we start saying things we'll regret."

Darla laughed. "I'd say that's a great idea."

One of Roxie's more pleasant experiences on this ridiculous tour was the return trip to Salt Lick without Darla. Even the crappy food at Hogg's Drive-In had been half palatable. Now, back at the shack of a house where they were staying, she had put on sweat pants and a tank top to work out, which she did faithfully every night. She was in a Pilates stance, but she was watching her husband closely. He had been sitting on the edge of the bed talking on the phone for ten minutes in an animated, fun-type conversation with a female. Roxie knew he was speaking to a female because men talked differently to women, especially women they had a fondness for.

Darla. He had to be talking to Darla.

Roxie smiled to herself. She couldn't keep from thinking of how good it was going to feel when she walked out on his ass—after telling him his aging body disgusted her, and just in general, he made her want to throw up every time he touched her. Everyone knew why she had married him and it damn sure hadn't been for his bedroom prowess. She no longer even tried to deny it. She found it comical that he seemed to be the only one ignorant of the facts.

Her marriage to one of music's well-known managers had given her a leg up in the music business, for sure. Roxie Denman's time was so close she could almost feel the adoring eyes of her fans, the crush of the media, the pressure of the paparazzi. She was the next Mariah Carey, Beyoncé and Britney, all rolled into one. She had been told by a few of Nashville's best that she had the pipes and the style.

She changed positions, lying flat on her back. As she brought her knee tightly up to her chest, she let her thoughts drift into another one of her fantasies. The first thing she would buy when she made it was a Ferrari California GT with retractable roof. She had been looking at pictures. It would be a hot red number that no one could miss.

She switched knees. The second thing she intended to do was get rid of the current lover in her life who was starting to be demanding. He was good for a quick ride and getting things done for her in Nashville when Bob wasn't looking, but he wasn't good enough to ride in her Ferrari.

"Okay, well, you girls be careful and don't get into any mischief," her husband said into the phone. "Don't drink so much that you miss tomorrow night." He paused for the reply, then chuckled. "Don't worry, I'll make sure you get there. Sleep tight."

Flipping the case closed, he turned to Roxie, smiling. "Darla and those crazy Salt Lick girls are spending the night together. I thought she was just riding back to Salt Lick with them, but I guess they decided to make a party out of it." He shook his head slowly. "That Darla. She's never met a stranger. I've never known anyone who could turn a bad situation into a celebration better than she can."

"My, my, just listen to you gush," Roxie said, feeling the heat of anger climb up her spine. "If I didn't know better, I'd think you were still married to her. The blessed Darla. Saint of Lost Souls. *Old* lost souls."

Bob sighed deeply. "There's no need for that kind of meanness, Roxie. She's no older than I am. We have a lot of history together. We were just kids—"

"Oh pu-*leez*." Roxie got to her feet and wiped her brow with a towel. "Don't give me that worn-out speech again. Why don't you just admit you're still in love with her? Like I give a shit. You can't possibly think you're sparing my feelings by not saying it. In fact, why don't you go join her little party tonight and leave me the hell alone?"

"Rox, don't be that way. Tell you what. When this tour's over, we'll take a nice long vacation. Maybe go back to Bora-Bora, where we honeymooned."

"Humph. Is that supposed to be your big seduction move, dragging up memories? As foreplay goes, that's pretty lame."

Bob's face took on a pinkish hue and his back went rigid. "Roxie, listen to yourself," he said. "If I didn't know and believe better, I'd think you're the coldest, meanest woman who ever drew a breath."

"Really? Don't have the guts to just outright say that's what you really mean, Bobby Boy?"

She saw a tic in his jaw and malevolence in his eyes. "How's this for what I really mean, Roxie? I wish I'd never laid eyes on you. How's this to finish that thought? When this tour's over, instead of Bora-Bora, how about divorce court? You and I are done."

Roxie had expected him to be pissed. In fact, that had been her intention. But she hadn't expected he would go so far as to threaten an end to their marriage. He had never said anything like that to her. The anger she had first felt turned into fury. How dare he beat her to the punch. She picked up her nightgown and casually tossed it over her shoulder. Then she brushed past him, trailing a finger across his neck as she headed for the bathroom. "Now that's better, Bobby. Talk dirty to me. That's my idea of *real* foreplay."

She stopped at the door and looked back at him. On a sardonic laugh, she said, "And if you think it's *done* when the tour is over, you're wrong again. It's done *now*, big shot."

She slammed the door and locked it. "Bastard," she said.

But at least she was rid of him for the night. As for him leaving her, that was a joke. She had always been sure he felt lucky to have her even pay attention to him, much less marry him. He would come crawling back. They always came back.

Bob heard the click of the bathroom door lock. His first inclination was to kick down the door, but as always, his rational thinking overcame his reflexive thoughts. He was no kid and he wasn't sure he could kick in a door without injuring himself. And if *that* happened, what would Darla do for the remainder of the tour?

He couldn't say his heart was broken at having Roxie lock the door against him, but something was at work within him. Pride, ego, regret? Probably all of that. He contemplated calling Darla and asking if he could join the all-nighter she and those two women were sure to pull. Sharing drinks with salt-of-the-earth people was enticing. He might have had the shit stomped out of his pride, but it was only bruised, not dead.

He walked up the hallway to the room where Darla had slept the previous night. He laid his keys and phone on the table beside the bed, pried off his boots and undressed. Stretching out, he yawned and rolled over, grabbed the extra pillow and pulled it to his chest. A fragrance that he knew all too well sneaked into his nose. Joy. God knew he had bought enough of that pricey stuff to know it was Darla's favorite perfume. The fragrance was one he could never associate with anyone but his ex-wife. A hodgepodge of old memories wandered through his mind like lost children.

Children. He and Darla should have had kids. A woman with as much heart as she had would have been a great mom. They had loved each other enough, but there had never been time. From the beginning of their marriage, Darla had been on a fast track to stardom. Her career had cost everything, and not just for her. It had cost *him* everything too. "Shit," he mumbled.

He sat up, picked up his phone and opened it, keyed in a number and listened to the burrs. He was about to hang up when Darla's voice was suddenly on the other end.

"Hey," he said. "How would you gals like some extra company for a while?"

chapter twelve

Debbie Sue listened as Bob Denman repeated the directions she had just given him to her house. Was he bringing his wife with him? He didn't sound as if he was. And that took Debbie Sue to wondering what was going on with Roxie and why Bob might want to crash a hen party that included no one but his ex-wife and two strangers.

But, setting her dithering aside, she said, "That's it. It's real easy to get here. From town, it shouldn't take you fifteen minutes. But if you get lost just holler. We'll leave the front porch light on."

Still unable to precisely figure out a situation where Darla was touring around the country in the close quarters of a bus, accompanied by her ex-husband and his trophy wife, Debbie Sue closed the phone and handed it back to Darla. "Well that's a surprise, isn't it?"

Darla smiled wanly and looked down, avoiding Debbie Sue's eyes.

Guilt if she had ever seen it, was Debbie Sue's first thought. And stunning. She had expected a spirited denial. "Or is it?" she said.

"It's more than a surprise," Darla said. "It's unheard of altogether. I haven't known Bob to leave Roxie's side since they married two years ago. *She's* left *his* side plenty of times, though."

"They must've had a fight," Debbie Sue said. "He sounded down in the dumps."

"Bet it was over you," Edwina said to Darla, smacking her gum and measuring a jigger of tequila.

"Me?" Darla said, pressing a hand against her chest. "Why would it be over me? I haven't done anything."

"She treats you like you're the other woman," Edwina said all-knowingly.

Oh, hell, here we go again. Debbie Sue rolled her eyes. But she had to admit that when it came to men and women and relationships, Edwina was usually right.

"She treats every woman like the other woman," Darla said with a false laugh. "She hangs on to Bob like she cares about him and every female is a threat."

"But she looks at you different from the way she looks at the others. She has hate written all over her face when she looks at you."

"I've never done anything to her," Darla said, shaking her head slowly. "I don't take crap from her, but I've never harmed her."

"Darla, I forgot to tell you," Debbie Sue put in, "that we call Ed here the 'Dahlia Lama' of Love and the Pope of Passion.

She has a patent pending on the ingredients that make up that elusive thing called chemistry between males and females. She even writes an 'Advice to the Lovelorn' column in Salt Lick's newspaper."

"Oh, hell, Debbie Sue," Edwina said. "I don't know the Dalai Lama from Tony Lama or the Pope from soap on a rope. But I do know what I'm talking about when it comes to the opposite sex." Edwina drowned out further conversation by turning on the blender.

"Just go ahead and laugh at me," she said after she had quieted the blender. "But I know what I'm talking about. Bob still loves you, Darla, but he doesn't know it. All the feelings he has for you he dismisses as nostalgia and marks them up to friendship. Every time those feelings come creeping in he's sure to say"—Edwina lowered her voice to mimic a man's voice—" 'We have history together.' "

"Well we do have history together," Darla said defensively. "We got married as kids. Lord, we practically raised each other, but you can't call that love."

Edwina skillfully ran a lime wedge around the rim of a mason jar, then turned it upside down in a little pile of coarse salt. Then she carefully filled the jar half full from the blender. "Oh, okay. Then what's the word you'd use?"

"I'd use . . . ummm . . . I'd have to say it's . . . oh, hell, I don't know what it means. My God, I've been married four times. Does that sound like I'm an expert?" She sipped from the jar Edwina handed her, then licked her lips. "Hey, this is good."

"Come on now. What was the word you were trying to think of?"

"Ed, leave her alone," Debbie Sue said. "Can't you see she

doesn't want to talk about it? Besides, what difference does it make? Bob's got a wife."

Darla sipped again and held up her right hand. "That's okay, Debbie Sue, I don't mind." She turned her attention to Edwina. "You want to hear a word, oh Pope of Passion? I'll give you one. And the word is *love.* You can't endure all that Bob Denman and I have gone through together without a little love. By God, I do love Bob. I always have and I always will, whether he's married or not. There. I said it."

Edwina let out a whoop and pumped the air with her fist. "I'm right again. I knew you were still in love with him. I knew from the very start."

"Oh, hell," Debbie Sue said. "You'd better stop drinking those margaritas, Darla. I think Ed forgot to mention she laces them with Everclear. They're sure to bring out confessions better left as secrets. That's why I only drink one. Or two at the most."

"It doesn't matter, Debbie Sue," Darla said. "Even if I hadn't screwed up royally all those years ago, you're right. He's taken. And as far as I know, he's happy."

Roxie walked out of the bedroom and checked both of the other bedrooms. Not finding anyone, she moved on into the living room, where Mike, Eddie and Valetta Rose were sprawled all over the furniture watching TV. "Where's Bob?" she asked.

Everyone looked at her, but no one answered.

"Are all of you deaf? Turn down the damn TV. I'm talking."

Valetta Rose picked up the remote and reduced the volume to a barely audible level.

Roxie could always count on Valetta Rose to do what she

was told. "That's better," she snapped. "Now. I asked where Bob is."

"He left," Eddie replied.

She strode to the front door and looked out, didn't see the black pickup truck. She turned back to the group. "Did he leave in the pickup?"

"Sure did," Mike said. "Didn't say where he was going."

She gasped. "That ass. Just who in the hell does he think he is, leaving me stranded here? Leaving all of us stranded."

"Where've we got to go?" Eddie asked.

"Or maybe he should've asked where've *you* got to go?" Mike said.

"Don't get smart with me, Mike. I know enough on you to make Bob send your skinny ass back to Nashville. He won't stand for drugs and you know it."

"Roxie, don't," Valetta Rose said.

"Shut up, Valetta Rose. I could tell your secrets too. Then where would you be? Back in a damn funeral home slapping pancake shit on dead people, that's where."

"A little weed ain't drugs," Mike said, laughing. The others joined in.

Roxie fixed them all with a heated glare. How dare they laugh at her expense. She walked out onto the patio where night noises that weren't city noises surrounded her. She hated this damn town. Why any sane human being would want to live in a shithole like this she didn't know. She strode back into the house and began to pace.

"Is there anything we can do for you, Roxie?" Eddie asked.

"Like what?"

"I don't know. You're just so uptight. There's beer in the fridge."

"Who bought beer? I thought you were all broke."

"What difference does it make? If you want one, help yourself."

"You don't have anything stronger?" She knew Eddie had a long history of drug use. Everyone said he had tried everything. He might no longer be on the hard stuff, but she suspected he always had something.

"You just said Bob didn't cotton to drugs," Mike said. "I think he'd consider anything stronger than beer a drug, What do you say, Eddie?"

"I say there's beer in the fridge. And I don't want to get in the middle of this."

"Shut up!" Roxie yelled. *Jesus Christ*, they were driving her crazy. "All of you! Just shut the fuck up!" She stamped to the refrigerator and pulled out a cold beer.

Just where the hell had Bob gone? He was beginning to show some balls and she didn't like it one bit. She didn't care if he was fed up, but now wasn't the time. Before she left the room, Eddie's voice stopped her.

"You know, Roxie, you're so beautiful, I can't help but think if you just smiled more or tried to be nicer to people, things would be easier for you. You can tell Bob to fire me, but I think somebody needs to tell you what a negative, mean person you are. I thought it was because Darla sings better than you, but—"

"Shut your mouth!" she screeched, barely restraining herself from hurling the full can of beer at that damned old dope addict's head. "She does not sing better than me. She doesn't do *anything* better than me."

The room sat in silence. Finally, she regained control of her temper. "After Sunday, you're all finished," she said icily. "I'm telling Bob how things got out of hand while he *left* me here with a bunch of drugged-out perverts. I'm telling him how I came out to get a beer and disrupted your drug fest. Knowing our keyboard expert's past, Bob won't even give any of you a chance to defend yourself."

"Bullshit. He won't believe you," Mike said.

"Maybe not at first, but trust me, Mike. I can make his life a living hell until he does. I know how to handle Bob Denman, and don't ever think I don't."

"Don't get ahead of yourself, Roxie," Mike said, and she thought she heard fear in his voice. "The tour can't go on without music."

"Get hold of yourself, fool. I can get on the phone and have new musicians here tomorrow night and you know I can. You might as well face it. You're all finished."

"That doesn't include me, does it, Roxie?" Valetta Rose asked meekly. "I mean, I didn't do or say anything."

"I'm done with all of you." She turned and gave them a condescending smile over her shoulder. "I'm going to bed. Keep the TV down so I can get my beauty sleep."

"Bitch," she heard Mike mutter under his breath.

She whirled and stamped back into the room. "Fuck with me, Mike, and I'll tell Bob you tried to rape me."

"That's uncalled for, Roxie," Eddie said, shaking his head.

"Really? Well if you think I can sing, you old doper, wait until you see me act."

"I've said it before and I'm saying it again," Eddie said. "One of these days, you're gonna get what's coming to you."

She chuckled. "Damn straight. And when I do, I won't even know your names. In fact, when we get back to Nashville, I'm going to make a few phone calls. And after I do, it'll be a cold day in hell before either one of you sits in a band for anyone again."

Roxie flipped her hair and started out of the room.

"Oh, yeah? Well don't look now, missy, but this is hell and it's snowing outside."

"Eat shit, Eddie." He had a lot of nerve.

The Overstreet dogs began barking outside and Debbie Sue heard the sound of a truck engine she recognized. She walked to the window and looked out. "Bob's here. Guess those directions I gave him were good enough."

"Listen, both of you," Darla said. "Promise me you won't say a word about what I just said. I mean it. Promise me right here, right now or I'll ask him to take me back to the house."

"Scout's honor," Debbie Sue vowed.

"When were you ever a Scout?" Edwina asked Debbie Sue. To Darla she said, "Don't worry about it, hon. I talk a lot, but I know when to keep my mouth shut."

Debbie Sue looked at Darla and Edwina. She believed Darla's confession was safe with Edwina, but she wondered if Darla herself might break the promise.

She opened the door to Bob and led him into the kitchen, where Darla and Edwina sat at her square yellow Formica table. He walked over to Darla and dutifully gave her a peck on the check. To Debbie Sue it appeared to be as casual as the nod he gave to her and Edwina. But she had no doubt Edwina was visualizing something entirely different.

Edwina jumped up from her chair and went to the blender on the kitchen counter. "Bob, you wouldn't turn down a Texas-style margarita, would you?"

"Texas-style? Dare I ask what makes it Texas-style?"

"Tequila, Grand Marnier and a splash of Everclear. If it doesn't kill you, it'll clean your teeth. If you swish it around in your mouth a little, they'll practically dazzle."

"Lord, is that what was in the two I've had?" Darla asked, wide-eyed. "My God, Edwina, I don't think even antifreeze is a hundred and ninety proof."

Edwina frowned, pressing a crimson-nailed finger against her chin. "Really? Well then. Now you're all set for the coming winter months."

Bob laughed. "I'll take the margarita, but no Everclear please. I don't drink much and I think anything that's a hundred and ninety proof might do me in."

"Okay, Bob, I'll leave out the Everclear," Edwina said. "I don't want to make anybody sick."

Everyone laughed more and Bob took a seat adjacent to Darla at the square table. "Hey, look at this," Bob said of the table. "An antique."

Darla smoothed her hand over the top of the table. "This is what they used to call a cracked ice pattern." She twisted in her chair that matched the table and ran her hand over the silver upholstery tacks. "How old is this dining set? I haven't seen one like this since I don't know when."

"We had a red one, Darla, when we were first married," Bob said, and sipped his drink. "Don't you remember? We bought it used at a Salvation Army store."

Darla beamed a huge smile at him.

There was no missing the smug look on Edwina's face.

"Debbie Sue, how long have you had this?" Darla asked.

"It was my grandmother's. My mom used it her whole life before she moved out of this place. She wrote many a country song right here at this table. It has to be from the forties or fifties, I'd guess."

"As long as you're guessing, guess how much it would cost to buy this set now," Bob said.

"Oh, I don't know. Three hundred dollars?"

"Ohhh, *The Price Is Right*," Edwina said. "I love that game. Let me guess, too. Hmm, I'm going to say two hundred. You'd be a fool to pay more than that."

"Darla, you want to take a guess?" Debbie Sue asked.

"What does the winner get?" she countered playfully.

Debbie Sue looked around the room, then left her chair and headed for the cupboard. "A jar of genuine home-canned pickled peaches. Made 'em myself." She brought out a pint jar of golden peaches. "I can't cook worth a damn, but one of the customers at the beauty shop taught me how to make these."

"They're beautiful," Darla said. "And I love them. I'll say seven hundred dollars."

Edwina gasped. "Y'all are nuts. Why, I can practically taste those peaches now."

Darla grinned. She appeared to be having fun with the game.

"The table is in perfect condition," Bob said. "I think it would go for about eight-fifty. The chairs are probably worth about a hundred and fifty each."

Edwina's jaw dropped. "My God. As I live and breathe."

Debbie Sue quickly did the math in her head. "That's fourteen hundred and fifty dollars. Lord, I don't think everything in this house combined is worth fourteen hundred and fifty dollars." She, too, gently ran her palm over the table. "When I think of the saddles I've thrown on this table. And I mean big, heavy saddles."

"Not to mention the times Buddy has thrown *you* on it," Edwina added, laughing.

"Ed, no one needs to know that."

"Just don't do it anymore," Darla said. "The saddles, I mean."

They all laughed together, then fell silent, as if they had run out of anything to say. Debbie Sue had purchased three enormous sacks of candy bars at Sam's Club for the candy bowl in the beauty salon. She dragged a bag out of the cupboard and found a deck of cards in the hutch on one side of the small room. "Okay, everyone, since we're having a slumber party, how about a little poker?"

Everyone agreed.

"Here's how we usually play. A Snickers is worth five dollars. Almond Joys are ten and a PayDay's worth twenty, M&M'S are—"

"Oh, hell, forget the M&M'S," Edwina said. "I'm eating those."

A couple of hours later, little piles of candy lay in front of Bob and Edwina both. Debbie Sue and Darla had only a few pieces.

"This is so much fun," Darla said. "I can't remember when I've laughed so much."

"Wish y'all were going to be around to meet Buddy and Vic. Bob, you and Darla should come back and—" Debbie Sue stopped herself, realizing she had inadvertently made a couple out of Darla and Bob.

Edwina grinned like a cat that had swallowed the world's only canary, and Darla blushed.

"Oh, hell, I'm sorry," Debbie Sue started.

"Don't worry about it, Debbie Sue," Bob said. "It happens all the time, doesn't it, Darla?"

"All the time," Darla answered. "But at least they don't ask if I'm your daughter." Her hand flew to her mouth and Debbie Sue could see she was genuinely embarrassed by what had popped out of it. "Oh, Bob, I'm so sorry. That was a lousy thing to say. Can I blame it on the tequila?"

Bob placed his hand on top of Darla's. "Don't worry about it, darlin'." He looked at her intently. "That's something that just tonight I decided to do something about. When this tour is over, if I can wait that long."

Oh, my God, holy cow, Debbie Sue thought. They were on the cusp of something. Debbie Sue wasn't sure how she should react. Did Bob intend to leave Roxie for Darla? And if that happened, would it be a big cataclysmic explosion or nothing more than a tiny pop? She almost felt sorry for Roxie, remembering the pain she had experienced when she and Buddy were divorced and Buddy was hanging out with a schoolteacher from Odessa.

The jangle of the wall phone made everyone jump. Debbie Sue stumbled out of her chair to get to the phone. She checked caller ID and saw Maudeen Wiley's name. Maudeen was her favorite octogenarian and a loyal Styling Station customer. "Hey, Maudeen, what's up? Are you okay? You're not sick, are you?"

"Why, lands no," Maudeen answered. "Why would you ask?"

"Sweetheart, it's after ten. And you told me you made yourself sick on homebrew."

"Oh, that," she said dismissively. "Why, I didn't even think about the time. I was just watching 'Lustful Co-eds in Cancun' on the Playboy Channel, and I saw this girl with the prettiest red hair. And it reminded me, I think I missed my appointment to get my hair trimmed and colored."

"No problem, Maudeen. Just come in tomorrow. Around eleven."

"I didn't drag you away from that pretty husband, did I?"

"No, no," Debbie Sue said. "He's out of town until Monday."

"Honey, that man spends too much time out of town. Just think what you could be doing if he was *in* town."

Debbie Sue didn't need to be reminded of that. "Oh, we'll catch up when he gets back."

"Well, I'll see you tomorrow. Sorry to call you so late, honey."

"That's fine, Maudeen. That's okay. Don't apologize. We'll see you tomorrow. Cut, curl and color."

Debbie Sue hung up and returned to the group. The spell surrounding Bob and Darla had been broken. "Everything okay with Maudeen?" Edwina asked.

"She lost track of the time."

"I don't wonder, as dark as she keeps that apartment all the time."

"Oh, Ed," Debbie Sue said. "She says that's the secret to her lasting beauty."

"One of our elderly customers," Edwina explained to Bob and Darla, stacking the cards and slipping them into their box.

"Bless her heart," Darla said.

"Bless her heart," Bob added.

"Oh, don't worry about Maudeen. As the old-timers around here would put it, she's a ring-tailed tooter."

"Anyway she's coming in tomorrow," Debbie Sue said. "Her hair won't take us long."

Bob rose from his chair. "Guess I'd better be getting back to the house. I've got to make sure everyone is present and accounted for tomorrow and not cavorting around doing something they shouldn't. I swear, sometimes keeping up with a bunch of musicians is like running a day care."

"Well, rats," Edwina said. "I was winning, too. Do I get to keep the candy?"

"It's going to the shop, where you'll end up eating half of it anyway," Debbie Sue said.

"True enough," Edwina countered.

The three of them accompanied Bob to the door. As they stood on the front stoop and watched him walk to Vic's pickup, Debbie Sue remembered the *Price Is Right* game they had played earlier. "I never renege on a bet, dammit." She hurried to her kitchen pantry, pulled out a jar of pickled peaches and returned to the porch. "Bob, wait," she called to him.

He stopped mid-stride and turned toward them.

"I'll take it to him," Darla said, snatching the jar from her grip.

chapter thirteen

Darla felt self-conscious walking the jar of peaches out to Bob. The closer her steps took her to him, the more she realized he was watching her intently. She felt giddy, almost girlish, as she handed him the jar.

"Thanks," he said. "You didn't need to bring these out. I could've come back and gotten them."

"I wanted to," she said, then ran out of words.

Darkness surrounded them like a black cape. No light could be seen anywhere except from the countless stars twinkling down at them from the heavens. "My God, look at all those stars," she said, gazing upward. "I can't remember when I've seen anything so pretty. Or for that matter, the last time I even looked."

"Me either," Bob replied.

She turned her gaze to him and realized he wasn't looking

at the stars, but was instead staring at her. The next thing she knew, his arms were around her and their lips had met in a homecoming kiss that sent a million different emotions racing through her. They kissed for a long time, with her hanging on to the jar of peaches between them. He murmured words of sweetness. Tears sprang to her eyes, but still she kissed him.

At last they parted and he set her away. "I've got to go," he said, his voice rough.

"I know," she said in a tiny voice.

He turned away from her and opened the pickup door. She wanted to grab him, beg him to stay, but she didn't dare. Instead she stood there hanging on to the jar of peaches. *Oh, my God. The peaches.* "Bob," she said shakily.

He turned back to her. "Yes?"

She thrust the jar of peaches toward him. "You—you forgot your prize."

"No. I didn't, baby. I never did."

Though driving in a virtual black box with only his headlights to show the way, Bob had never seen things more clearly. He didn't belong where he was. Being Roxie's husband was as laughable to him as it was to everyone else. Why hadn't it been two years ago, before he had said those vows?

Maybe it was because when he first met her, Roxie had brought back memories of a youthful Darla—fresh, beautiful and talented as all get-out. Like Darla, she had known exactly what she wanted and had gone after it. The difference was, Darla hadn't stepped on toes and feelings and, in some cases, hearts to get to the top. Roxie, on the other hand, in her attempt to climb the ladder of fame, had strewn human beings behind her as if they were trash, never bothering to wonder what might become of those she disposed of. To Roxie, no-longer-needed people were someone else's problem.

Bob held no doubt that at some point, he too would become one of the disposables. And because he was convinced of that, the telethon performance would be her last under his management.

He felt an instant relief and freedom at the thought. In high spirits for the first time in a long time, he began to hum a Darla Denman song especially dear to his heart. He had helped her make up the lyrics one evening when they were wrapped in a blanket in front of a roaring fire . . . *humm-hmm . . . we loved all night . . . humm, hmm . . . Now it's daylight and time we both went home . . .*

Pulling into Salt Lick, he made the first turn on the right, another left and parked in the small house's driveway. No lights were on in the house, which was just as well. He wasn't in the mood for late-night chatter. He opened the front door quietly and tiptoed inside.

Snores came from the dark living room. A figure was on the couch. He couldn't make out who it was, but the snores told him the sleeper was dead to the world.

He slipped off his boots and in stocking feet started for the master bedroom. He found the door closed and heard sounds. Unmistakable sounds. Someone was having sex. Roxie? With whom? Mike or Eddie? A new acquaintance she had met earlier in the day? He suspected Mike. He had seen that Roxie seemed to have a connection with him that she didn't have with Eddie.

An odd feeling stole through him. His brain told him he should be furious and indignant, but the only feeling he had was to marvel that she would be so bold as to do it right under his nose. Whoever she was with, the two of them must be having a good laugh about what an old fool Bob Denman was.

Well, he wouldn't give her the pleasure of walking in on her and making a scene. She would enjoy all of that melodrama too much. He quietly stepped backward, went to Darla's room and shut the door, where at least his wife's activities wouldn't disturb his sleep. He wanted to be rested and alert tomorrow when he told her to take a hike. Literally.

Sunday morning's light came way too early for Debbie Sue. The last Texas margarita had been one too many and she felt the ill effects.

The unmistakable aroma of fresh-brewed coffee and something baking tickled her senses, and the sound of someone in the kitchen piqued her curiosity. Buddy? No way. He would be out of town for another day at least, and even if he was fooling around in the kitchen, he wouldn't be baking.

Then she remembered that Edwina and Darla Denman had stayed over. She was pretty sure Edwina wouldn't be baking either. Padding barefoot to the kitchen, she saw Darla standing at the sink, busily washing dishes and stacking them on the dish drainer to her left.

Darla looked up. "Why good morning, pretty girl. I thought you were going to sleep the day away."

Debbie Sue squinted toward the clock on the wall. "What time is it?"

"Eight fifteen. Hope I didn't wake you up too early."

"Heck, no. Eight fifteen is sleeping in for me. How long have you been up?"

"Must have been around seven. I tried to be quiet. When I'm a guest in someone else's home I try to follow their routine, but I was so hungry I took the liberty of rummaging through your cupboards. I found everything I needed for a cinnamon coffee cake. I haven't made it in years. I thought I'd forgotten the recipe, but it all came back. Hope you don't mind."

"Mmm, yummy," Debbie Sue said. She poured herself a cup of coffee and carried it to the table. "You actually found the ingredients for cinnamon coffee cake in *this* kitchen? Lord, something that good hasn't been cooked in here since my mom moved out. The only thing I ever find in the cupboards are excuses not to make something. Buddy does most of the cooking. I've never been very good at it."

Darla slipped an oven mitt on her right hand and opened the oven door. As an even more intense scent of cinnamon filled the kitchen, Debbie Sue's mouth watered. Darla set the square pan on the stovetop, pulled off the oven mitt and, as if she knew right where to go, went to a drawer and found a knife. Then she opened the cupboard door and dragged out plates.

"Marriage is a whole lot more than just who does the cooking, you know." She sliced the coffee cake into squares. "I've heard you talk enough about this Buddy of yours to know he's your soul mate." She lifted out two pieces of the coffee cake and placed them onto the plates. "Take a lesson from me, babygirl. Do not *ever* let anything come between you and that man. I mean, *nothing*."

"You know, I did do that for a while and Buddy divorced me. And while we were apart, he took up with a schoolteacher who was hearing wedding bells. That was a very bad time in my life, on top of a previous bad time. So, no, ma'am. I will never again let anything come between me and Buddy."

Darla set a piece of steaming coffee cake in front of Debbie Sue, who inhaled the heavenly aroma of warm cinnamon, then sliced off a bite and popped it into her mouth. "Oh, my God, this is good."

Darla tasted her own piece of the warm cake. "Hmm. It isn't bad. I haven't totally lost my touch. I learned to cook as a child." She brought her plate and coffee to the table and sank to a chair adjacent to Debbie Sue's. "What was it that came between you and Buddy?"

"Rodeo. And barrel racing. I won some ProRodeo championships on the circuit."

"Really," Darla said, her eyes large and rounded with surprise.

"Yep. I had a great horse, so I got bigheaded and thought I could go all the way. I made a balls-out effort, too." Debbie Sue made a gesture with her fist. "That's one of my big flaws. With me, it's all or nothing."

"Oh, my God," Darla said. "What happened?"

"Nothing much. I never made it to the national finals in Vegas, so Buddy wanted me to give it up. We argued about it a lot and he finally told me we were through if I didn't quit. My hard head took control of my common sense and I said, 'No way am I quitting.'"

"You mean he refused to support you?"

"It was more complicated than that, but that's the short version. It's a really long story. I never talk about it."

"Hmm, I understand," Darla said. "Well, it doesn't matter who's right and who's wrong. Never lose sight of how much you love him and what your life would be like with him gone from it." She stared into space, seemingly lost in her own thoughts. "I wish Bob and I could have another chance. Believe me, the second time, I'd be the kind of wife he deserves. The kind of person he should have in his life. I've been so damned wrong so many times on so many levels, I almost can't stand to think about it."

"You know what?" Debbie Sue said. "Ed thinks you still have a chance with Bob. I might be talking way out of turn here, but I think she could be right. That marriage of convenience he's in appears to be real *inconvenient* for him."

"Is it that obvious to strangers? I've been thinking the same thing, but I'm afraid to believe it."

"Afraid to believe what?" A rumpled, sleepy-eyed Edwina walked into the kitchen, wearing Debbie Sue's robe, the hemline and sleeve length way too short. Her hair was still plastered to her head from wearing a hat all day yesterday. "Hmmm," she said bending over the coffee cake and inhaling. "What is this?"

"Cinnamon coffee cake," Debbie Sue answered.

Edwina opened a cupboard door and took out a plate. "Darla, that looks scrumptious."

Debbie Sue huffed. "Dammit, Ed, how do you know I'm not the one who baked it?"

Edwina gave her an arch look. "Because I know you. You haven't put anything in the stove since you were seven and got an Easy-Bake oven for Christmas."

"Oh, hell, you're right." Debbie Sue left her chair and placed another slice of the coffee cake on her plate. "I can't even make it work with those Pillsbury things you whack against the counter edge."

"Now, back to the subject I missed out on," Edwina said, taking an oversized slice of coffeecake. She took an oversized mug from the cupboard, filled it with coffee and began adding teaspoons of sugar.

Darla watched wide-eyed.

Debbie Sue had counted eight teaspoons of sugar. She

frowned at Edwina's cup, but to Darla, she explained, "Edwina doesn't have to worry about what she eats. She never gets fat."

"Wow," Darla said. "Fat's the least of it. If I put that much sugar in a cup of coffee, I'd zoom out of here like a rocket."

"Darla, you said something about being afraid," Edwina said, bringing her cake and coffee to the table. "Afraid of what?"

Debbie Sue filled Edwina in on the previous conversation she and Darla had had. Edwina listened intently.

"What I didn't tell Debbie Sue," Darla said hesitantly, "is that last night Bob and I kissed, really kissed for the first time in years. The chemistry's still there. I almost told him I still loved him."

"Great balls o' fire," Edwina gushed. "I knew it. I just knew something happened between you two." Having finished both her coffee and her slice of coffee cake, she rose from her chair and took another huge slice of the coffee cake, poured another cup of coffee and added eight teaspoons of sugar. "Let me tell you what I think—"

"No. Let me tell you what *I* think," Debbie Sue said. "That coffee you're drinking is like swallowing syrup. I kept my mouth shut for the first eight teaspoons, but now I have to ask, what in the hell are you doing?"

"Listen, I'm gonna be just fine. I read somewhere that P. Piddy or some such somebody does this the day of a performance. After the high passes, massive amounts of sugar can have a calming affect." Edwina brought her coffee cake and coffee back to the table.

"Edwina, I've heard everything imaginable for revving up to perform," Darla said. "Uppers, downers, cocaine, booze, sex, you name it. But I've never heard of anyone using excessive sugar."

Debbie Sue shook her head slowly, incredulous. "And have you taken into consideration that everyone's body reacts differently? Eating a pound of sugar might work for P. Diddy, but you don't really know what it might do to you, do you?"

"Well, no. . . . I'm just assuming that by tonight when I'm ready to perform, I'll be fine." Edwina swallowed a great gulp of her coffee.

"Or in a diabetic coma," Debbie Sue said.

Edwina emptied her mug and cleaned her plate again, even pressing her fork against the crumbs to get every last one, then she got to her feet, grabbed a dishrag and began wiping down the counter, one foot tapping the floor as she worked.

"Look at you," Debbie Sue said. "You're already so wired you can't even stand still. You're going to be so jacked up you're going to take off somewhere and we won't be able to find you for a month, much less get you settled down for tonight."

"And how long does it take this high to pass?" Darla asked with a skeptical tone.

"Relax, will you?" Edwina flopped her hand at Darla. "What was I about to say? Oh, yeah. I think that after tonight Roxie will be gone."

"What do you mean by gone, oh all-wise one?" Debbie Sue asked.

"Well, hell, Dippity-do. I only know one meaning for the word *gone*. Out of the picture. Absent. No longer around."

"And where would she be going?" Darla asked.

Edwina moved to the opposite counter with her dishrag and began wiping it, too, her feet doing a dance while she wiped. "She's got a voice like I've never heard. Once it hits the airwaves she'll be gobbled up by adoring fans or agents or producers or whoever it is who makes people big stars. The only thing better than her voice is her face. Running a close second to that is her body. Ol' Bob's going to be left sucking hind tit."

"Ed!" Debbie Sue said.

Darla broke into laughter. "It's okay. I know what that means. Because I grew up in Texas around agriculture people."

"It's a simple explanation for a common occurrence in the animal kingdom," Edwina said in a condescending tone.

Debbie Sue rolled her eyes.

"He'll come running back to you, Darla," Edwina said. "You'll be the one he turns to for support after she dumps him. Thank God for rebounds, huh?"

Debbie Sue smacked her forehead with her palm, wishing she had a cork for Edwina's mouth. All of that damn sugar-caffeine combo had her talking a mile a minute. Words were just tumbling out. And her theory about Bob and Roxie and Darla didn't sound even close to right. One had only to glance in Darla's direction to see that it hadn't set well with her, either. Her backbone had gone straight as a rail.

"Rebound?" Darla tossed her head ever so slightly. "Darla Denman is *no one's* rebound. If Roxie's future is clear to you, Bob has to know it too. Looking for a soft place to fall, is he? The bastard. Well, I'll show him."

Debbie Sue winced and shot a look of consternation in Edwina's direction.

"Did I say something wrong?" Edwina asked.

"No, Edwina," Darla answered sharply. "You're talking sense, which is something I needed to hear. What time are you two going in to your shop today?"

"We need to be there before eleven, for Maudeen," Debbie Sue said.

"Do you think y'all can work me in today? I want everything you offer."

"Everything?" Edwina perked up. "Even the lip and eyelid tattooing?"

"You do that?"

"Ed's about the best I've ever seen," Debbie Sue said. "Just because we live at the end of the world doesn't mean we don't do good work. Ed's worked wonders."

"Hmm, I'd rather do that than Botox," Darla said. "I've been self-conscious of my chicken lips the past couple of years. They've gotten thinner and thinner. Unfortunately, my thighs didn't notice. Okay, put me down for the lips, but I'll pass on the eyelids. I don't want anything coming at my eyeballs."

"You could always go see Tatts by Matt," Edwina said. "He's probably more qualified than I am."

"No, thanks. And Debbie Sue's testimony is good enough for me. I trust you. Hell, I'm feeling better already."

"And by the time the show starts tonight you'll be looking better, too," Edwina said. "Think I'll have another slice of that coffee cake and some more coffee."

"No!" Debbie Sue exclaimed, getting to her feet and standing between Edwina and the coffee cake. "My God, you'll be so revved up, Darla will end up with a zigzag lip line."

"Everything is perfectly under control," Edwina said indignantly.

Darla suddenly slapped the table with her palm. "If Bob Denman wants me, he's going to have to prove it *before* Roxie makes her big debut and bails on him. Right or wrong, I'm telling him how I feel tonight. I'm drawing a line in the sand. It's me or Roxie. Make your choice, Bob Denman. You choose me now, not after she's walked out on you."

"You go, girl," Edwina said. "I think he'll choose you."

"Me too," Debbie Sue said. "Don't you think so?"

Darla sighed, her bravado already declining. "I don't have a clue. Seems like I never do. I'm lousy with men. Edwina, Debbie Sue's right. Stop eating that coffee cake and drinking that coffee. If I'm going to get my man back, I need you to have a steady hand."

chapter fourteen

Bob stood at the living-room window sipping his second cup of morning brew and taking in the sunlit morning. Eddie had gone out to the patio attached to the back of the house to smoke while Mike cooked breakfast. Mike's behavior this morning appeared to be no different from what it always was—absorption in the music from his earpiece and indifference to almost everything else.

Bob set his suspicion aside. Roxie's antics meant little to him anymore. Even after what he had learned about her last night, he had slept as if he had been cradled in the arms of angels, couldn't remember the last time he had rested so well. Amazing how things coming into focus could clear the mind.

An elderly woman coming out of the cottage across the street caught his attention. She crossed the street, coming toward the house carrying a newspaper. As she shuffled up the driveway, he walked to the front door and opened it. "Good morning," he said cheerily.

"Morning," she said. "You must be the new renter."

"Well, no—"

"I'm Koweba Sanders. Debbie Sue called me and told me you was here. I brung you the paper." She handed over an edition of the *Odessa American*.

No doubt Debbie Sue had asked this Mrs. Sanders to keep an eye on things at her house, though he wondered what the woman could see. She looked to be a hundred years old, wore huge black-framed glasses so round and thick the sheer weight of them kept them sliding down her narrow nose. Bob smiled as he took the paper. "Hey, thanks."

"I used to have a freezer full of casseroles and I'd bring one of them to new neighbors," the elderly woman said, "but Debbie Sue's had so many renters I've used 'em all up."

He stepped back for her to come into the house. "I'll be sure to return the paper."

She waved the suggestion away as she came into the living room. "Nah. Don't bother. I haven't read that paper in years. Don't give a damn what happens in Odessa. I've kept up my subscription so my kids will have something to read or a puzzle to work when they come for a visit."

"It's no problem for me to bring it back to you after I've read it, Mrs. Sanders," Bob promised. "And I won't touch the crossword. I'll leave it for your kids to work."

"Oh, that's all right. You go ahead and work it if you want to. I've got stacks of newspapers saved up. Those kids live over in Austin. They haven't come to see me in years." She turned and limped back to the front door. A wave of pity washed over Bob as he watched her totter back to the tiny, neatly kept house across the street. "Do you need any help over there?" he called out.

"No, thanks," she yelled back. "I haven't been to the fair in years. Too many people."

"Bless her ol' heart," Bob mumbled.

"Bless whose old heart?" Roxie asked when he returned to the kitchen. "Darla's?"

Bob felt an uncustomary rush of anger. Putting up with his wife's nastiness and snide remarks had already sent his blood pressure off the chart. He leveled a fierce look at her. "What would you know about someone else's heart, when you don't seem to have one of your own?"

Roxie's eyelids narrowed. "What did you say to me?"

"You heard me. Not only do you have a heart of stone, my dear wife, you've got the morals of an alley cat. You're not fit to say Darla Denman's name."

"Well, look at you. You've finally decided to grow a pair. What brings on this sudden . . ." Her words trailed off and her lips eased into a reptilian smile. "You came home last night after all. I figured you'd stay all night with the sweethearts of the rodeo. You should've brought Darla home with you. You'd have been welcome. I have no problem with a threesome."

"Shut your mouth. I don't even want to know who you were screwing last night. It doesn't matter. If he's got any sense he'll get as far away from you as he can." Picking up the truck keys from where they lay on the table, Bob said, "Mike? Eddie? Valetta Rose? Y'all grab your stuff. I'll wait for you in the truck."

The three left the room. Bob turned to leave through the front door, but Roxie moved to block him. "Where do you think you're going?"

"To Hogg's for breakfast and then to Midland, as if it's any of your business."

"But I'm not ready."

"That's okay." Bob clasped her shoulders and moved her aside. "You're not invited."

"But how am I supposed to get to Midland?"

"I don't know. But knowing you and your resourcefulness, you'll figure something out."

"Hey, Bob," Mike said from behind him. "If it's all the same with you, I'll stay here. I've still got gear to get together."

Bob stopped and gave him a long, hard look, but the drummer didn't flinch. Finally, Bob broke away and left through the front door, with Eddie and Valetta Rose trailing behind him.

"You worn-out old man," Roxie yelled after him. "You'll be sorry. All of you'll be sorry. After this, the only way you'll see me again is if you buy a ticket to my show. Do you hear me? A three-hundred-dollar ticket to *my* show!"

Roxie watched the pickup back out of the driveway, reverse and disappear up the street. *Crap.* She had really messed up this time. She didn't care what Bob thought. But the timing was all wrong. She needed to sing on TV tonight. Her voice and her looks were her ticket out and if Bob Denman thought he was going to stop her, he was out of his mind. Having national television time, even if it was a chicken-shit local show, was gold. It could cut years off the exhausting trail of finding another manager.

"You didn't have to stay here with me," she said to Mike.

"I'm not staying with you. I want to talk to you about last night." He walked outside to the patio.

Double crap! Was he mad, too?

"As far as I'm concerned there's nothing to talk about,"

Roxie said, addressing him through the screen door. "We've both got good reasons to keep our mouths shut, so I suggest that's exactly what we do. In the meantime, we've got a show to put on."

As she turned away from the door, her thoughts veered back to her husband. She would love to just let the chips fall where they might, but she couldn't. She would be the one to decide when her marriage ended and now wasn't the time for it. She needed another chance to get him alone and sweet-talk him. She knew the buttons to push and when to push them.

But first, she and Mike needed a ride. Slipping her phone from her robe pocket and a business card from the other, she keyed in a number, pressed the phone to her ear and listened to two rings. "Hey, hot stuff, can you pick me and Mike up and give us a ride to Midland?"

At the Styling Station, Debbie Sue unlocked the back door for Edwina and Darla and they followed her inside. "You'll be meeting our very most favorite customer today," Debbie Sue told Darla as she flipped on the lights and raised the shade covering the front door's window.

"The older woman who called last night who was confused about the time?"

"Ooh, yeah. That's her," Edwina groused. "Sometimes she's a big pain in the ass. I just hope she doesn't bring a bunch of cackling old hens from that nursing home with her."

Debbie Sue could tell Edwina's sugar high had worn off. Instead of the calming effect Edwina claimed to have read about, the overload of sugar and caffeine had had an opposite result. She was cranky as an old maid watching *The Bachelorette* on TV. "Ed! Bite your tongue. You love Maudeen. And those cackling old hens are a big part of our livelihood. If it wasn't for the ladies at Peaceful Oasis we might have to shut our doors."

"Oh, I know that. And you know I love them. And I do love Maudeen like my own mother. Shit, I'd kill for a Snickers bar about now."

"That whole sugar thing was dumb. I didn't figure you could count on being calm once those cocktails you were guzzling wore off."

"Or a Butterfinger. God yes, I want a Butterfinger. Did you bring that candy with you that we were playing poker with last night?"

"No, I forgot it."

"Well damn it all to hell, Debbie Sue. How could you forget it when you know I need sugar? Now I'm gonna have to go to the Kwik Stop."

Debbie Sue stepped in front of Edwina and clasped her shoulders. "Ed. Please don't buy any more sugar. You need something with protein or complex carbs to level out your cravings."

Edwina twisted away from Debbie Sue's grip, frowning. "And just how do you know this?"

"You're not the only one who reads, Ed. Except you rely on P. Diddy and I read stuff from legitimate health sources."

"Whatever," Edwina said, readjusting her purse on her shoulder. "Lard and what else?"

"*Carbs*, Ed, complex carbs. Pasta. Whole-grain bread. Even potatoes would be better than sugar. Proteins would be meat, cheese, dairy products—"

"I got it, I got it," Edwina grumbled. "So I'll get a milk shake and some potato chips."

Debbie Sue let out a gasp. "You're hopeless, Ed."

"Y'all want anything?" Edwina asked.

"Thanks, but nothing for me," Darla answered, preening in front of the large mirrors that hung at the workstations and studying her own profile. "God, I have to lose ten pounds by tonight."

"You could bring me a Baby Ruth," Debbie Sue said to Edwina. "One of the giant ones, not the regular size. And Ed, if you get your customary Dr Pepper, make sure it's sugar free."

"Bite me, Debbie Sue," Edwina retorted as she made her exit. The door slammed behind her.

"I have *never* seen her like this," Debbie Sue said to Darla. "And she has *never* talked to me like that. Next time I need to be a real bad-ass I'm loading up on sugar."

"Debbie Sue, have you ever used one of those slimming body suits they advertise on TV all the time? You know the one. The model looks like a sack of grapefruit and she goes into the dressing room and comes out smooth with her tits shoved up under her chin?"

"I haven't, but Ed's worn one."

"Of course you haven't. You're young and you're built like an Olympic swimmer. And Edwina's a rail. Why would she use one of those?"

"About a year ago she was convinced she was getting fat and she bought one. It turned out she was allergic to whatever it was made of. She broke out in hives all over her torso and had to go to the doctor. It's remarkable how soothing *and* smoothing Calamine lotion can be."

Darla laughed. "I want to try one. Where do you think I could get one around here?"

"Walmart, maybe," Debbie Sue said. "It's practically the

only place to buy anything anymore. There's one of their superstores in Odessa."

"Can we go today?"

"Sure. We'll just have to leave Salt Lick a little earlier," Debbie Sue answered.

"Do you know I haven't been to a Walmart store since I was a kid. And back then, it was nothing like it is now."

"Well you're in for a treat, Miz Darla."

Just then the Christmas bells tied to the front door jangled and Maudeen hobbled in. She had used a cane to hold the door open and an ace bandage was wrapped around her right ankle.

Debbie Sue rushed to the door to assist her, at the same time glancing out into the parking lot to see if she had driven herself in her ancient Cadillac or if her granddaughter had brought her to the shop. The granddaughter rolled down her window and yelled, "I'll be back for her in about an hour and a half."

"That'll work," Debbie Sue yelled back and turned her attention to her elderly customer. "Maudeen, what in the world happened to you?"

"Oh, hell, honey, I twisted my ankle. I was showing the ladies how to do the funky chicken and I got my high heels tangled up. Don't get old, honey. Your body turns on you. It refuses to do anything you tell it to."

Debbie Sue made a little gasp and planted her fists at her waist. "And what have I told you about wearing mile-high shoes? I can't even wear them myself."

The diminutive woman brushed her away. "We've been through this before, honey. Now you know I love my high heels." She looked at Darla and winked. "Makes me taller and the men can't get enough of 'em."

Darla laughed and it occurred to Debbie Sue that she hadn't told Maudeen a celebrity was going to be in the shop. "Maudeen, there's someone I want you to meet," she said enthusiastically, taking her by the elbow and guiding her gently to where Darla stood.

"You don't have to introduce me, honey," Maudeen replied. "I practically watched this one grow up onstage. Hello, Mrs. Denman, it's nice to meet you. I thought you were dead, honey. I'm glad to see I was wrong."

"Maudeen," Debbie Sue said, "I thought you'd be a little more excited. It isn't every day we have a star in the shop."

"Don't be offended, Mrs. Denman," Maudeen said. "When you reach my age, just waking up each morning is my excitement for the day. Anything else comes in a distant second."

"No offense taken, darling," Darla said, taking her hand and covering the top of it with her own. "And please, call me Darla."

Coloring, trimming and curling Maudeen's thin, wispy hair took Debbie Sue only a short time. During the process, the elderly woman regaled them with tales of her romances. She was under the dryer when Edwina returned.

"What took you so long?" Debbie Sue asked.

"Oh, you know me. I ran into people and got to talking. Everyone in town has heard about us backing you up, Darla. They asked me a million questions. Is she nice, what does she look like with her makeup off, can she still sing as good as she used to."

"I hope you had a positive answer for all those questions," Darla said, smiling.

"Oh, I did, I did. But I didn't tell them you're over here at the shop. They'd have followed me back for sure."

"That was good thinking, Ed," Debbie Sue said. "Looks like you got your sugar high under control. You seem more like your old self."

"Debbie Sue, you are so smart. Remind me the next time I ask you if you were born stupid that I told you on this date that you're smart. I ate a jumbo hot dog with lots of cheese piled on. Carbs and protein, right? I ate two egg, cheese and potato burritos, a container of yogurt, gag me, and I washed it all down with a sugar-free Dr Pepper."

"Good Lord, Edwina," Darla said. "I'd have put on ten pounds if I'd eaten all of that. And speaking of weight, Debbie Sue's taking me to Walmart this afternoon to buy one of those body-slimming thingamajigs."

"Did she tell you what happened to me when I wore one?"

Darla laughed. "She mentioned it."

"Just be careful is all I'm saying. Okay. Now that I'm fortified with real food, get over here and let me take a gander at those chicken lips."

A couple of hours later, Darla was leaning in close to the mirror, turning her head from side to side, pursing and relaxing her lips. She couldn't believe the difference. She had always drawn her upper lip with lip liner and in a photo it could pass. But in person it looked just like what it was—an upper lip drawn with lip liner. But this was perfect. Edwina had used a shade natural to her own lips, with just a hint of color. That woman was truly an artist and Salt Lick was lucky to have her. She could teach Valetta Rose a thing or two.

"Try not to move your lips too much for another hour or so," Edwina said. "You don't want that ink to spread. Here, put this ice pack on your lips. It'll help keep any swelling down. Come back to the sink so I can put a conditioner on your hair."

Dutifully Darla followed Edwina to the shampoo bowl. Relaxing on the chaise chair, she felt more alive than she had in years. She was happy to the point of giddiness. Tonight was the first night of her new life. She would do the Darla Denman comeback tour for a year, maybe cut a new album, and then she would happily retire as Bob's wife. The wife she should have always been but never was. She had a lot to make up for where Bob was concerned, and she was ready and willing to do it if she just got the chance.

With that sweet plan on her mind she settled back and drifted off, hoping for Edwina to work another one of her miracles.

chapter fifteen

Sitting in a bar near the civic center, Bob watched Eddie and Valetta Rose play pool.

"Damn, Valetta Rose," Eddie grumbled, digging three crumpled bills from his jeans pocket and slapping them onto her outstretched hand. "You shoot pool better than anybody I ever seen, man or woman. You should go to Vegas to those tournaments or something."

"I don't like playing for money," she said shyly.

"You sure don't seem to mind taking *my* money," Eddie said.

"But this isn't money that I'm going to keep." She smiled as she laid the bills on the table. "This is for the next game. Rack 'em, Eddie."

Eddie picked up a bill and fed it into the table and the sound of dropping balls thudded in the dimly lit room.

Valetta Rose strolled over to where Bob sat, reached for

her Coke and took a long drink. She appeared to be the only member of the group who didn't drink.

"You're whipping Eddie's butt," Bob said, as she set her glass back on the table. "Where'd you learn to shoot pool that well?"

She ducked her head, not looking at him. "Ever hear of Clyde, Texas?"

Bob shook his head. "Can't say that I have."

"It's a little town outside Abilene. It's where I grew up. I've got three older brothers. My mom used to make them take me with them everywhere. They figured the only way to handle it was to treat me like one of the guys. The only pool table in town was in the back room of a convenience store. So they took me to the convenience store when they went to play pool. If they couldn't come up with a way to get rid of me and if there was nobody else to play with, they let me play. After I got older, I took to practicing by myself, mostly to stay out of their way if they were flirting with girls or if they got in a fight. And if that didn't work I always had a hold on a cue stick I could use for a weapon." She laughed, a shy, self-deprecating sound. "Mom hoped having me there would keep them from getting into trouble."

Valetta Rose was becoming a more interesting person all the time. Bob read a dozen scenarios between the lines of her story. "And did it?"

She sipped her Coke. "My brothers were outlaws in those days. They took after my dad. They loved to start fights, end fights and jump in the middle of one that was already going on. There weren't three tougher boys around. 'Course they had to be to survive living with my dad. I always felt safe with them."

Bob angled a look at her. "How in the world did you end up in the world of stage makeup? I've seen a lot of people in that business, some good and some so-so, but you're really good."

She smiled again. "Promise not to tell?"

Bob crossed his heart with his index finger. "Absolutely. Anything you tell me is safe."

"Okay, don't laugh. I used to work in a funeral home in Abilene."

Bob gave a belly laugh. "I heard that, but I didn't know if it was true."

"You laughed," she exclaimed.

Bob could see he might have hurt her feelings. "I'm not laughing at you, Valetta Rose. I'm laughing *with* you."

"But it isn't funny. It's sad. We'll all be in that position someday."

"You're right. I'm sorry I laughed. But you're so young. How did you get a job like that?"

"I helped to pick up and deliver dead people from wherever they fell. Hospitals, streets, wherever. One night we brought in the woman who had been doing the makeup on the dearly departed at that funeral home for years. With two upcoming funerals, the director just about lost it. He ordered me to step in and do her makeup and I did. As they say, the rest is history."

"You must have made those corpses look good."

"Let's just say the one who died an old maid wouldn't have if I'd been fixing her face. She looked beautiful lying there in her coffin. Her family complained that she didn't look anything like herself and they were right. To heck with them, I thought. A girl deserves to meet her maker looking her best. Don't you think?"

"Absolutely," Bob answered, no longer grinning.

Eddie had finished racking the balls and was leaning on his cue stick. "You're up, Valetta Rose."

She smiled and walked away. Bob had never had a conversation of more than a few words with Valetta Rose. She seemed like a different person from the one he had first met. He had mistaken her quiet demeanor as snooty, but he could see a more accurate word was *guarded*.

She chalked her cue and shot, but missed. Stepping back, Eddie approached the table and leaned in for his turn. He began a run on the table and Valetta Rose returned to Bob's side.

"So tell me," Bob said, "how did you come to meet my wife?"

Valetta Rose hooked a sheaf of her blond hair behind her ear, still watching Eddie at the pool table. "It was an accident. I went to Nashville to visit my brother a couple of months ago. He took me out one evening and we wound up at the club where Roxie was singing."

"Nashville Nights?"

"Yeah, that's it. When she finished her set, she came over to the bar for a drink. I commented that she'd look less harsh if she used a different shade of makeup. And if she went a little lighter on the eye shadow and used blush better."

"You said that to Roxie?" He chuckled. "I'm surprised you survived."

"Oh, she was plenty pissed, but you know Roxie. Anything that might make her look better got her attention. She must have thought about what I said because later she asked me to come back the next night and do her makeup before the show. I did and I figured I'd never hear from her again, but she kept calling me. Then she called and asked me to come on this tour with her, all expenses paid. I didn't even have to think about it. I've never been anywhere that my brothers didn't take me."

"I remember the transformation; but she never told me it was you who was responsible. I thought she went to some high-dollar salon. You should feel proud of yourself."

"I do. That and shooting pool is about all I know how to do."

"But working on the living has to be a lot different than working on the dead."

"It is," Valetta Rose said with a laugh. "The dead don't call you names and throw things at you. But I was used to that treatment."

"Your dad?"

"He was mean. Let's just say I learned how to cover bruises early." She took a long drink of her Coke. "First my mom's, then mine." She shrugged. "I learned early to take advantage of what life throws your way, even if it's shit."

Darla snapped her cell phone shut. "Bob says we go on at eight thirty. I told him we'd be there by seven o'clock."

Debbie Sue stopped chewing on her thumbnail long enough to look at the clock. Four hours. She had only four hours to steel herself.

Edwina had finished tattooing Darla's lips and had put a shining coppery color on her long hair. Now Edwina lazed in a chair, examining the Chili Pepper No. 5 nail polish she had applied to Darla's toenails minutes earlier.

"Works for me." Darla bent over to smooth a smudge.

"Tell me what will be going on," Debbie Sue said, having added pacing to her case of nerves. "Step by step. I don't want any surprises."

Darla smiled. "You really are nervous, aren't you? I thought maybe you were kidding."

"I wish I was," Debbie Sue said.

"But when you barrel raced, you rode out into an arena packed with people and every eye on was on you. And only you."

"She had Rocket Man with her," Edwina said, shaking the nail-polish bottle. "Isn't that right, hon?"

"Rocket Man is my horse," Debbie Sue explained to Darla. "He's so big and strong, such a great athlete. I felt like every eye was on him, not me. All I did was sit on his back and have fun."

"All right, then, you can let me be your Rocket Man," Darla said. "You enjoy yourself and I'll try to keep every eye on me."

"You're right. You'll be the focus, just like Rocket Man was."

"Except you won't swish at flies with your tail and throw your head back and whinny," Edwina added.

"God, let's hope not," Darla muttered.

Debbie Sue laughed and shot Darla an appreciative glance. "Thanks. Now, tell me the routine. Yesterday, we didn't exactly rehearse it in the right order."

Darla explained that Bob would come out first with a big welcome to the audience. He would talk about the tour and invite everyone to buy CDs that would be strategically located in the lobby. He would then ask Darla to come out to the stage and give everyone a big hello. Then he would introduce Roxie, who would sing the opening number.

"Will he say he's married to her?" Edwina asked, still preoccupied with the nail polish and her toenails.

"Oh, no. There'll be no mention of that."

"Doesn't she have the same name?"

"Well, yes, but—"

"Then the audience is gonna assume she's your daughter."

Darla's eyes bugged and she stared at Edwina. "Oh, my God! Do you really think they'd think that? Do I look old enough to be her mother?"

"Of course not," Edwina said. "Forget I mentioned it. They'll think she's your sister. You know like Loretta Lynn and Crystal Gayle."

"Actually," Darla said, twisting her mouth, "Loretta *is* old enough to be Crystal's mother."

Debbie Sue saw a need to change the subject—and quick. "What about the band? Will he introduce them?"

"They'll be onstage, but I'm the one who does their intro. I'll introduce them and you ladies after about three songs."

"Do we have to say anything?" Debbie Sue asked.

Edwina suddenly became animated. "Oh, oh, I want to say something."

"You can't. Just a small wave or a smile will do."

"Darla, whatever you do, do not let Edwina get the mike," Debbie Sue said. "The government would have to write a new law stripping her First Amendment rights just to get her off the stage."

"Whatever," Edwina said. "Tell you what. Before we take off for Midland, let's go over to Hogg's and eat. I'll buy."

"Super," Darla exclaimed. "But Edwina, you can't possibly be hungry."

"Yeah, Ed, what are you thinking?" Debbie Sue said.

"I'm *thinking* I haven't eaten since this morning, I'm *thinking* of a double meat cheeseburger with all the trimmings. Fries or maybe onion rings. One of Aunt P's apricot fried pies and an ice cold Dr Pepper."

"Oh, my," Darla lamented, "I'm thinking I agree one hundred percent. All of that all sounds too good to pass up." She pressed her sides, then her stomach with her palms. "Dammit, I bet there's not enough elastic in the world to hold this shape together after a meal like that."

Debbie Sue removed her smock with a flourish, went to the front door, turned the sign hanging in the window from OPEN to CLOSED and declared, "Ed, if you're buyin', I'm tryin'."

They set off on foot to Hogg's. Debbie Sue couldn't help but marvel at the turn in events in a mere forty-eight hours. She had been expecting a slow weekend, with Maudeen in the salon and nothing but free hours to spend with Buddy after that. Now she was walking side by side with a celebrity, readying herself to perform on TV in the evening. Anyone who said there was nothing to do in a small town hadn't spent enough time in her small town.

"Say, Edwina," Darla said, looking across Hogg's parking lot, "isn't that your pickup?"

"Sure is. We must not be the only ones who're hungry."

Debbie Sue held the door open while Darla and Edwina entered Hogg's before her. They were met with hearty greetings from Valetta Rose and Eddie, and the heartiest of all from Bob.

A huge grin spread across Darla's face. "Bob, you scoundrel. I just talked to you. You didn't tell me you were over here. I thought you were in Midland."

"We came back to see how things are going with you. We just sat down. I was just about to call you back." He moved over to allow for room. "Here, sit by me. We're starving. I've probably got just enough of a balance left on my credit card to buy a round of burgers." He turned her shoulder away from him. "Hm, love the hair color. That'll pop on camera. Did the Styling Station girls do that?"

"Sure did. Edwina is an expert colorist."

"What have y'all been up to today?" Debbie Sue asked.

"Shooting pool," Bob answered. "Darla, you should see this little lady shoot pool," he said, gesturing toward Valetta Rose. "She's as good as that Asian girl we watched in Vegas. Remember that?"

"Yes, I remember," Darla said. "Where's Roxie and Mike?"

"I left them at the house."

"All day long?"

"Yep."

"Good Lord," Edwina said. "From what I've seen of that woman, she'll be madder than a wet cat. Anybody had the nerve to check on them?"

"They might be hungry, too, Bob," Darla said.

"They're all right. She called that guy Tatts by Matt to pick them up."

"Roxie's with a tattoo artist?" Valetta Rose asked.

"When I called her earlier, she and Mike were planning on hanging out with him at his tattoo parlor, then riding to Midland with him."

Valetta Rose sat for a minute expressionless, then looked away. Something was going on inside her head, but Debbie Sue couldn't figure what.

"Speaking of tattoos," Edwina said, "look at Darla's lips."

Valetta Rose studied Darla's lips closely. "You had your lips tattooed?"

"Edwina did it," Darla said, faking a smooch. "Aren't they fabulous?"

"They really are," Valetta Rose replied, leaning in for a closer look. "They're as good as any I've ever seen, Edwina."

"Thanks," Edwina gushed. "It's just a little something I took up. Most women my age are gardening or knitting baby blankets. Or God help me, scrapbooking. I decided to take up tattooing lips and eyelids."

"Do you mind telling me about your technique?" Valetta asked.

While the two women gabbed, Debbie Sue studied the traveling makeup artist. As far as she could tell, Valetta Rose wore no discernable makeup and except for bleach, her hair appeared to be free of hair products. Maybe she was trying for that less-is-more look, which wasn't for Debbie Sue personally, but it worked for the younger woman. She was attractive in a fresh-scrubbed way.

Darla stood. "If y'all will excuse me, I'm going to visit the ladies' room. Y'all order me whatever you're having. Cheeseburger, fries, the whole works."

"Uh, Mrs. Denman," Valetta Rose said timidly. "You need to be careful eating anything greasy for twenty-four hours. Your pores could absorb some of that oil and smear your lips permanently."

Darla delicately touched her newly tattooed lips with her fingertips. "Really? Oh, my God. Edwina, did you know that?"

"Nope. Looks like we learned it together. It makes sense. And it explains a lot to me."

"Like what?" Debbie Sue asked.

"Well, for one thing, why May Dean Gantt won't speak to me anymore. I thought she was wearing the wrong color of foundation all this time because it made her lips look like they had spread all over her face. I didn't know about the oil. I must've been late the day they went over that in class. I must've missed that lesson."

"It's a wonder she didn't sue you," Darla remarked.

"Or the shop," Debbie Sue added, alarmed.

"It's a wonder she didn't kill me," Edwina said. "You don't know May Dean and her husband."

"Hmm, y'all just order me a glass of iced tea," Darla said. "That will be the best. I can put Plan B into operation if I don't overeat."

"Plan B?" Bob asked.

"Walmart and body armor," Debbie Sue answered. "We're going to stop off there on our way to the civic center."

"They have Spanx at Walmart?" Valetta Rose asked.

"Maybe Kymaro or Lipo in a Box," Edwina said. "I'm sure they'll have one or the other."

"See there," Bob said to Eddie. "I've always known women had a secret language and this proves it. I didn't understand a damn word they just said."

Eddie, who Debbie Sue had never heard utter a word, suddenly spoke. "Me neither, boss, but if somebody's getting spanked at Walmart, I wouldn't mind seeing that. In fact, I think I could sell tickets."

The group was laughing when Valetta Rose's phone warbled. Without looking, she flipped open the cover and pressed the device to her ear. Though Debbie Sue couldn't hear the caller, she could see that Valetta Rose's mood changed instantly.

"Just hanging out," she said into the phone. "No, we weren't laughing at you. Why would you even think that?"

Roxie. Had to be Roxie, Debbie Sue thought. For the first time she felt sorry for Valetta Rose. Valetta Rose closed the phone. As she returned it to her pocket, she stared intently at her menu.

Debbie Sue watched the color in Bob's face slowly rise to a reddish hue but before he could speak, Valetta Rose's phone warbled again.

"Is that Roxie?" Bob asked sharply. Debbie Sue had never heard him use such a demanding tone. He had been the consummate gentleman the past couple of days and clearly this phone business was pushing him to another side.

"Is that Roxie?" he asked again.

"Yeah," Valetta Rose answered dully.

"Give it to me," Bob ordered, his hand extended to accept the phone. He pressed it to his ear and listened. "We're having a meal," he said. "When we're finished we'll head for Midland, and . . . Well, no . . . No, not before . . . Oh yeah? Well, back at ya, sweetheart. I'll see you dead too."

Bob returned the phone to the young woman. "Sorry y'all heard that. I apologize for the disruption."

"What disruption?" Darla asked, returning to the table.

"Roxie," Edwina answered. "And I'd say her *place* is going to be six feet under if that phone rings again, am I right, Bob?"

"Shut up, Ed," Debbie Sue said.

Bob didn't answer.

chapter sixteen

After everyone had eaten, the group divided into two—Bob, Valetta Rose and Eddie piled into Vic's pickup and headed for Midland. Debbie Sue had left home this morning carrying her black dress and red shoes in a big leather shoulder bag that showed a ProRodeo logo. Now she drove Edwina by her mobile home to grab her dress and shoes. Edwina came out with a suitcase the size of a carry-on flight bag and placed it in the pickup bed.

"What is all of that?" Debbie Sue asked. "I mean how much room does a simple dress and a pair of shoes need?"

"It's my makeup, girlfriend. You know I'd never make an appearance onstage without my makeup. I brought several types to make sure I've got the right stuff."

"I should have known," Debbie Sue said, now on the way to

the house for Darla to pick up her makeup and her costume for tonight's performance.

As soon as they were on the road, butterflies hit Debbie Sue again. Her hands began sweating on the steering wheel. "Oh, God, Ed, here we go. We're really gonna do this."

"It's what we said we'd do. Don't think about it."

"You'll be great," Darla added.

"Just keep thinking that this time tomorrow it'll all be over and our lives will be back to normal," Edwina said.

"I don't know if anyone would call our lives normal, but this time tomorrow it'll certainly all be over," Debbie Sue replied.

It'll be just like riding Rocket Man into the arena for a barrel race, she told herself. *I'll just smile and do my part and all eyes will be on Rocket Man, or uh . . . um . . . Darla. All eyes will be on Darla Denman. She's the star.*

Debbie Sue repeated this mantra until the Odessa Walmart parking lot came into view.

"Okay, I don't want to get recognized in here," Darla said. "If I got trapped doing autographs or something and wound up being late getting to Midland, they'd have to go on without me."

"No problem," Edwina told her and fished a huge pair of rhinestone-encrusted sunglasses with black lenses from her monstrous purse. "Put these on. If anybody says anything, I'll tell them you're my sister from Big Spring. She's in management. Once they hear that, they won't bother us."

Debbie Sue parked and they ambled into the store, found the sought-after garment and purchased it. Everyone stared at Darla with those I-know-you-from-somewhere glances, but no one approached her. And soon they were headed for Midland again.

The enormous civic-center parking lot that had been virtually empty during rehearsals now looked like an ocean of cars and trucks. Debbie Sue had forgotten the coliseum's seating capacity, but seeing that there were no parking spaces left wasn't difficult.

"Debbie Sue," Edwina screeched, "you missed the turn in. Stop!"

Debbie Sue slammed on the brakes and pulled to the curb.

"Back up and turn in," Edwina said. "Damn, girlfriend."

"Debbie Sue, are you going to be all right?" Darla asked. "If this is really bothering you this much, I can do it with one person. I really can. Just say the word. Now's the time."

"Yeah, hon, don't make yourself sick," Edwina said in a sympathetic tone. "Nothing's worth tossing your cookies over."

"I'm fine, just fine. I'm a little shook up, but I'm fine."

Debbie Sue backed up and turned into the parking lot, only to find herself behind Vic's pickup carrying the rest of Darla's entourage and their instruments. She followed them toward the secure area in back of the arena, presented her pass to the guard at the gate and found a parking spot. Darla had brought her makeup and garb for the show in a large rolling suitcase. Debbie Sue and Edwina helped her lift it out of the pickup bed. Edwina's suitcase came next. Finally, Debbie hooked her own bag on her shoulder and they set out for the auditorium.

This time they entered the civic center from the back, behind the stage area. Everyone suddenly seemed to be going off in different directions. Eddie struck up a conversation with another group that was entering the building at the same time. Bob went left and Debbie Sue assumed Valetta Rose, veering to the right at a jog, was going to the dressing rooms or the restrooms.

The hustle and bustle stirred a memory within Debbie Sue of her rodeo days and waiting behind the chutes to hear her and Rocket Man's names called. An unexpected calm began to steal through her. Just like dozens of times before her ride in the arena, she began to inwardly focus on the job she had to do, shutting out all negative influences. Maybe this evening wasn't going to be so bad after all.

"Where in the hell are Roxie and Mike?" Darla asked Eddie. "Have you seen or talked to either one of them?"

"Mike should be setting up his drums. I'll go check," Eddie said, and then he was gone.

"Y'all come with me to my dressing room," Darla said to Debbie Sue and Edwina. "You can change in there. It's a lot bigger than the space they cleared out for Roxie."

Leading the way, Darla looked back over her shoulder. "Debbie Sue, you okay?"

Debbie Sue could hear the emcee talking to the audience and the crowd's laughter. "I'm fine. I'm fine. Don't worry."

In a matter of minutes the women were in Darla's dressing room, changing clothes. Debbie Sue and Edwina had little to do. A plain black dress was a plain black dress. Debbie Sue's shoes were plain red pumps and Edwina's were the Jimmy Choos she had been wearing when she and Debbie Sue had run from a bad guy through Central Park in New York City.

Darla, on the other hand, glittered from head to toe. She had on black western-style slacks, sleek black patent leather cowboy boots and a white leather western-cut jacket. Lord, it had foot-long fringe, silver and gold embroidered roses, all accented with spangles and rhinestones. The contrast with the shiny copper color Edwina had put on her hair was stunning and the body-sculpting device was doing its job.

"Hmm-hmm," Edwina said to her. "You look prettier than a new puppy. Fabulous jacket."

"Thank you, Edwina. I had it made several years ago in Nashville. Back when I still had some money."

"I'm guessing you spent a sizeable chunk of whatever you had on that jacket," Debbie Sue said.

"I'm embarrassed to say how much," Darla replied, "especially given my present circumstances."

Debbie Sue thought they had finished with time to spare, but before she could believe it and before she was ready, a rap sounded on the door and a voice called from the other side. "Ten minutes, Miz Denman."

"You ladies need to go on out," Darla said. "I'll stop by Roxie's dressing room and make sure she's ready. Mike and Eddie will be onstage with you. I don't come out for a few more minutes, after Roxie sings." Taking Debbie Sue's hands, she said, "Now, remember the drill. Bob will be first. Then I'll come out and say hello and introduce Roxie. Then she sings. One song."

"I remember," Debbie Sue said with more confidence than she felt. "While she's singing we sit in a couple of chairs they've put behind the mikes and when you come onstage we stand up."

"That's right. You just sit and enjoy the show from a really good seat." She turned to Edwina. "How are you, Edwina?"

"Me? Oh, hell, I'm fine. We'll *both* be fine," she added, grabbing Debbie Sue by the arm and urging her toward the door. "You knock 'em dead or break a leg or whatever you show-biz people say."

Darla smiled. "Thanks. I will."

A deafening thunder came from the stage and Debbie Sue assessed that the cloggers were finishing up their number.

"This is really cool, isn't it?" she yelled in Edwina's direction.

The dancers made their exit. Stagehands immediately began moving props to the stage, including the two microphones for her and Edwina and the two chairs they would sit in while Roxie sang. Mike positioned and repositioned his drum set and Eddie set his guitar on a stand, then took a seat at the keyboard, his back to them. Debbie Sue found herself wondering just how many instruments he played.

Bob appeared, with a broad grin plastered across his face. "Well, kids, this is it. Y'all go ahead and get in your spots and in about one minute the curtain rises and we'll get rolling."

Debbie Sue felt an adrenaline surge, familiar from the days when she competed in barrel racing. Anticipation and eagerness replaced nervousness and terror and she entered another realm. She was sitting astride Rocket Man. She had a tight grip on his reins. The horse was prancing and straining to go, waiting for the signal. Only the costume was different. Hell, she was so fired up she could have done the entire telethon solo. Teetering on her high heels, she started for the stage. "Come on, Ed. Let's make Salt Lick proud."

A hand grabbed her arm and spun her around. Edwina was white as a sheet. "I can't do it," she said in a tremulous voice. She had a death grip on Debbie Sue's arm with one hand and the velvet stage curtain with the other. "I think I'm gonna pass out."

"What? Dammit, you can't pass out, Edwina Perkins-Martin. You're the one who talked me into this."

"I know, I know. But do you want to see me sprawled on the floor?"

"Ed, are you that nervous? Why didn't you tell me you got stage fright?"

"Hell, I didn't know it until now, Debbie Sue. Me, of all people." She closed her eyes and swallowed hard. "God almighty, it's hot in here. Darla's gonna hate me. What will I say to her? What'll I do? Tell her I'm sorry. Now I gotta—"

"Oooh, no, you don't. You're not doing anything but going out on that stage with me."

"But Darla said it could be done by one person. So you can do it."

She turned to walk away, but Debbie Sue stepped in front of her. "Edwina Perkins-Martin, now you listen to me. You are going out on that stage. With me."

"I feel lightheaded. I think I'm gonna faint. Or throw up. Or worse yet, have diarrhea."

"Then grab a trash can and a roll of TP, because you're going onstage."

"Ladies," Bob whispered urgently, "get in place."

Debbie Sue moved behind Edwina and pushed her one painstaking step at a time to their chairs behind the microphones. "Just sit still for a second," she instructed. "I'll go find a trash can in case you hurl."

Debbie Sue moved as quickly as she could in the high heels, taking mincing steps so as not to land on her butt. She grabbed the first small trash basket she saw. She was within a couple of feet of Edwina when the curtain slowly started to rise. Edwina looked truly ill. Before Debbie Sue could reach her side, Edwina lay her forehead against the microphone and said into what was supposed to be a dead mike, "Hurry up, Debbie Sue. I really mean it. I think I'm gonna puke."

The declaration bounced off the walls and hung in the air. The audience went silent, then began to murmur and titter. Bob came onstage smiling broadly, the consummate professional. "Spoken like a true professional, huh, ladies and gentleman? Let's give a big West Texas welcome to your own friends and neighbors, Debbie Sue Overstreet and Edwina Perkins-Martin from Salt Lick, Texas! These two brave women have agreed to be Darla Denman's backup singers this evening!"

The crowd erupted with whistling and hoots and rose to its feet, clapping and whistling more. Debbie Sue stopped, trash can still in hand and gave a little curtsy. Edwina managed a small smile that grew wider as her shoulders squared. Debbie Sue knew the outward signs. Edwina was going to be okay. Thank God. "Let's get going before something else happens," she whispered.

Bob completed his introductions and then said, "Let's bring out the little lady you all came to see. Darla wants to introduce her opening act, a new talent she just discovered this year. A young lady meant to go places. Ladies and gentlemen, I give you Darla Denman!"

The musicians started one of Darla's signature swing hits and the crowd went crazy. Continuing to stand, they applauded for several minutes.

Bob re-approached the stage. "Have we got ourselves another case of stage fright?" The audience laughed. "Darla, honey, come on out. We've got some people here who want to see you. And our opening singer is waiting for an introduction."

The band started again. The audience continued to stand, but Darla Denman didn't appear.

Bob caught Debbie Sue's eye and gave his head a jerk, indicating for her to go backstage and check on the performers.

Debbie Sue slipped out of her shoes and made a hasty exit. Tatts by Matt strode ahead of her and she followed close behind him. He went straight to a janitor's closet and opened the door.

As if he had been shot, Tatts by Matt swayed and crumpled in the doorway.

"Matt!" Debbie Sue stopped, staring down at his supine form. She looked around her immediate area. "Hey, hey, somebody! We need some help over here! Somebody's sick!" Then she remembered she had to get Roxie and Darla headed to the stage.

She stepped around Matt, peered into the tiny room and stopped in her tracks.

Darla Denman stood there all right, staring down at the floor, nail file in hand. At her feet in a pool of vivid blood lay the lovely Roxie, her eyes fixed in a permanent stare. Debbie Sue didn't have to be an EMT to know Roxie Denman was not headed for the stage. The only place she was going was to the morgue.

Darla looked up, an eerie emptiness in her eyes, her mouth ajar.

"Oh, sweet Jesus," Debbie Sue gasped, her mind gone blank.

chapter seventeen

Time stopped. The stench of blood and death filled the small windowless space. Debbie Sue's stomach wobbled and she clutched at it. She felt weak in the knees and cold all over. *Buddy, I need you! Help me!*

She and Darla stared at each other. "Darla?" she said in a reedy voice. "What happened?"

"Hey, Debbie Sue," the singer said with no tonal inflection, "are we on now?"

The woman must be, *had* to be, in shock. "Uh, no," Debbie Sue answered feebly.

She glanced down at the long nail file clutched in Darla's bloody hand. Was that item significant? Could a nail file have killed Roxie? If it looked like a stiletto, perhaps it could have. And the fact that Darla had it in her hand and both it and her hand were bloody spoke volumes. All of this was swirling inside Debbie Sue's brain as she scanned the room, desperately hoping to see a plastic bag or something to put the nail file in. If fingerprints were on it, they needed to be preserved.

Spotting a plastic sack, Debbie Sue reached for it and opened it fully. "Darla, listen," she said softly, "you're getting your clothes messed up. Why don't you drop that nail file in here."

Darla blinked. "Oh, okay. Let me clean it first."

"No, don't—" But before Debbie Sue could make a move to stop her, Darla had folded the cuff of her shirt sleeve around the narrow metal file and wiped it clean. "Oh, no, Darla—"

An ear-piercing scream startled Debbie Sue and made her jump. She jerked around and saw an ashen-colored teenager standing in the doorway staring at Roxie's lifeless body. All at once, people were everywhere, pressing to peer into the room and gasping and chattering.

The only thing that kept them from coming inside was Tatts by Matt's collapsed form blocking the doorway.

"Darla, listen to me," Debbie Sue said urgently. "Drop that nail file in this sack. Right now."

Darla complied and Debbie Sue started to tie the top of the sack when Bob Denman's voice pierced the noise of voices. " 'S'cuse me, 's'cuse me, please." He was trying to part the throng of oglers. "Let me pass, please."

Then he was there, his big physique filling the doorway and his face a mask of horror. "Oh, my God. Roxie." He looked from Roxie to Darla, to Debbie Sue and then back to the floor. "Dear God in heaven, what has happened? Is she . . . she's—" He faltered. His fingertips flew to his forehead.

"Dead, Bob." Debbie Sue's voice broke, but she fought back

the tears that wanted to spring forth. True, she hadn't liked Roxie, but that was different from finding her murdered. "Did someone call nine-one-one?"

"Oh, my God," Bob said, a look of pure horror on his face. His upper body leaned forward as if to come into the room, but Tatts by Matt's unconscious form stopped his feet. He glanced down. "What's wrong with him? Is he dead, too?"

"I think he fainted," Debbie Sue answered weakly.

Bob stooped and dragged Tatts by Matt inside the tiny room and closed the door against the looky-loos, his hands visibly shaking. Then he straightened and faced Darla. "Oh, God. Darla. Sweetheart. What happened?"

Darla's head tilted to the side as if she were a rag doll. She looked up at him and blinked.

Bob stared at her. The dawning seemed to be hitting him that Darla Denman had lapsed into another world. He turned to Debbie Sue. "Are you the one who found her?"

His tone was so sharp Debbie Sue felt a need to defend herself. "Matt got here first. Then he fainted. I was behind him."

"Oh, my God," Bob said again and drew his hand down the side of his face.

"Listen, Bob," Debbie Sue said. "If someone called nine-one-one, the police should be here any minute." She grasped Darla's forearm, striving to get her attention. "Darla, you've got to talk to me before they get here."

"Wait a minute," Bob said. "Why does she have to talk to you?" He stepped between Debbie Sue and Darla.

Debbie Sue raised the plastic sack and opened it wide. "Because she was standing here holding this when I came in."

Bob stared down into the sack, now bloody inside from the nail file. "No, no, that's not true," he said with finality. He turned around and gripped Darla's shoulders. She looked up at him with a dreamlike light in her eyes. "Darla, sweetheart," he said, "tell me what you saw. Did you see someone leaving the room? Did you hear something?"

Darla touched his cheek, leaving a smudge of red on his face. "We need to get in place, Bob. Roxie isn't going to be able to sing tonight."

A loud, madder-than-hell female voice overrode the din emanating from the throng of people who had gathered outside the door. Debbie Sue had no trouble recognizing it. "You short-shit sonofabitch," Edwina shouted. "If you shove me back one more time, the next thing you'll be doing is pushing up daisies! Let me in there! I'm part of the act!"

Debbie Sue yanked open the door and Edwina was catapulted into the room. Debbie Sue slammed the door behind her. The brunette's eyes bugged at Roxie's body, and then with equal horror she reacted to Matt's apparently lifeless body at her feet. She screamed like a banshee and started to run in place, her knees pumping up and down, her arms sawing.

The scene was growing more bizarre by the second and now all Debbie Sue could think was, *Where are the cops? Where are the cops? C'mon. C'mon. Oh, dear Lord, Buddy, where are you when I need you?*

A man's gruff voice brought her around. "Get back. All you people get back. And by get back, I mean get all the way back and out of the way. Take a seat along this wall. No one is to leave this building. Sergeant, put a man on every door, every exit, no one leaves until we talk to everyone here tonight."

The door opened and the entrance was filled by a large man dressed in the dark blue of the Midland Police Department. Debbie Sue could tell from his uniform that he was a captain.

She could also see that he was very unhappy at the sight of a small, cramped murder scene butt-to-butt with people and with one in particular running in place.

He did a quick assessment of the deceased. "I'm Captain J. D. Fuller," he said and placed a hand on Edwina's arm. "Ma'am, I'm going to have to ask you to stop that."

Edwina slowed her pace and finally stopped altogether. "I'm sorry. It's a nervous response. I get a little crazy when my mind gets blown."

He looked her up and down suspiciously. "Just what blew your mind, ma'am?"

"That," she said, pointing shakily at Roxie's body. "And that." She pointed at Matt, who still had not revived. "I've never seen two people murdered at the same time."

The captain squatted next to Matt and tapped his cheeks a couple of times with the back of his hand. "Matt, Matt. You all right?"

Tatts by Matt's eyelids fluttered open. Recognition came into his eyes. "Captain Fuller, did you see?"

"Yes, I did, Matt. Let me help you to your feet." Captain Fuller got to his feet, pulling Matt up by the arm. "Who found the body?"

"I think I did," Matt said.

"Matt did," Debbie Sue said at the same time. Always ready and looking out to learn new detecting methods, she asked the captain softly, "How did you know Matt wasn't dead?"

"'Cause I've sent officers out to his parlor about a dozen times when he's keeled over. I know he can't handle needles and the sight of blood and whatever went on in that room must have spooked him pretty good."

"But he's a tattoo artist," Debbie Sue said, puzzled. "Or at least he said he was." She wanted to ask more questions, but now wasn't the time. She reined in her curiosity and held her tongue.

Captain Fuller gave orders to a swarm of police officers to question everyone sitting along the wall in the hallway. Then he turned to the group. "The detectives will want to question all of you."

No sooner had he said the words than another giant of a man stepped through the doorway. He had on starched Wranglers, a starched pale blue shirt and a silver-belly, Gus crease hat.

"This is Detective Finley," the captain said.

"Let's get these people out of here," the new arrival firmly ordered, fixing all of them with a no-nonsense blue-eyed gaze.

He motioned for a young police officer, who quickly stepped up. "Yessir."

"Stay with these folks, Brian," the detective said, "until I tell you different. Don't let them speak to each other and you don't converse with them."

Brian herded the group into a vacant room next door. Everyone stood by anxiously waiting for what might happen next.

"Who the hell is that guy?" Edwina whispered.

Debbie Sue knew many in area law enforcement from the days when Buddy was a sheriff, and those she didn't know, she had heard him mention. But she didn't know Detective Finley. "The one in charge I'm guessing," she answered.

"How the hell could somebody that good-looking live within a hundred miles of me and me not know it?"

"Ed, shut up. You're not supposed to talk."

"What the hell happened in there, Debbie Sue?"

"Ed, shh."

Before Edwina could ignore instructions further, Detective Finley and Captain Fuller came into the room. "I want to speak to each of you separately," the detective said, "so I'm going to ask you to wait in the hallway and don't leave until we tell you you're free to go." He called in a younger beat cop and at the same time grasped Tatts by Matt's arm and held him back. "Matt, we'll start with you."

The group filed out to the hallway and waited in heavy silence. Soon Tatts by Matt came out, ashen-faced and shaken. "Don't speak to anyone about this," the captain told him.

Matt only nodded and disappeared up the hallway.

Captain Fuller addressed Edwina. "You, Running Man. Detective Finley wants to hear your part in this." He took her by the elbow, guided her into the room and closed the door.

Debbie Sue's heart had been beating at a rapid pace ever since she had walked into the janitor's room behind Tatts by Matt. Adrenaline—she recognized it. Seeing Edwina led away by a police captain made it beat a little faster. Having the woman questioned by the police was a scary proposition.

It seemed Edwina was gone forever, and with each passing moment, Debbie Sue's worry was amplified. God, what would Edwina tell? She was so high strung that for all Debbie Sue knew, her partner might have gotten caught up in the high drama and might have confessed.

Debbie Sue glanced over at Darla, who stood quietly and unmoving, leaning against the wall with her head down, not making eye contact with anyone. Bob stood beside her and picked up her hand. She looked up at him tenderly. "It'll be all right, Bobby."

"Quiet, please," Brian said.

Bob released her hand and Brian moved to stand between them. Still, Bob occasionally stole glances at Darla.

Edwina soon came out of the room and took a place beside Debbie Sue. She said nothing, so Debbie Sue made no attempt to talk to her. When the captain motioned for Bob, he defied the police order, reached over and squeezed Darla's hand.

Bob returned after what felt like forever and stood beside Darla again. Captain Fuller motioned to Debbie Sue. "Ma'am, you're next."

Debbie Sue felt a strong protective surge for Darla and didn't want to leave her. "Sir, I don't want to . . ." She waggled a finger between herself and Darla " . . . Couldn't he talk to both of us? My husband is James Russell Overstreet, Junior. He's a Texas Ranger and—"

"Mrs. Overstreet," the captain said politely, "I've known your husband for a number of years. I respect him as much as I do anyone in law enforcement. But I can't let that sway the way you're treated. Now, if you'll just come with me."

Reluctantly, Debbie Sue walked to the doorway. Before passing through it, she looked across her shoulder and smiled wanly at the woman who had planned to make this night her big comeback performance. "Darla, will you be okay?"

A long moment passed and Debbie Sue wondered if Darla was going to answer her at all. Suddenly she raised her head and smiled. "I'll be fine, Debbie Sue, really. Go on. When it's my turn I'll tell him all about how I killed Roxie."

"Darla!" Debbie Sue cried. "You don't mean that!"

"Darla!" Bob cried, his face a mask of stunned disbelief.

"Mrs. Denman, don't say another word," the captain said. "Sergeant, please escort Mrs. Overstreet to one of the patrol cars outside. We'll talk to her at the station." He gestured for Darla to turn around. Drawing her hands behind her, he removed a pair of handcuffs from his belt. "Mrs. Denman,

I'm placing you under arrest. You have the right to remain silent—"

Debbie Sue shot a can't-you-do-something look at Bob.

He stepped toward the captain. "But officer—"

"Wait," Debbie Sue protested. "She's in shock. She can't be Mirandized. Why, she doesn't know if you're reading her her rights or a cookie recipe."

"That's not my concern, ma'am. It's my duty to inform her of her rights. We'll let the lawyers fight over her state of mind."

As the captain led Darla away, he resumed the familiar warning, "Anything you say can and will . . ."

Debbie Sue had never felt so helpless. "Darla," she called out, "don't say anything else. I'll be right behind you."

No way in hell had Darla committed murder. But *someone* had and maybe with good reason. Roxie practically wore a sign that said KICK MY BUTT. But Darla hadn't done it. Debbie Sue was sure of that much. Why, she was counting too much on her big comeback. She was excited. She had plans. She had a new future. No one would commit murder minutes before those plans came to fruition.

As Debbie Sue left the room with the uniform, she saw both Mike and Eddie in the hallway looking grim. Eddie was smoking. Mike had a bandaged hand. What had he done to his hand? The two musicians quickly turned away. Debbie Sue thought she saw Mike's shoulders shaking, thought she heard him break into sobs as he rubbed his bandaged hand. Again Debbie Sue wondered, *What has he done to his hand?*

Walking alongside the young officer, she reached inside her purse and found her cell phone. "May I make a call?"

"Er, yes, ma'am, I guess so." He looked around as if he wished someone would come to his rescue. "You're not under arrest. The captain just wants me to take you so you can give them your statement."

Debbie Sue had already started to key in Buddy's number. But she paused. She could hear Buddy's voice now, "Debbie Sue, how do you and Ed end up in these messes?" *Fuck!*

Dammit, this time she and Edwina truly hadn't done anything. They and the band had been patiently waiting onstage when someone jabbed a nail file into Roxie's neck. Where had everyone been during that time? Darla? Or Bob? Or Valetta Rose? Debbie Sue and Edwina had been with Darla in her dressing room, but not for fifteen or twenty minutes. Could you kill someone in fifteen minutes?

She thought back on her own brief encounters with the now deceased Roxie Denman. She had wanted to throw her under that tour bus within a minute of meeting her *and* drive the bus over her. But that didn't mean she wanted to kill her.

With her own eyes she had seen Darla angry enough to throw articles at Roxie in Hogg's. She had heard Darla's sniping remarks about her. But no one could ever make her believe Darla had killed her, no matter what she had said. A new idea began to form in Debbie Sue's mind. If Darla was confessing guilt to a murder, she was covering up for someone else. It had to be someone important to her, someone for whom she had strong feelings. Was that someone Bob Denman?

Bob. He was the type to be right in the middle of things, but seeing Darla handcuffed and arrested seemed to have left him speechless. Debbie Sue wondered what he might be doing now. He was, after all, the grieving spouse. She supposed it would be only logical that he would be somewhere grieving or talking to relatives of the deceased.

As she and the young officer exited the civic center, she

dropped her phone back into her purse. She would put off calling Buddy until she knew more. She needed to talk to the one person who could read people as well as Buddy could, the one who, in spite of her initial hysteria, had probably already sized up the situation and would know exactly what was going on. She needed to talk to Edwina.

chapter eighteen

By the time the police officer drove Debbie Sue back to the civic center and she was able to catch up with Edwina, hours had passed.

"How's Darla?" was Edwina's first question.

"A basket case," Debbie Sue answered. "Listen, Ed, she confessed that she did it. Right there in front of me and Captain Fuller."

"She did not!"

"I heard her with my own two ears."

"Oh, Debbie Sue, that's more shocking to me than Roxie being dead."

"I know. We haven't known her long, but I just don't think she's capable of killing someone. What keeps sticking in my mind is that she was so excited about this tour. Making a comeback meant everything to her. A woman intent on reviving her career wouldn't kill someone, would she?"

"Haven't you ever heard of a crime of passion? Maybe Roxie said the wrong thing one time too many and ol' Darla just snapped."

"I don't buy that."

"Okay. Then, if she didn't do it, she confessed to cover up for somebody."

"My thought exactly."

"And I can think of only one person she'd make that kind of sacrifice for."

In unison, Debbie Sue and Edwina said, "Bob."

"Where *is* Bob?" Debbie Sue asked.

"He was here a little while ago," Edwina answered. "After the cops talked to him, he said they told him he could go back to Salt Lick to collect some phone numbers. He wanted to call Roxie's parents. He said he's never met them. She hardly ever spoke of them. All he knows about them is that they're separated and live apart somewhere in the Los Angeles area. He said Roxie had an address book in her suitcase, but if her parents' numbers aren't in it, he doesn't know how to reach them."

"For some reason, Darla must feel the need to cover for him," Debbie Sue said. "But my gut tells me he didn't do it either."

"My gut says the same thing. Female intuition. You should never sell it short."

"That's exactly what I tell Buddy."

"God, Debbie Sue, we've got to help Darla. What are we gonna do?"

"We should try to reason with her if we're ever allowed to talk to her. But who knows? Maybe forensic evidence will clear it up." Debbie Sue paused a few beats. "Ed, you didn't tell the police you thought Bob did it, did you?"

"How could I? *Why* should I? Until you just now said it, I didn't know Darla said she did it. Did *you* tell them?"

"No, and I'm not going to. I told them there were several people who might've done it. And that's the truth."

A few beats of silence passed. Then Edwina asked the question Debbie Sue knew she would ask. "Have you called Buddy and told him?"

"I don't want him knowing we're involved in the case."

"We aren't involved in it."

"Of course we are, Ed. The cops may have forensics and even DNA on their side, but we can trump them."

"How?"

"We know all the players and we have that good ol' female intuition. With the experience and resources we have, we—"

"Forensics and DNA are science stuff. Intuition and being acquainted with somebody doesn't trump science." Edwina shook her head. "And even if that weren't true, Buddy will never stand still for us to even go close to a Midland police investigation." Edwina shook her head again. "I don't know how you're going to convince him otherwise."

"Maybe he'll never know about it."

"Listen to yourself, girlfriend. A famous person is sitting in a Midland jail facing a murder charge. And a murder in Midland is a big deal even for an un-famous person."

"Oh hell, you're right, Ed. Buddy's probably already heard about it."

"And he knows we were supposed to be performing with these people. They're staying in your house, for crying out loud."

Debbie Sue bit down on her lower lip. "Fuck. I'm pretty sure him and his Ranger buddies are already talking about it in Austin. I haven't checked my cell phone because I'm pretty sure he's called with a million questions."

"Oh dear," Edwina lamented.

"What are you oh-dearing about?"

"We're gonna end up in trouble. Again."

"Darla's the one in trouble. Why do you think trying to help her is going to get us in trouble?"

"Just call it that good ol' female intuition, laced with a shot of having a really good memory."

Darla Denman released a breath that could extinguish the candles on a centennial birthday cake. Last night seemed a million years ago. The sight of poor Roxie's corpse was still a vivid picture in her mind. Indeed she hadn't liked the girl, but she hadn't wished her a horrible death. She had lapsed into some kind of shock and had been slow to come around, but now she was fully functional and completely aware of everything. And like it or not, the picture of her future wasn't pretty.

She had been hauled to jail in the back of a police car, handcuffed, bawling her eyes out and clinging to the tiny bit of dignity she had left. Not exactly the splash she had meant to make in Midland, Texas. Not only had her life taken a downward turn, she would need a bulldozer to dig a hole deeper than the one she now found herself in. How had her big comeback ended up like this? She was supposed to be signing autographs and new recording contracts, sipping champagne in the back of a limo and embracing her loyal fans.

Captain Fuller had been patient and kind to her, but when she said she didn't have an attorney, he had abruptly stopped everything and brought her to this cell, promising that a court-appointed lawyer would come by to see her soon.

The lawyer hadn't shown up yet and that was fine with her. She didn't want to talk to anyone. She wanted to be left alone.

When they first brought her in, they had put her in a stark room with green walls and no windows because they thought she might hurt herself. Later they moved her to the cell where she now sat on the edge of a cot, which was really nothing more than a thin, smelly mattress thrown on a concrete bench. She looked down at her clothing—an orange jumpsuit her jailers had ordered her to wear. Her eyes watered with new tears. Her beautiful bespangled leather jacket and her custom-made cowboy boots floated into her mind. She had no idea where they were. She tugged at the jumpsuit's waistband, which was too tight around the middle. But she wasn't about to ask for a larger size.

Jumpsuits. Now who in God's name came up with that idea? And in neon, glow-in-the-dark orange? She had red hair, for God's sake. Redheads didn't wear orange.

Besides that, this outfit was meant for someone much taller than her five-foot-barely-three-inch frame. Bending over, she rolled up another inch of one pant leg, but even that gesture revealed another source of distress. The shoes. She couldn't remember the last time she had worn canvas shoes, or tennis shoes, as she had always called them.

And the laces had been removed. What in the hell did they think she would do with the laces? Two tied together wouldn't be long enough for her to hang herself, even if she were so inclined—and she wasn't. She supposed she could tear out the aglet and poke her eye out, but then she'd be a one-eyed, middle-aged, heavyset woman in an unflattering jumpsuit, wearing ugly shoes with no laces. She could attempt to swallow the aglets, but instead of strangling her they'd probably add more weight to her body.

At this point all of her choices were bad ones.

Sighing again, she lay back on the cot and hid her face with her forearm, hoping to discourage her neighbor, who had begun to stir, from talking to her. The middle-aged woman had been brought in last night drunk and belligerent. She had fallen across her one-inch-thick mattress and was snoring before the cell door could be locked again.

"Hey," a raspy smoker's voice said now. "You awake over there?"

Darla didn't respond. The last thing she needed at this point was a talkative stranger.

"Hey," the woman bellowed. "Did I miss breakfast? I'd kill for a cup of coffee and a cigarette."

Darla winced at the word *kill*. She was torn. She didn't want to develop a jail buddy, but she didn't want to be confronted because of her silence, either. Keeping her arm in place over her eyes, she muttered, "They haven't brought anything yet."

"The last time I was in," the woman continued, "they came at around seven o'clock. Wonder what time it is."

Great, Darla thought. Her neighbor had been in jail enough times to have the schedule down pat. Not a comforting bit of news. "Don't know. I don't wear a watch. And even if I did, they probably would have taken it."

"God, I feel like hell. I must have tied on a good one last night. The last thing I remember was someone saying, 'Hey, wanna come back to my trailer and party?'" Her laughter ended in a smoker's cough. "Guess I must have."

Darla detected more movement, but didn't open her eyes.

"Man, I gotta pee."

That announcement was followed by the sound of a shower curtain—the only form of privacy in the cells—sliding on its metallic rings. Darla cringed even further into herself.

A flushing of water and more metallic ring sliding told Darla the woman had finished. Darla moved her arm and opened her eyes.

"Yep," the woman continued, "this place ain't bad, but if you ever want to get tossed in a really nice place you should get picked up in Andrews County. The sheriff's wife is the cook, and man, she can really dish out a great meal. Not like this powdered eggs-hard baloney-stale bread crap they give you everywhere else. She makes meat loaf and mashed potatoes, yeast rolls and desserts to die for. She's got a good heart beating in her chest."

Darla didn't know which was worse—the vision of the food making her stomach growl from intense hunger or the fact that she appeared to be stuck with the Travelocity spokesperson for West Texas jails.

"My name's Judy," the woman said. "Judy Jones. What's yours?"

Darla looked at the hand that was extended toward her, a strong hand that showed manual work and nails bitten short. Considering herself a coward, Darla decided getting along was the best approach. She sat up and cleared her throat. "Darla," she said, returning the handshake with limp fingers.

"Seems like I've seen you before," Judy said.

Darla smiled faintly. "I don't know where it would've been."

"Let me guess why you're in here, Darla. I kind of pride myself on reading people. It's a skill I've developed over the years. You got to have it in my line of work."

"Really? What's your line of work?" Darla asked, trying to sound interested but half fearing what she might hear.

"I'm a bail bondsman." Judy laughed to the point of coughing again. "Ain't that a hoot? I make my living getting people out of jail, and here I am. Life's a schizophrenic bitch, ain't she, Darla? There's days she's on her medication and everything's fine, and then boom, she gets all weird."

Perhaps Judy Jones's knowledge of the area jails came from hearing about them from her clients as opposed to first-hand experiences. Besides that, she was earthy and likeable. Darla began to warm to her.

Judy seemed to be studying her intently with watery no-color eyes. "Okay, now lemme think." After a few uncomfortable minutes of scrutiny, she said, "It's easy to see you're well kept. Hair dyed, manicured nails. Face looks like you get facials two or three times a week. Hey, your lips were recently tattooed. Someone really did a good job, too. And judging from the tan lines on your fingers you had some pretty big rings on."

Darla gave her a look. All of that was true.

"Your eyes are swollen from crying," Judy continued, "so I'm guessing you're not accustomed to being in jail."

Tilting her head, Darla stared at her.

"So I'm close, huh?" Her tone was laced with pride, as if she knew just how close she was.

Darla gave a bitter chuckle. "You must be good at your business, Judy."

"Oh, I am, honey. I got clients all over West Texas. It's a damned lucrative business, I'll tell you that. Another thing, you don't need to be afraid of me. I'm just an ol' party gal that don't know when to stop or say no."

Darla made a bitter huff. "The truth is, Judy, I've been in that spot a time or two myself."

"Have you now?" Judy braced a hand on her knee and cocked her head. Her eyes scrunched into a squinty stare. "I'll bet you're in here because of some man, am I right? You just look like the type that'd have a man hanging around. Ninety-nine percent of the women I help are in trouble because of a man. Maybe not directly, but somewhere along the way a man had his hand in it."

"Right again." Darla sighed, feeling tears welling up behind her eyes.

"Did he beat you? Force you to give him money, take everything you got, then put out a peace bond on you?"

"No, no. Nothing like that. Bob's a wonderful man. I thought we had a chance. . . ." A sob broke through and Darla pressed her face into her hands.

"Come on now, honey. Things look bad now, but tomorrow's another day. And that means you got another chance to make things good. After all, it ain't like you committed murder."

Darla's sobs became wails and she dropped her face into her hands.

"You didn't, did you? Murder someone, that is? Damn, darlin', did you murder ol' Bob?"

"No," Darla wailed. "I wouldn't harm a hair on his head. I've been in love with him my whole adult life. I can't even hurt his feelings."

Judy sighed. "Well that's a relief. You had me going there for a second. I thought you were going to tell me you murdered somebody."

"I did, but it wasn't Bob."

"Well, I'll be damned. Who was it?

"His wife. I confessed to killing his wife."

"The hell you say." Judy hesitated, then stood up, walked over to the bars and yelled toward the door at the end of the hall, "Hey, could we get some coffee in here?" She turned back to Darla. "We both need some good, strong coffee, don't we?"

Darla didn't answer, she just cried harder. She felt a touch on her arm and opened her eyes, saw Judy holding out a business card. "You're gonna need my help, sugar."

Whimpering, Darla took the card and stared at it.

"They'll get that coffee in here in a minute," Judy said.

Darla slipped Judy's card into the breast pocket of her county-issued jumpsuit. It was going to take a lot more than coffee to raise her spirits. A lot more.

chapter nineteen

Debbie Sue lay in bed, but she had been awake for what seemed like hours. She was so wired she could scarcely be still. She and Edwina had made it back to Salt Lick around midnight. Then she'd had a phone conversation with Buddy, which had been enough to set her mind to churning. He had called the minute she got home last night to make sure she was safe, and once that had been confirmed, he had forbidden her involvement in the case.

Forbidden!

She glanced at the clock on the bedside table and was surprised to see that it was seven o'clock, much later than she would have guessed.

Coffee. She definitely needed some strong coffee. Throwing back the covers, she walked barefoot from her carpeted bedroom and across the braided rug in the living room to the cold linoleum of the kitchen floor. Her nerve endings seemed to be on fire and she reacted to each change under her feet with a start.

She removed the cake cover from the plate it covered and stared at the cinnamon coffee cake left from yesterday morning. Had it been only twenty-four hours since Darla Denman, confessed murderess, had baked this coffee cake in this kitchen? Twenty-four hours since Darla, Debbie Sue and Edwina had sat and shared it, laughing and talking about their lives and what the evening ahead might hold?

No one could have imagined all that had unfolded, and even now, Debbie Sue had to question if she was in the middle of a terrible, grotesque dream.

"The Eyes of Texas" bleating from her cell phone startled her and she grabbed her purse, which was hanging from the back of a kitchen chair. She dug out the phone and without looking at caller ID, answered.

"I'm on my way to your house," Edwina informed her without saying hello. "I stopped and bought a newspaper. Do I need to bring anything else?"

Debbie Sue ran her finger along the side of the cake plate, capturing a crumb and bringing it to her mouth. "I guess not, Ed."

"Do you still have coffee? I don't mean enough for a cup or two either. I'm talking about a lot of coffee. I haven't slept all night."

"Yeah, I've got more than half a can. I haven't slept either."

"What about food? You got anything to eat?"

"Umm," Debbie Sue said, looking around the kitchen. "I still have some coffee cake left over from yesterday, but I wouldn't object if you picked up something greasy. You know, sausage biscuits, bacon biscuits, plain biscuits with gravy. Brain food."

"Greasy. Got it. But why do we need brain food?"

"We're going to be doing a lot of thinking."

"We are?"

"I hope to shout we are. We've got a murder to solve. Get here as soon as you can."

"Now Deb—"

Debbie Sue closed her phone. She didn't want to hear about practicalities. She'd been through all of that already on the phone with Buddy. The word "forbidden" was still stuck in her brain.

She sighed as she filled the coffeemaker with water. Buddy's penchant for forbidding her to do a thing had been a bone of contention throughout both their former marriage and their present one. That very thing had gone as far as divorce court years back.

She had vowed never to allow her stubbornness to get so out of hand again, but dammit, this was different. The woman in trouble was someone she had spent two days with and she didn't believe for a minute she was guilty of murder. Buddy had demanded that the Domestic Equalizers not interfere with the Midland police. *Demanded.* They were plenty capable of catching a killer, he had assured her.

Okay, she accepted the part about the capabilities of the Midland Police Department. But that didn't mean she couldn't watch very closely from the fringes and make sure Darla Denman's big day wasn't an appearance on death row.

A glance at the wall clock told her she had just enough time to jump into the shower before Edwina arrived. She quickly added coffee to the coffeemaker basket, clicked the ON button and dashed from the kitchen, pulling her Dallas Cowboys T-shirt over her head as she went.

Twenty minutes later she emerged from the bathroom towel-drying her hair. The hot water had loosened the tight muscles in her neck and across her shoulders. The lavender body wash had rejuvenated her senses. She was ready to get to work.

Walking into the kitchen, she came upon Edwina filling a mug with coffee. "I feel one hundred percent better after that shower," she said brightly.

"Hmm, I had a shower, too, but only got to seventy-five percent," Edwina said.

"Did you use lavender body scrub? That's the extra twenty-five."

"I'll keep that in mind. Now what is it we're gonna work on?"

She watched Edwina dump a teaspoon of sugar into her mug. "You're not still doing that sugar thing, are you?"

"Nah," Edwina said. "I decided that didn't make sense. And Vic told me it could damage my kidneys."

"And no telling what else," Debbie Sue said.

A brown-paper grocery sack sat on the table. Debbie Sue dug in it and came up with a sausage biscuit.

"You must have stopped by Kwik Stop. There's only two biscuits in here. Did you already eat?"

"Had a double-sausage biscuit with a fried egg and cheese on the way out here."

"Then you can grab that yellow legal pad by the phone while I fix myself a cup of coffee."

Edwina complied, picking up the pad and going back for a pen before she sat down. "I assume we're going to be writing something."

Indeed they were. Debbie Sue intended to copy how Buddy analyzed crimes, the method he said helped him bring everything into focus on complex cases. Debbie Sue intended to dictate her thoughts for Edwina to write down—not to force her involvement, but to allow Debbie Sue the chance to eat.

"Okay, what am I supposed to do with this?" Edwina asked.

"Draw a line down the middle of the page," Debbie Sue instructed, unwrapping her sausage biscuit.

Edwina followed the directive, adding a curlicue at the end of the line. "Now what?"

"Okay, let me think." Debbie Sue sipped her coffee. "At the top of the first column, write 'People Who Wanted Roxie Dead' and at the top of the second column, write 'Where Were They?' "

"Okay, but I'm going to need a longer piece of paper." Edwina began to write, but suddenly stopped. "This won't work."

"Come on, Ed. I've seen Buddy use this method and—"

"It's not the method I'm questioning. I think this list could get pretty long."

"That's pretty smart of you, Ed. See? This greasy food is working already."

"Well, I did have that biscuit with *double* sausage." Edwina tapped the top of her pencil on the yellow pad. "Do we really know *how* Roxie died? Has anybody said?"

"We already talked about it, Ed. That nail file punctured her jugular and she bled out. That's why there was so much blood all over everything."

"Eeww," Edwina said, curling her upper lip. "I just ate."

"You asked the question."

"I know you must have talked to Buddy. What did he say?"

"I talked to Wyatt Earp last night. He told me not to interfere with the Midland police. He knows Captain Fuller and

Detective Finley both and he said if we get in their way, the outcome will be a lot different from what it was when we dealt with the sheriff in Jones County. He said those guys wouldn't stop with just calling us clowns like that Jones County asshole did."

"Food for thought, girlfriend. With Vic five hundred miles away, I don't know who'd bail me out of jail."

"Buddy doesn't understand." Debbie heaved a sigh. "But I told him we'd stay out of the Midland Police Department's way."

"That's probably a wise plan, Debbie Sue. Have you heard from Bob?"

"He called last night, too. He said Mike and Eddie are all torn up. He said he'd found the phone numbers he needed and called Roxie's folks."

"That's good. How is Valetta Rose taking things?"

"He didn't mention her." Debbie Sue shook her head. "God, Ed. He just sounded so damned sad."

"Did he say if he's taking Roxie back to Nashville?"

"No and I didn't feel I should ask. Hell, I don't even know if Nashville is where she's from. The whole thing's just sad, isn't it? I mean she might have been an ass, but she had a whole lot going for her."

"Yep. Beauty and talent is a helluva lot more than most of us get to start out with." Edwina shook her head. "But apparently, she just couldn't rein in that hateful tongue. I only knew her a couple of days, but she pissed me off enough for a lifetime."

"Hmm, I think you're onto something, Ed. She pissed everyone off, but who did she piss off bad enough for them to actually kill her? I mean, you don't kill someone for being a smartass, do you?"

"I don't. And if everyone did, we'd all be stepping over bodies. It takes a whole other kind of riled to kill another human being. Maybe there's another motive we don't know about yet."

"Maybe. Unfortunately, we don't really know any of these people." Debbie Sue sank to a chair at the table. "Okay, how many names on the list?"

Edwina counted down the page. "Nine."

"Holy cow. I thought you'd say three or four."

"Well, I included you, me and Tatts by Matt."

"You can mark you and me off. I'd say that's a safe bet."

"Now who's being a smartass?"

"Why did you add Matt? I never saw him and Roxie together but for a minute. And he's local."

"Remember? She spent yesterday afternoon at Tatts by Matt's tattoo parlor. That dude's a little odd. There's no telling what happened there."

"You're right, so that's seven. And that's about six more suspects than we've dealt with before."

"Not necessarily. When Pearl Ann was killed we had the whole state of Texas to consider."

Debbie Sue took a sip of her coffee and pulled her robe tighter to her body. "You're right. Good Lord. Wouldn't Pearl Ann and Roxie together have made a handful of trouble?"

"Clearly, neither one of those women ate enough fat," Edwina said.

Debbie Sue leaned forward and patted Edwina's hand. "I'm going to dry my hair and get dressed. We're going to Midland, Ed."

"We are?"

"Yep. Buddy will be home tonight and he might handcuff

me to a chair. Before that happens, we need to see what we can find out."

"And how are we going to do that?"

"Why, Ed, by doing what we do best. Talking, listening and spreading some bullshit around."

Bob Denman sat at the kitchen table in the home he was borrowing in Salt Lick, Texas. He felt low. Just about as low as he had ever felt in his entire life. Making funeral plans for his wife while the woman he loved sat in jail for her murder was, hands down, the worst thing he had ever faced.

Roxie, just a year earlier, following the funeral of a friend, had said, "If something should happen to me and you're still around, just roast me. I don't want to be planted like some damn tulip bulb." In terms of money, that was really the first break she had ever given him and she wasn't even aware of it.

Despite the early hour, he had already reached Roxie's mother in Los Angeles. The woman, Bob observed, had not been overcome with grief. She and her daughter hadn't spoken to each other in more than five years. She told him to forget about locating Roxie's father. After losing his last dime at the tables in Las Vegas, he had disappeared. The man couldn't be found and Bob shouldn't even worry about it.

She had no argument over cremation, had no interest in helping plan a memorial service in Nashville. All she asked was that Bob ship her daughter's ashes to her in L.A. Normally he wouldn't think of not delivering the urn personally, but he had a mission involving the living that took precedence in his mind. As soon as he did his duty to Roxie in Nashville, he would have to get back to Texas and see to Darla's well-being.

Simply shipping the urn to Roxie's mother and forgetting

about a funeral made the most sense, but the few friends and acquaintances Roxie had were in Nashville. She had considered Nashville her home. His and Roxie's marriage might have been a joke to everyone who knew them, and she might have treated him like something she would scrape off her shoe, but he couldn't deny her a decent exit—visitation, words from the Bible, music. In Nashville.

Thus, he had made a list of what was needed for a small, simple memorial service. He had dealt with each item in his usual, methodical fashion, taking care of every last detail, leaving nothing forgotten or overlooked. Decorum and decency dictated as much.

He'd had a long morning.

All plans in place, Bob did a mental countdown for the week ahead. Darla's arraignment wouldn't occur until tomorrow, Tuesday. For sure, he would be present. An autopsy would take place tomorrow morning, then Roxie's body would be released. A Midland funeral home would carry out the cremation, and then on Wednesday, Bob would travel to Nashville with his wife's ashes.

He had set the visitation for Wednesday afternoon at a funeral home in Nashville, followed by a simple service in the chapel. He didn't know who might be present. He assumed Mike, Eddie and Valetta Rose would be there simply as a result of their association with Roxie, but it was anyone's guess who else would show up.

Today he had to pay a visit to Darla.

chapter twenty

Debbie Sue drove toward Midland without talking, which was just as well. Edwina's mouth was moving at ninety miles an hour, yakking and cracking her gum between sentences. "Why are you avoiding my questions?" she finally asked.

Debbie Sue's mind was busy. She was trying to decide where to start once they got to Midland. She shifted her position as she adjusted the vent to blow cool air directly on her. "I'm sorry, Ed. I was thinking about something. What did you ask me?"

"I asked about Buddy. You haven't told me what he had to say about all of this, except that he warned us to stay out of it. He must know something that nobody else knows."

"He doesn't. All he had to say was the usual Buddy stuff. Be careful, don't get involved, yada, yada. I told him we were only going to observe the Midland PD so we could learn a few things about police work. I said we'd only jump in if needed."

"And what did he say about that?"

"He said he couldn't see why we would be needed. He said for us to let the professionals do their jobs."

"The professionals, huh? Not silly ol' us."

Since more often than not, Edwina started out agreeing with Buddy, her tone of annoyance sent Debbie Sue's thoughts off in a new direction. Why couldn't Buddy have said, *Darla's going to need your help. Let me know if I can do anything.* Or why couldn't he have said, *Good thing you two are there to make sure things run smoothly.* Would that have been so hard? Sometimes men could be so damned maddening.

No matter if Buddy did throw cold water on her plans, Debbie Sue knew that in the end, she could always count on her good friend Edwina for support. "Ed, do you ever get really mad, I mean *really* mad at Vic?"

"Of course I do, hon. I'm living proof that men and women weren't meant to coexist. I mean, think about it. God knew Adam and Eve couldn't live in close quarters, so He gave them the whole damn Garden of Eden. No borders, no boundaries, separate bathrooms. He knew they'd need lots of space."

"I never thought of it that way," Debbie Sue replied. "Sunday School skimmed over that part."

She saw in her peripheral vision that Edwina was studying her closely. Finally, her partner, who knew her almost as well as she knew herself, said, "Are you mad at our sweet Buddy?"

"Not really mad," Debbie Sue answered. "Just a little irritated."

"Hm. We all get a little irritated. Just don't let it take you down a road that makes no sense."

"Oh, don't worry. I've already been down that road and I don't want to travel it again."

The William Anders Justice Center and Law Enforcement Building's parking area loomed ahead. As Debbie Sue turned into it, she saw it was nearly empty of cars. "Where is everyone? This place should be humming with activity. I don't see a soul."

Edwina scanned the empty lot. "Shit-fire, Debbie Sue, it's a holiday. I totally forgot about Labor Day."

"Oh, hell," Debbie Sue said, smacking the steering wheel. "There won't be an arraignment today."

"Shit," Edwina said, then sighed. "Well, we've driven all the way over here. Let's go into the jail and see if they'll let us talk to Darla. I'm sure she'd welcome the company."

"Good idea." Debbie Sue parked, killed the engine and checked her image in the rearview mirror. "Now remember, if we should happen to strike up a conversation with someone inside about the case, keep it casual. No nosy questions. That way, I can tell Buddy we were just being friendly."

"Gotcha," Edwina said. "He won't see through that at all."

They walked across the parking lot and entered the building that housed city and county official offices as well as the jail. Just inside the front door, Debbie Sue laid her purse on the conveyor belt that scanned for prohibited items and walked through the metal detector without incident. Edwina's purse, on the other hand, set off the alarm and the two cops who were monitoring the system asked her to step aside.

Debbie Sue watched with mortification as Edwina explained that the gun-shaped object they found inside her purse was a personal massage device. She could see that the two deadly serious cops doing the inspection were having a hard time keeping straight faces.

Once they cut Edwina loose with her *personal item* still inside her purse, Debbie Sue dragged her up the hallway. "Jeez Louise, Ed. What in the hell are you doing with that thing in your purse?"

"It's a gag gift Vic brought me from California. But, turns out it feels really good along my shoulders."

"May I help you girls?" A deep baritone voice interrupted them and they both turned toward it.

Detective Finley stood two feet away. He gave them a look that clearly relayed the message that he brooked no tomfoolery. The man looked just as delicious as he had yesterday at the civic center when he had shown up to investigate Roxie's demise. He wore basically the same outfit—starched cotton covering hard muscle. *Yum.*

"What are you girls doing here?" he asked.

Before Debbie Sue could answer, Edwina pushed her aside. "Hi, I'm Edwina Perkins-Martin. Remember me? We spoke yesterday." Still hanging onto his hand, she stared up at him. "Gracious goodness, you're tall, aren't you? I don't think I noticed that yesterday."

"Ed, shh!" Debbie Sue gently pushed her a step to the side.

Extending her own hand to the detective, Debbie Sue said in an even tone she hoped conveyed professionalism, "I don't think I mentioned it in our conversation yesterday, but we're the Domestic Equalizers, private investigators from Salt Lick. We came to visit Darla Denman. I might add that we feel she's been wrongly incarcerated. Perhaps you can tell us where we can find her."

His stark blue eyes squinted. "Why do you say wrongly?"

Edwina pushed past her again. "Well, you see, this all started a few days ago when Darla—"

"Ed." Debbie Sue glared at her. "Ed, *we* do not need to explain anything."

"Mrs. Overstreet, I'm sorry," their new acquaintance said, "but yes, you do need to explain. Now that you're here, I'd like to talk to you and your friend again. Would you please come with me?"

He walked off with the confidence of a man who had not a shadow of doubt that others would take his direction and follow him. His boot heels thumped a steady rhythm on the tile floor.

Edwina's elbow gouged Debbie Sue's arm as they fell in step behind the detective. "See what you've done?" she stage-whispered. "Now we're in trouble."

"We are not in trouble," Debbie Sue whispered back. "He only wants to talk to us. And where do you get this *we* stuff? I'm not the one carrying around a damned dildo that looks like a pistol."

"It's not a dildo," Edwina stage-whispered.

The detective turned his head and looked at them across his shoulder, his brow arched.

Edwina gave him a Colgate smile. As soon as he turned away from them, she whispered from the side of her mouth, "Trust me. Anytime a man that good-looking is around, *I'm* in trouble."

"You think he's good looking?" Debbie Sue asked.

"Hell to the yes."

"Hell to the yes? So now you're a rapper?"

"See? Being around a man that looks like that brings out another side of me."

"A side Vic wouldn't like, I should point out."

"Shit, Debbie Sue. Just because I think he's good-looking

doesn't mean I'm going to *do* anything about it. I'm like a diabetic. Maybe I can't have candy anymore, but I can sniff it."

Lying on her back on the concrete bunk attached to the cell wall, her mind in turmoil, Darla stared at the ceiling. Her cellmate, Judy Jones, snored loudly. Darla envied her ability to sleep in these surroundings, but she figured she must be used to them. Judy had made it clear that being in jail wasn't all that new to her.

It would take more than loud snores and rumbles to deter Darla from her thoughts. Less than twenty-four hours had passed since the horror of finding Roxie's body. Walking into that janitor's room and seeing that girl lying on the floor in a pool of blood had been so shocking and Darla had been so rattled that the confession of guilt had come out of her mouth before she had even been aware she was speaking.

Darla had first convinced herself that saying she did it was no big deal. Nothing but her confession tied her to Roxie's death. But today, with coherent thought returning, she realized she might have been wrong. Now that she'd had more time to reconsider events and think more clearly, she could see that even without her confession, *everything* tied her to Roxie's death. Tatts by Matt had seen her standing over Roxie holding that damn bloody nail file. Why had she even picked it up?

Everyone who knew her and her team had heard her and Roxie argue and trade insults.

Then there was the fact that Roxie was married to Darla's ex-husband, who, even while being divorced from Darla, had continued to manage her career for years. Debbie Sue and Edwina knew she had kissed Bob just the night before the murder.

Yep. Probably any clear-thinking person would say Darla Denman's goose was cooked. *Dear God.*

It was all Darla could do to contain herself when she desperately wanted to scream to the top of her lungs, *This is a huge mistake! Get me out of here! I'm innocent!*

Of course she had enough sense to know that declaring you had committed murder wasn't like changing your order to the waiter. Once out there, those words were taken seriously by people with no sense of humor, and no matter how hard or vehemently you tried to explain, they wouldn't allow you to simply say you were kidding and take it back.

She had a perfectly good reason for making the confession. She knew the killer's identity. Bob Denman. But Darla believed to the bottom of her soul that he wasn't capable of deliberately hurting a fly. She had never known a kinder, gentler human. He had somehow accidentally killed his wife.

Or possibly, he had been driven to it in a fit of anger. Perhaps Roxie had finally found his tipping point, piled on that last straw, pushed him to the edge. And he had snapped. The expression on his face when he had walked into that room and looked down at his wife's corpse had told Darla all she needed to know. She had been reading that face practically her whole adult life. He had conveyed to her without words exactly what had happened.

Darla had to wonder about her own role in what had happened. Had she unwittingly driven him to commit murder? She had bad-mouthed Roxie at every opportune moment. And she had flirted with Bob, even stolen a kiss.

She had to make amends. This time, it was she who had to come to the rescue, as he had done so many times for her in the past. She wasn't about to let him face a murder charge in Texas, a state that prided itself on dealing out harsh punishment to law breakers, in particular murderers. It was unthinkable. So she had taken the blame and even made sure any fingerprints left by him were removed from the weapon.

A knee-jerk reaction had compelled her to do this for him. For more than thirty years he had done everything for her, while she had done almost nothing in return but expect more from him. He had devoted his life to her career and even married a younger version of her in an attempt to recapture the life they once had together. Deep down, Darla had always believed that was why he had married Roxie. But even if she hadn't believed that, she knew Bob so well she figured he would soon come to the police and turn himself in. He wouldn't let Darla Denman stay in jail for his offense. Throwing up a smoke screen to cloud the issue and allow him time was the least she could do.

The Monday holiday had everything on hold, even justice. Her arraignment wouldn't take place until tomorrow. Thank God West Texas was in the middle of nowhere. The press apparently hadn't yet learned the bad news. The good news was, a lot of people in the press didn't even know where West Texas was.

Darla had yet to see the court-appointed attorney Captain Fuller had promised, but she sensed it was still early in the day. Maybe he or she would show up soon.

"Darla Denman!" A female voice boomed her name. It had come from the area where she had been processed the evening before.

Ah. The attorney. Darla stood up quickly and moved to the cell door. "Here," she called out and immediately wanted to laugh. Under the circumstances, where else would she be?

A very large woman dressed in civilian clothing—khaki pants and a white shirt—approached from her left. "You got visitors. Step back from the door, please."

Darla obeyed like a good little prisoner. Her hands immediately flew to her hair, attempting to straighten it. She hadn't seen a brush or a comb since last night. She smoothed her jump suit. A habit of always appearing at her best carried over even in jail.

The large woman opened the door and motioned for her to step forward.

Darla departed the cell, and turned in the direction from where the woman had appeared and waited until the cell was locked again. Together they walked to the end of the hallway, where Darla was ushered into a stark gray room holding a gray metal table with two gray metal chairs on one side and a single chair on the other. She saw a large reflective window on one wall. She had watched enough cop shows to know it was a one-way mirror, a window for watching all that happened on the other side.

"Have a seat, Mrs. Denman. Your visitors should be here shortly. You've got thirty minutes."

Visitors? As in more than one? Darla sat down on the side of the lone chair and, forgetting the real purpose of the mirror, began to fuss with her hair with her fingers. She didn't know who might come in the door but she intended to be poised and ready.

Edwina was right on Debbie Sue's heels and ran into her when she stopped at the closed steel door. "Go on in," she urged.

"Hold on, will ya?" Debbie Sue groused. "Are you sure this is the right door?"

"Detective Finley said the first door on your left. This is it."

Debbie Sue opened the door a crack and peered in. "Darla?" she said softly. Seeing the singer, a sense of relief passed over her. She rushed in. "Oh, it's so good to see you. Are you all right?"

Darla stood and before Debbie Sue could wrap her arms around her, a voice crackled from the intercom. "No physical contact. Please stand apart from each other and sit in the chairs provided."

"Damn," Edwina said looking around. "Big Brother's watching. Can he listen, too?"

"I think protected speech applies to conversations with her attorney only, but I'm not sure," Debbie Sue said. "Darla, you should be careful what you say. You have called your lawyer, haven't you?"

"Heavenly days, I don't have a lawyer. Lawyers are expensive. Captain Fuller promised someone would come to see me, but I haven't seen him or her yet."

"Oh, my God, Darla. That sounds like . . . Are you talking about a court-appointed lawyer?"

"Why, yes. I have no money."

"Does Bob know? Is he trying to find someone for you? Surely some lawyer owes you a favor. Darla, you need a good lawyer."

"Yeah," Edwina said. "A *criminal* lawyer."

"Thanks for the advice, girls, but I'm not worried. I don't have anything to hide."

Debbie Sue exchanged glances with Edwina, but decided to not waste any more of their visiting time discussing lawyers. "We'd have been here sooner," she said, "but this detective wanted to talk to us and we've been with him for over an hour."

"Was it Detective Finley?"

"Yeah, good-looking cuss, ain't he?" Edwina answered.

"I couldn't tell you. I barely remember talking to him. I was crying so hard when he came in to see me he gave up asking me anything. He said he'd talk to me later. What did he ask y'all about?"

"What *didn't* we talk about?" Edwina grumbled. "He asked us everything. I kept wondering what I'd do if he asked for our phone numbers, being a happily married woman and all."

"He did ask for our phone number, Ed, and our addresses. And we gave them to him." Debbie Sue turned to Darla. "He did ask a lot of questions about what we knew and conversations we had before we all went to Midland. I felt like he was trying to figure out who Ed and I are mostly. He's thorough. A good detective needs to be. He's probably as much in the dark as we are."

"But you don't have to worry, hon," Edwina said gently. "We told him there wasn't a chance in hell you killed anybody. And even if you did, it would've been an accident—"

Debbie Sue gasped. "Shut up, Ed."

"Oh, you're right," Darla said. "I didn't do it."

Debbie Sue sat back in her chair momentarily stunned. "Then why did you say you did?"

"I was covering for Bob."

Debbie Sue leaned forward, her chin only inches from the tabletop, and spoke softly. "But Darla, if Bob had done it, wouldn't he have said so? I can't see him ever allowing you to be arrested for something he did."

"He had no choice. Once I confessed there was nothing more to say. I'm sure it was an accident. Bob Denman is no murderer and they don't have any proof to convict me."

"You don't think a confession is enough?" Debbie Sue asked, amazed.

"Bob will come in and admit to the murder," Darla said, looking at the two women as if they weren't quite tuned in to the real world. "There won't be any evidence to hold him and they'll release us both."

"Darla, I don't know what courtroom TV series you've been watching," Debbie Sue said, "but that isn't how it works."

"At least not on planet Earth," Edwina added. "And sure as hell not in the nation of Texas."

"What she's trying to say, Darla, is that both of you admitting guilt either makes it look like you're covering for each other or . . ." Debbie Sue sat back in her chair, mulling over what to say next.

"Or? Or what?"

"Or that you're in cahoots and you're both guilty. They could decide to charge you both."

Darla sat up straighter. "What? But there's no proof."

"Darla," Debbie Sue whispered, "I saw you wipe that nail file that looked like a stiletto. I had to tell the detective that. Just that alone makes you look guilty."

"That's why I wiped it off, in case there were fingerprints, which could have been proof that Bob did it. Honestly, you girls are confusing me. I feel like I'm talking to the wall."

"Hell. This conversation is affecting me worse than that," Edwina said. "I feel like a hamster racing in a wheel."

"It didn't cross your mind that Bob didn't do it?"

Darla looked at Debbie Sue and blinked hard. Her gaze swerved to Edwina. "Why, uh, no, I never . . . I mean, the way Bob looked at me . . ."

"Maybe he was in shock. We all were," Edwina said. "If

you'd held a mirror up to my face I'm sure I looked like death warmed over. No pun intended."

Darla clasped her cheeks with her palms. "Oh, my God. What have I done?" Debbie Sue saw a glister of tears in her eyes. "I'm in a lot of trouble, aren't I?" she said in a tiny voice.

Edwina snorted. "You think?"

"You two believe me, don't you?" Darla said.

Debbie Sue looked at Edwina for assurance. "Oh, hell," Edwina said. "We discussed it, already said we don't believe you're guilty."

"See?" Debbie Sue said. "But you have to admit it looks bad."

Darla broke into sobs. Debbie Sue shot a look at the door. A noisy emotional outbreak might bring the jailer in. She was pretty sure that prisoners getting too emotional made the people in charge edgy.

"Darla, don't cry. Listen to me. We're going to help you. Ed and I have this detective agency, the Domestic Equalizers. I think we told you about it. We've solved crimes before. We'll use our resources to help you."

"We have resources?" Edwina said, drawing back and looking at Debbie Sue.

"*Yes*, Ed, we have resources."

The female jailer's unmistakable deep voice came from the hallway.

Fuck. This visit is over, Debbie Sue thought. "Look, we'll be here tomorrow at your arraignment and just in case they're willing to release you, we'll find a bail bondsman—"

"I've already taken care of that," Darla said, wiping her eyes with the back of her hand.

"How is that possible?"

The door opened and the female jailer appeared. "Time's up. Mrs. Denman, come with me, please. Ladies, please stay here until I come back."

As Darla stood to be led away she looked at Debbie Sue. "My cellmate owns a bonding company. She and I have already worked it out."

As Darla was led away, Edwina whispered, "How lucky is that?"

"I don't know," Debbie Sue said, her brow squeezing into a painful crease. "Let's hope it's for real and hope it continues. 'Cause, Ed, luck, and lots of it, is what that woman's gonna need."

chapter twenty-one

As they left the building, Edwina didn't talk, for once, and Debbie Sue was grateful. Crossing the parking lot, she knew if she looked in her partner's direction the blah-blah-blah would start and she wouldn't be able to think, so she stepped up her pace to stay two strides ahead.

"Hey," Edwina said. "Hey, don't think walking ahead of me is gonna keep me quiet. We'll be in the cab of your pickup soon enough. You can't escape me there."

Yep, Edwina's silence was too good to be true. On a big sigh, Debbie Sue stopped and turned to face her. "I know you've got a mouthful to say. So let's have it."

"Do you think they were listening to our conversation?"

"I don't know. But we didn't say anything that hasn't already been said."

"I don't recall that anybody's accused Bob of being the killer. That would be new information."

"Ed, Bob and Roxie were married. Husbands are always the first people they look at. Don't you remember the questions Detective Finley asked us about his and Roxie's relationship? If Darla hadn't popped off and confessed, Bob would be their number-one suspect. He might be the one in jail instead of Darla."

Edwina shrugged.

"We've got to help her," Debbie Sue said.

"Why? You said you told Buddy we were going to observe the Midland PD and jump in only if needed."

"I know, Ed, but we have resources. We—"

"What the hell does that mean? What *resources*? I think we'd better do what Buddy said and leave this to real cops."

"Ed, I had no idea how badly Darla's screwed herself with this confession and all. I only suspected that saving Bob was the reason she confessed. Until this visit, I didn't *know* it. And I didn't know the reason she cleaned that nail file was because she was trying to wipe off *his* fingerprints. I thought she did it because she was in a one hundred percent wigged-out state of shock."

"So?" Edwina said.

"So she's in big trouble, Ed. Since she gave them a confession, I'll bet they won't look very hard for anyone else. And if Bob steps up now and says *he* did it, my God, that makes them both look guilty, like they planned it together or something. Just like I told her in there."

"I don't believe either one of them is guilty."

"I don't either. But who's the killer then? The next closest people to Roxie were the ones in Darla's entourage. Were any of them capable or motivated to kill her?"

"Possibly," Edwina replied. "If you recall, that girl wasn't exactly Miss Congeniality. Hell, she could piss off the Pope. But since I didn't spend much time with any of that bunch except Bob and Darla, I don't have a read on all of them."

Debbie Sue bit down on her bottom lip. "Me neither."

"Is this when we turn to our *resources*?"

They reached the pickup, and as Debbie Sue bleeped the door unlocked, she said, "You're being tacky, Ed. But yeah, I think it is."

"Good. What are they?"

Debbie Sue counted the items off with her finger. "Intelligence, perseverance and the absolute total refusal to take no for an answer."

"Uh-*huh*," Edwina said.

"What we need to do, Ed, is spend some time around Mike, Eddie and Valetta Rose. They've got to be the key to solving this. Roxie had some kind of relationship with Valetta Rose. I want to find out what kind it really was. And I'd sure as hell like to find out something about the bandage on Mike's hand."

"Uh-*huh*," Edwina repeated.

"Ed, will you stop being shitty? Detective Finley told us those three have been ordered not to go any farther than Salt Lick, so we need to get back there and—"

"Uh-oh," Edwina said, looking across Debbie Sue's shoulder. "Here comes Bob Denman now."

Debbie Sue turned to look behind her and Bob raised his hand in a wave as he circled the lot and brought Vic's pickup to a stop in a parking space beside them. He scooted out and came toward them.

"Shit," Edwina said. "He looks like something the cat drug in."

Edwina was right. His face looked drawn. His step had no spring. "Are y'all leaving?" he asked.

"Hi, Bob," Debbie Sue said. "Yes, we're leaving."

"You saw Darla? How is she?" He glanced anxiously toward the jail cell windows. "I can't believe this has happened. It's like a bad dream."

"I hear you," Debbie Sue said. "Are you just now getting here?"

"I've been putting Roxie's funeral arrangements in place."

"It's hard to believe this time yesterday we were talking about what shoes to wear in the show," Edwina said, "and now we're discussing funerals. When's the service?"

"Wednesday afternoon in Nashville." He looked down and shook his head.

"I know Darla confessed," Debbie Sue said, "but Bob, you know she didn't do this, don't you?"

"Of course. Darla isn't capable of hurting anyone."

"It could've been an accident," Edwina said.

Debbie Sue shushed her, but the skinny brunette planted a hand on her hip and gave Bob a direct look. "Do you think Darla could've killed her accidentally?"

Bob glared back at her, his eyes hard. "I know who the guilty party is, Edwina."

"Who?" Debbie Sue and Edwina asked in unison.

"*I* did it," he said, his jaw taut.

"Oh, Jesus H. Christ," Edwina said, rolling her eyes and throwing up both hands. "This is getting sillier by the minute. You did not kill your wife."

"Bob, I have to agree with Ed," Debbie Sue said. "I don't

believe you. I think you're saying that just to protect Darla, the same way she's trying to protect you."

Bob's face softened. Debbie Sue thought she saw his eyes glisten with moisture. "Did she say that? Did she say she confessed to murder to protect me?"

"That's what she said. Less than thirty minutes ago."

A single tear slid down his cheek. His head shook back and forth. "That crazy redhead. I can't believe she did that for me. I don't think anyone has ever thought that much of me in my whole life."

"And we don't doubt you feel the same way," Edwina said. "Just tell us you're not going in there to confess too."

Bob looked down at his shoes. "I intended to earlier, but then I realized all that I had to get done for Roxie. So now I'm planning on coming back here after Roxie's funeral. I'll confess then and get them to release Darla from jail."

"Forevermore," Debbie Sue exclaimed, incredulous. She too threw her hands in the air. "What's wrong with you music people?"

"Yeah," Edwina said. "Have too many drum beats affected your brain?"

"This isn't a kid's game," Debbie Sue said. "We're not playing hide-and-seek. You can't yell olly, olly, oxen free and all come from their hiding places. Cops don't play games, and when you confess, they take that to the bank. Or to be more precise, to the DA. And they stop looking for other suspects."

"Olly, olly oxen free?" Edwina asked, frowning. "Are you sure? All this time I thought it was golly, golly, smell my feet."

Debbie Sue gave her friend a flat look. "Ed, are you nuts? That makes no sense at all."

"Oh, and olly, olly, oxen free does? What the hell is olly and what does it matter if oxen are free?"

"Ladies," Bob broke in, "could we please get back to the issue at hand? I'm trying to think of a way to get Darla out of there."

"Until tomorrow that's not possible," Debbie Sue said. "This is a holiday, you know. The county has appointed a lawyer for her. Tomorrow he'll enter her plea at the arraignment and they'll set her bond—that is, if they let her. Texas is tough on killers. I'm not sure they'll let her bond out after she's confessed to murder. Since she doesn't live here, the judge might consider her a flight risk. But I'm going to ask my husband about all of it when I talk to him later." Debbie Sue sighed. "But at least she's already talked to a bail bondsman, so that's one less thing to deal with."

"Where did she find a bail bondsman?" Bob asked.

"Her jail mate is her bondsman."

"Wow," Bob said, an expression of amazement on his face. "I'm beginning to see why people love Texans. You truly are the most accommodating people I've ever met."

"Thanks," Debbie Sue said sarcastically, "but it's just happenstance that Darla's sharing a cell with a bail bondsman. What we really need right now, Bob, is for *you* to *not* go in there and make matters worse."

"Matters could get worse?"

"They can if you go in and try to help Darla by confessing," Edwina replied. "Hell, Bob, they could accuse the both of you of plotting to off your wife so you can be together."

Bob slowly shook his head again. "I can't just stand aside and do nothing when Darla's in this kind of trouble."

"Listen, this is where the Domestic Equalizers can come in," Debbie Sue said. She dug in her purse, found a business card and handed it to Bob. "You know Ed and I are detectives, right?"

"I heard something about that."

"We're licensed by the great state of Texas and everything. We've already told Darla we're going to take the case and help her."

"And at no charge," Edwina added. "Usually we get fifty bucks an hour, but for you—"

"Shut up, Ed." Debbie Sue glowered at her partner. She turned to Bob. "Forget all that. We're going to help her because we're friends. And we think she's innocent."

Bob studied the card for a few seconds, then looked up at them. "How do you plan on helping her?"

"Don't you worry, Bob," Edwina said. "We've got *resources*."

"We have to find the real killer, Bob."

"I agree. What can I do to help?"

"Until we find out the time of death, the cause of death and some more stuff, we can't make much progress," Debbie Sue said. "But that doesn't prevent us from talking to Mike, Eddie and Valetta Rose. Can you arrange some time we can spend with them?"

"Actually, no. They're gone."

Debbie Sue's eyes bugged. She all but shouted, "What do you mean *gone*?" Then she calmed herself and said in a reasonable tone, "They can't be gone, Bob. Darla just told us the detective ordered them not to go any farther than Salt Lick."

"That's news to me," Bob replied. "Mike called me late last night from Hogg's. The three of them stopped there after they gave statements. They ran into a trucker who's a big fan of

Darla's. They told him what happened and he agreed to give them a ride back to Nashville."

"Shit," Edwina said. "Just like the backup singers. What are the odds of that? All I can say is, those damn truckers should stay out of Hogg's."

Debbie Sue stared at Edwina, who stared back.

"Uh, what about their musical instruments?" Edwina asked, turning away from Debbie Sue. "I thought that was the reason they didn't haul ass back to Nashville when the backup singers hitched a ride with a trucker a couple of days ago."

"I promised I'd get their instruments back to them," Bob said absently. He rubbed his forehead. "Jeez, I specifically asked Mike if they were supposed to stay around, but he said they'd all been given permission to leave."

"Hah," Edwina said. "I guarantee you Detective Finley didn't say that. And if you go inside and tell him anything, it needs to be that those three skipped town. Hell, they not only skipped town, they left the whole damn state. With that to chew on, maybe he'll divert his attention from Darla and start to look at those guys as suspects."

Bob stared toward the entrance to the building for a long time. "You're right," he finally answered. "They could be suspects, couldn't they? And I've grown really fond of those three. It hurts to know one of them might be guilty of killing my wife."

In the back of Debbie Sue's mind, nagging notions danced. She read Detective Tom Finley as a man who lacked a sense of humor when it came to murder. If he told Debbie Sue Overstreet not to leave town, she most likely would comply without question. Yet Eddie, Mike and Valetta Rose had just hitched a ride willy-nilly and ridden out of Dodge. Was one of them hiding a secret? Or were all three?

Mike's bandaged hand weighed on her mind. She still wondered if that was significant. Could he have cut himself in a scuffle with Roxie? The only way to find out was to confront all three of them. And now it appeared that she and Ed would have to travel to Nashville to do that. *Fuck.* How in the hell would they ever get Buddy and Vic to let them take off for Nashville? Neither of those guys had quite gotten over her and Edwina's trip to New York City a few years back.

She laid her hand on Bob's forearm in a show of support. "Try to remember, Bob, like Edwina said, perhaps it was a terrible accident."

"Yeah," Edwina said. "It'd take a real monster to shove a metal file into somebody's jugular on purpose."

Debbie Sue slapped her forehead with her palm. "Ed, forgodsake."

Bob said nothing, just looked at Edwina with pain in his eyes for a few beats. Then he said, "I guess I'll go inside and see Darla. Don't forget to call me if I can do anything to help you."

"We will," Debbie Sue said. "Okay if I call you this evening and get the addresses and phone numbers for Mike, Eddie and Valetta Rose?"

"Sure. You want them now?"

"No, that's okay. I don't have anything to write on. I'll call you this evening."

Edwina nudged her arm. "Here's a pen and some paper."

"No, that's okay."

"I'd better get in there," Bob said, already backing away. "I'll be waiting for your call."

As he strode across the parking lot, Edwina said, "Why didn't you write down the addresses and phone numbers?"

"I don't want to be too optimistic. When I tell Buddy we

have to go to Nashville, I don't want him to think I already planned it."

"Nashville? We're going to Nashville? The one in Tennessee?"

"If the suspects aren't here where we are, Ed, then we'll have to go to them. And it'll be worth the trip to see why Mike had a bandaged hand."

Debbie Sue could see gears grinding behind Edwina's eyes. No telling what she was thinking.

"And one more thing, Ed. In the future, could you please be a little more sensitive?"

Edwina frowned and opened her palms. "About what?"

Debbie Sue sighed. "Never mind."

Debbie Sue drove toward Salt Lick uttering an occasional "uh-huh" and "sure" to Edwina's non-stop blathering. Before starting back, they had stopped for a couple of burgers and Edwina had talked all through lunch. In fact, she hadn't *stopped* talking since hearing the word *Nashville*.

"If we're going to Nashville, we have to go to Ryman Auditorium and Tootsie's Orchid Lounge," Edwina said. "Patsy used to hang out at Tootsie's, you know. Oh, sweet Jesus, to walk where Patsy Cline walked. I get all atwitter just thinking about it." She heaved a sigh. "A camera, I've got to get a camera. One of those fancy ones, but simple to use. I don't want one I need a college degree to operate. What'll I wear? What are *you* gonna wear? When are we going? Lord God, I haven't been this excited since I found out HBO was gonna show all episodes of *True Blood* back to back."

"Ed, forgodsake, stop talking! We're not going on a sightseeing jaunt. I intend for us to get in and get out of there as quickly as possible. That is, if we can even get there. You know damn well Buddy Overstreet is going to throw a shoe over us going to Nashville to investigate Roxie's murder."

"As long as he doesn't hit you with it, I don't see the problem."

"This isn't funny, Ed."

Edwina fell silent. The only sound in the cab then was the hum from the pickup's diesel engine. Suddenly Edwina let out a shout. "I've got it!"

Debbie Sue jumped and veered out of her lane into the next and back.

"*Shit!* Dammit, Ed, don't do that to me!"

"But I've got it. We'll tell Buddy and Vic we're going to Roxie's funeral service. You know, to pay our respects. Neither one of them would tell us not to go to a funeral. They don't know we didn't like her. For all they know, we were best friends."

Instead of replying, Debbie Sue studied the road ahead. A plan was coming together in her mind.

"Well, say something," Edwina said.

"You know what you are, Edwina Perkins-Martin?"

Edwina sighed deeply. "Yes, I'm afraid I do. And I'm still waiting on a twelve-step program to remedy it."

Debbie Sue grinned, reached across the cab and pushed on her old friend's shoulder. "Silly, you're a genius, is what you are. We're going to Nashville. Definitely. Now get that paper and pen back out and start writing: Ryman, Tootsie's, Music Row . . ."

chapter twenty-two

Darla had barely gotten back to her cell when the jailer announced another visitor. She went through the same routine as before, anticipating that Mike or Eddie had come to see her, as she walked up the hallway and sat down in the room she had just left. When the door opened, Bob Denman entered. Her heart and hopes soared. To hell with the "no physical contact" rule. She sprang to her feet and rushed into his open arms.

The familiar voice rang out again. "No contact, please. Step apart and sit on opposite sides of the table, please."

"Whoa," Bob said, looking around. "Where did that come from?" He eased onto a chair on one side of the table.

"The mirror," Darla said, gesturing toward the reflective rectangle. "Someone's on the other side watching us." She sat down opposite him.

"Do you think they're listening to what we're saying?" he asked.

"Who knows? I think I'm supposed to be able to talk to my lawyer privately, but I don't know about other visitors. Listen, we've only got thirty minutes. What about the telethon?"

"Everyone was torn up, but they went on with it. You know how it is with a telethon. They can't forget they're trying to raise money for a cause. They had a lot of acts. They even had some local talent they called on."

"Has the press made a big to-do?"

"Nah," Bob said.

Darla gave him a wan smile. "I guess that's good news and bad news." Darla looked down at the tabletop. "I hate doing this to those telethon people."

Bob leaned forward and spoke in a low tone. "What in the hell were you thinking, Darla, making a confession? We both know you didn't kill Roxie."

She leaned forward too, her face a foot from his. "I was trying to help you, Bob. When you looked at me with that stricken, pitiful expression, it couldn't have been clearer that you and Roxie had a fight and you accidentally killed her in the heat of anger."

"You assumed that from an expression? Anger? My God, Darla. I've *never* been mad enough to kill anyone. You've got to quit reading those murder mysteries. I was just trying to keep myself together. I've never seen that much blood in my whole life. And the fact that it came from my wife overwhelmed me. I still can't stand to think of it."

A burn rushed to Darla's eyes. "Are you telling me that *I* told the cops that *I* committed murder because you looked like you were going to toss your cookies? Damn, Bob, I've done some foolish things because I still love you, but this one takes the cake."

"Because you still—"

"Love you. Yes, Bob, I still love you." She sniffled. "I don't think I've ever stopped."

Bob stared into her eyes for a few beats. Finally, he said, "I don't know what to say. I could say I still love you, too. And I *know* I've never stopped."

"Even after all I've done?" She sniffled.

"Don't cry, sweetheart. I won't be able to take it if you cry. Look, we've got to figure out what to do. Roxie's funeral is on Wednesday in Nashville. I was planning on coming back here to confess my own guilt afterwards and get you off the hook, but Debbie Sue and Edwina talked me out of it in the parking lot. What they said made a lot of sense. If I confess, hell, they'll think we're both guilty."

"I guess neither one of us is thinking too clearly." The room grew silent again. A full minute passed, then Darla cleared her throat. "Bob, I'm sorry about Roxie. You know there was no love lost between us, but no one should go out like that."

"Thanks, I appreciate it. You know, when we first married she was kind of sassy and full of herself, but she impressed me as being a sweet kid with a good voice. Then people began to hear her sing and the possibility of having real success changed her. She became obsessed with it. The closer she got to a breakthrough, the meaner she became."

"I've seen that happen in the music business more times than I want to count." Darla slowly shook her head. "I could name names and so could you."

"True enough."

"Who do you think did it?"

"There's no telling. That's sad isn't it? What kind of person gets murdered and there's a list as long as my arm of possible suspects?"

"A person who's burned too many bridges. Someone who's too young to think she's ever going to die," Darla said softly. She paused, her throat feeling as though it might close and cut off her breathing. "Where is everyone?"

"They left last night. Mike and Eddie and Valetta Rose gave statements to the police and hitched a ride back to Nashville with a trucker."

"You're kidding. Where'd they run into a trucker?"

Bob gave her a weak smile and shrugged his shoulders. "They went to Hogg's late last night and struck up a conversation with him. He was on a long haul form the West Coast and he offered to give them a lift."

Tears threatened her again. "Without even telling me goodbye. How can they just up and leave?"

"Mike said the police gave them permission, although Debbie Sue and Edwina said that couldn't be correct. Debbie Sue said Detective Finley told them not to leave town."

"And they left anyway?" Darla's heart began to race. "Then they must be guilty of something. My God, maybe all three of them are guilty."

"Don't worry, Darla. The authorities will find out who did this. Meanwhile, we can't leave an innocent person in jail. We need to get you out of here and clear your name."

"My name," Darla said bitterly. "None of this would have happened if it wasn't for me trying to bring my precious name back into the public eye. I've always been a fool. And now I'm an old fool." She sobbed into her hands.

"This is not your fault, sweetheart. None of this is your fault. Please don't cry. Everything's going to be fine."

"Oh, Bob, tell me something I can believe," Darla wailed, "something that will make all of this go away."

Bob patted her forearm and leaned closer to her. "The Domestic Equalizers are on the case. Debbie Sue is calling me this evening for the addresses and contact numbers for Mike, Eddie and Valetta Rose in Nashville."

Darla looked up, blinked once and broke into waves of loud sobs.

Darla had had an exhaustive day. And following a night of no sleep, too. She lay on her cell cot, her eyes closed, the day's events playing back in her mind.

Within minutes of Bob's departure she had been escorted to the visitors' room again. This time, she had found her county-appointed attorney waiting for her. He was chewing his nails when she entered the room and he looked to be no older than thirty. After a brief handshake he said, "Mrs. Denman, have a seat, please. My name is Rooster Perdue. I've been—"

"Excuse me," Darla said. "Did you say *Rooster*?"

"Yes ma'am. It's what they called my grandfather."

"Oh, it's a nickname then?"

"No, ma'am. It's my legal, birth-given name. May I continue?"

"Just a minute, Mr. . . . er, Rooster. I'm sorry, but this could be the most important day of my life and I want to be sure I understand everything. How old are you?"

"I don't see what that has to do with anything. I'm perfectly—"

"Just humor me, okay? You're going to know an awful lot about me before this visit is over. I think it only fair I know more about you than just your name."

"I'm twenty-six," he answered, looking at her through the thick lenses of black-framed glasses.

"You must be right out of school. Please tell me I'm not your first case."

"I finished in the top twenty percentile of my class."

"Good grief. I'm right." Darla dropped her forehead onto her palm and shook her head. She looked up then. "Oh, well, I don't guess it matters. Since I'm innocent, you don't need to be Perry Mason."

"Hm. He's unfamiliar to me. Where does he practice?"

"Sweet Jesus," Darla mumbled.

She and Rooster spent the better part of an hour together and when the interview was complete, she had even more mixed feelings about him. He had taken pages of notes, but she didn't know if that was to keep the session fresh in his mind or if he wanted to look up specific legal questions in his textbooks.

Now, Darla rolled to her side into a fetal position and moaned as she recalled asking her attorney if the cause of death had been determined. He had answered, "Homicide."

Maybe this was her punishment for years of traveling life's highway driving too fast and often times in the wrong lane. The gravity of her situation was settling in all around her and suffocating her. She had never been one to pray much, but if ever there was a time to start, she suspected now was the time.

Debbie Sue continued to strategize with Edwina until they reached Salt Lick. At her double-wide, Edwina invited Debbie Sue to come in, but she declined. She suspected Buddy was at home by now. But if he wasn't, there were dogs and a horse to feed.

When she reached home, to both her delight and dismay, Buddy's state rig was parked in its usual spot under the carport. She was happy to see he had come home, but dread cloaked her. In her evening phone conversations, she had hedged and simply neglected to tell him how close she and Edwina were to the situation in Midland. When the media reported that she had been on the scene soon after Roxie's death, she had downplayed that to Buddy as a mistake the press had made. After all, Tatts by Matt was really first on the scene.

In plain words, she had *lied* to her sweet Buddy. Consequently, he still believed that all she and Edwina had been doing was lip-syncing behind Darla.

Now she was caught like a rat in a trap. She would have to make a confession of her own. Not only would she have to tell her husband the whole damn story, she would have to add that she and Edwina had committed to Darla and Bob that they would find Roxie Denman's murderer. She would have to come clean on the reason for their desire to travel to Nashville. She would have to admit that it involved more than paying their respects to Roxie.

As soon as she entered the house, before he even said hello, he started asking questions. *Cop genes*, she grumbled mentally.

They took seats at the kitchen table and he sat stone-faced as she told him part of the truth. "I know Darla didn't do it," she said in conclusion. "And I know Bob didn't do it, but there's several who could have. I told you on the phone what kind of person Roxie was."

"You just met this Darla and Bob. You don't know them that well. What makes you think they're innocent?"

"I just feel it."

"They're the logical suspects, Flash. And if they don't have enough sense to not confess to a crime they didn't do, they must be guilty of something."

Frowning, Debbie Sue put her flattened palms together and shoved them between her knees. "Nooo, Buddy. They feel guilty because they're in love with each other and Bob is, or was, a married guy. They both say they committed murder to cover up for each other, when, in fact, neither one of them did it."

Buddy shook his head. Debbie Sue could see his mind was closed.

"Well it doesn't matter anyway," he said. "I'm sure the Midland homicide department's got everything under control. I've known Tom Finley for years and he'll get to the bottom of it. You're not getting involved, right?"

"Buddy, I can't abandon Darla, if that's what you mean,"

"Now, Flash," Buddy said gently, and Debbie Sue cringed. When he used that pet name in that tone of voice, her side of the battle was in trouble. He leaned forward, picked up her hand and placed a kiss on the back of it. "You know exactly what I mean. Let the Midland PD take care of it. You have no business even going near it."

"Dammit, Buddy, I visited her in jail and she looked so pitiful in that ugly orange suit and those tacky shoes with no laces." Tears stung behind Debbie Sue's eyes and she pulled her hand away from Buddy's. "All I could think was the day she sat in the Styling Station all glitz and glamour and sexy shoes and her beautiful glittery white jacket stained with blood and her shining coppery hair. Ed and I both told her we'd be there for her."

Buddy's tone softened more, as it always did when he feared she might cry. "I'm not saying you can't be there for her. All I'm saying is I don't want you to interfere with the Midland police."

"Oh, no. Of course not. . . . If I *hear* anything I'll report it to the police immediately. Any responsible citizen would do that."

Buddy straightened in his chair. His narrow-eyed look came at her like a hurled spear. "And how do you intend to go about *hearing* something?"

"Oh, you know. Just listening."

"Not asking questions, just listening? And where do you intend to do this listening?"

"In the shop. Around town. You know. People know me and Ed, Buddy. They know Ed and I were there when it happened. They'll be talking and we'll be listening."

"And *I* know you, wife of mine. If only that's all it would amount to, talking to people around town."

"Yeah, around town." Debbie Sue saw the opening and took a deep breath and leaned closer. "And at Roxie's funeral."

Buddy tucked back his chin, obviously surprised. "They're burying her around here somewhere?"

"Well . . . no, uh . . . it's in . . . that is, Ed and I thought we'd go to her service just to pay our respects." Debbie Sue winced inside at telling him the lie, but she plowed on. "Even Darla said everyone hated Roxie so much she doubted anyone would be there. Don't you think it's sad to have a funeral no one comes to? And it's kind of sad to be that young and no one—"

"Stop right there. *Where* is the funeral, Flash?"

"Wednesday," Debbie Sue said perkily, though she resented his using his cop tone in a conversation with her.

"I didn't ask *when*. I asked *where*."

"Nashville."

"Nashville! Is that in Texas? Has a new town sprung up that I don't know about?"

Debbie Sue almost bounced on her chair seat. "Dammit, Buddy, you know there's no Nashville, Texas. Listen, there's one Southwest non-stop flight to Nashville every day that leaves out of Midland."

"You've already looked up the flight schedules?"

"Well, I had some free time on my hands."

"Debbie Sue—"

"Buddy, please don't say you don't want me to go. Ed and I could go and come back the same day. We'd prefer staying a couple of days, of course. What I mean is we already made a list of places we'd like to see. And if you're going to be in Tennessee anyway, you might as well go see them, right?"

"Oh, well, as long as you've gone to the trouble of making a list."

"Sarcasm. All you can say is something sarcastic?" Debbie Sue tented her brow. "Just stop and think, Buddy. A poor young penniless girl with no one to mourn her is being laid to rest in a cold, dark grave—"

"Okay, okay," Buddy said and sighed. "I give up. I've seen enough victims laid to rest with no one present but the grave digger. You're right. It's sad. I don't know what you think you owe these people or what you've committed to, but I can see you're hell-bent on going. I'm not going to stop you."

"You mean that?"

"I mean it. I'm not going to stop you."

Debbie Sue couldn't keep from breaking into a wide grin.

Buddy's chocolate brown eyes drilled her. "But I *am* going with you."

"What?" Debbie Sue sat straighter.

Buddy slashed the air with a flattened hand. "After what happened in New York City, no way am I letting you and Edwina take off on an out-of-town caper again. I'm sure Vic will feel the same way. Besides, I've never been to Tennessee. I'd like to tour the state capital and check out the Titans stadium. And I'm due some time off."

Debbie Sue watched in stunned silence as Buddy rose, strode to the fridge on the far end of the kitchen, pulled out two bottles of cold beer and opened them. He returned to the table and handed her a beer. Looming over her, he touched his bottle to hers. "Here's to our trip to Nashville."

Shit!

"To Nashville," Debbie Sue mumbled.

Buddy's wary gaze came down at her. "You don't sound very excited. You don't want me along?"

"Oh, of course I do, Wyatt. We haven't had any time away in a long time and God knows you need a break from work. I just don't want you to go because you think I need a babysitter."

"It's your safety I worry about, not the amount of freedom you have." He bent forward, bracing his hand on the table, and gave her a fierce smack on the lips. "You can use that beautiful head for calculating and your perfect little nose for snooping all you want. I just want to know you're safe."

"I love you so much, Buddy," Debbie Sue said, getting to her feet and wrapping her arms around his waist and hugging him tightly.

"Prove it," he replied mischievously.

She angled a look up at him from beneath her eyelashes. "I can prove it. I could go run us a bath with lots of bubbles, light some candles and—"

"What are you waiting for?"

Buddy waited until he heard the bathwater running before he stepped outside the kitchen door to the deck he had built with his own two hands. He unclipped his phone from his belt, keyed in a stored number and waited impatiently as three rings passed. He was about to hang up when a voice on the other end picked up. "Detective Finley."

"Tom, Buddy Overstreet here. It's all set. I'm going to Nashville with them. Thanks for the tip. I'll report back later on."

"Right. Thanks for your help, Ranger."

"No problem. Glad to do it."

Closing his phone he stepped back inside, grabbed a couple more bottles of beer from the fridge and made his way to the sound of running water and his wife's voice singing a Darla Denman tune.

chapter twenty-three

Following a long, luxurious bubble bath that required adding water twice for warmth, Debbie Sue and Buddy dried each other with oversized bath towels and crawled into bed. She dozed in his arms, enjoying the heat of his body, the coolness of the air conditioner and the peace that surrounded her. She lay in a twilight state, the silence punctuated only by the mournful lowing of a distant cow. A question about why that cow sounded so lost and lonely was traipsing through her head when the jangle of the phone intruded.

Silently cussing a blue streak, she carefully reached across Buddy for the phone. "Hello," she whispered.

"Hey, girlfriend," Edwina said cheerily. "What's up?"

Getting to her feet, she tiptoed to the rocking chair and grabbed the afghan that hung across the back. "Just a minute," she whispered into the phone. She wrapped herself in the afghan and carried the phone into the kitchen. "Ed, I was in bed—"

"Still? It's been hours since you got home. Buddy was only gone three days. What do you two do when he's away for a whole week?"

"Never mind," Debbie Sue huffed. "What do you want?"

"I'm dying to know how Buddy took the news of the trip to Nashville. Are we going or not? I only have tomorrow to get packed. I can't wait 'til the last minute, you know."

"This is only Monday. Even *you* should be able to get packed by Wednesday."

Edwina squealed so loudly Debbie Sue had to hold the receiver away from her ear. She stepped back and looked down the hallway to their bedroom halfway expecting to see or hear Buddy. When he didn't emerge from the bedroom, she returned the phone to her ear. "Just settle down, Ed. There's more I haven't told you yet."

"I'm listening."

"Buddy's going, too."

"Uh-oh. How?"

"He's treating this like a getaway. He wants Vic to go too, but I'm sure Vic wouldn't be—"

"Why, Vic would love it. Second to me, the company he prefers most is you and Buddy. But what would we do with them while you and I try to unravel this Roxie mess? You know Buddy is gonna want to get right in the middle of it. I mean, he's a cop."

"I don't know yet. He said something about going to the Tennessee Titans stadium for a tour. I'm been thinking maybe you and I could beg off of that and make use of the time."

"The Tennessee Titans are in Nashville?" Edwina asked.

"Well, yes, Ed. I thought you followed football."

"I *do,* but only the Dallas Cowboys. I don't know anything about the other teams."

"Spoken like a real fan."

"This could be fun," Edwina babbled on. "We'll have to take one of your vehicles. Bob still has Vic's pickup and my old Mustang might never make it on a trip like that."

"Uh, Ed—"

"No. No 'uh, Ed.' We're driving, right? Please tell me we're not flying. You know how I am about flying."

Debbie Sue did know indeed. Edwina suffered severe air sickness for which she took copious amounts of Dramamine. The last time Debbie Sue had flown with her, Edwina had overmedicated herself and had to be brought on the plane semiconscious in a wheelchair.

"Ed, it's over a thousand miles. I did a MapQuest on it. It would take twenty hours to drive. We can fly in two hours."

"So?"

"So, we are not driving. If you'll take those air-sickness pills as directed you'll be fine. Thousands of people take them and I'll bet most of them don't have to be tied to an industrial dolly."

"Maybe I'll just stay here," Edwina snapped.

Debbie Sue huffed, but she knew how to handle her friend of so many years. "Well, if you want to do that, Ed, that's okay. I can't imagine going to the Grand Ole Opry without you, but that's okay. I'll be sure to take lots of pictures and bring you a souvenir from everywhere we go. What do you want from Tootsie's, a glass jigger with a picture of Johnny Cash or a Patsy Cline keychain? I've heard they have one that's a replica of her holding a microphone and it plays 'Crazy' when you squeeze her hand."

"Okay, you win. I'll go on a plane. I'll even let you be in charge of the Dramamine."

"But only if you promise not to have any with you and that you don't have Buddy and Vic giving you pills too."

"Hmm, do I have to promise that?"

"Without reservation."

"All right already." Edwina's tone changed. "Just think of it, Dippity-do. You and me in Nashville. I mean New York City was nice, but now we're talking Nashville, home of country music. This is *our* people. Does your mom know we're coming?"

"I haven't called her yet."

"This is going to be so much fun."

The word *fun* struck something deep within Debbie Sue. Her enthusiasm faded and she didn't reply to Edwina's comment.

"Debbie Sue, you still there? Hey, did we get disconnected?"

"I'm still here, Ed. I got a little carried away with the idea of the trip. Let's not forget the real reason we're going. A young woman who was brutally killed by someone is being laid to rest and we need to find out what happened to her."

"I haven't forgotten. Do you think I'm heartless? But you can't expect me to beat my chest and tear my hair. I only saw her a couple of times and both times she insulted us."

"I know you're not heartless, Ed. Look, I'll talk to you later. I'm standing in the kitchen naked."

Edwina had reminded Debbie Sue of her mother, Virginia, who now lived in Nashville. She would be thrilled at a visit from her only daughter and the man she looked upon as her son. She would line up a million things for them to do. Debbie Sue hated to disappoint her with the news that this would be a business trip.

Looking up the hallway again, she ascertained that Buddy was still sleeping. Still wrapped in the afghan, she stepped out the back door onto the deck. She sat down on the bottom step and began pulling weeds. "The Eyes of Texas" blasted from the phone and she keyed in to the call. A warm, familiar voice said hello.

"Hi, Mom," Debbie Sue said. "I was just thinking about calling you. Guess what? Buddy and I are going to see you Wednesday."

Debbie Sue left her house early on Tuesday, headed to pick up Edwina. She suspected everyone from ordinary housewives to evangelical preachers, not to mention the press, would be trying to get a seat in the Midland courtroom to get a glimpse of a fallen country-music star. The thought of the press gave Debbie Sue a jolt of anxiety. Absolutely no way did she want some reporter to get wind of what she and Edwina were planning.

Yesterday Edwina had called every booked Styling Station customer and rearranged appointments. Being a natural-born multi-tasker, Edwina could make the calls and pack for Nashville at the same time. She had rearranged the entire week so they could spend a couple of extra days in Nashville without feeling the pressure to get back to the salon. Even Buddy's captain, normally not one given to allowing time off without adequate notice, had encouraged Buddy to take all the time he needed. Everything was falling into place. Now if one of the suspects met them at the airport and provided a little hard evidence or confessed on sight, everything would be perfect.

Edwina appeared at last and climbed into the pickup. "Why are we going so early?"

"I want to get a seat, Ed. You know how it'll be. At the rate we're going, we'll be lucky to get a place in the hallway. Now remember, don't talk to anyone and don't let anything spill. We're just spectators, right? It wouldn't help Darla a damn bit if some reporter started following *our* every move."

"I got it, I got it. Mum's the word, as somebody said."

"When did Vic get back?"

"Last night around nine thirty."

"How did he react to going to Nashville?"

"You know Vic. He's up for anything. He does so much driving, flying is a nice change for him and you'll be glad to know he told me the same thing you did. Two pills, no more. But I think all I'll need is a dose of Vic sitting next to me."

"Trust me, Ed, between Vic and me, you'll get to Nashville just fine."

"And home again?"

"And home again."

Leaving Salt Lick's city limits, their talk turned to the pending trip: clothing that was being packed, weather that was expected and the places they would go. Then they were at the Midland County courthouse. Vehicles filled the parking lot. Debbie Sue had to make several circles before finding a spot.

When they finally reached the courthouse steps, they were stunned to be greeted by Darla and Bob coming out of the building. A young man wearing big glasses and an ill-fitting suit accompanied them.

"You're free?" Edwina exclaimed.

"Oh, my God, Darla, I'm so sorry," Debbie Sue said. "We wanted to be here for you."

Darla leaned in to hug of both of them. "That's okay, guys, don't worry about it. It was over in a matter of minutes."

"We weren't sure you'd get released," Edwina said. "What about your bail? Who came up with your bail?"

Darla gazed up at Bob lovingly, while he turned pink and looked uncomfortable. "Bob put up the deed to his office building in Nashville."

"And you pled not guilty?" Debbie Sue asked.

"Of course. Because I haven't done anything. My trial date is six weeks from today."

"That soon? When can you go back to Nashville?" Debbie Sue asked.

The young man made a step toward them. "The judge ordered Mrs. Denman to stay in the area until this unfortunate misunderstanding is cleared up and I've assured him that's not a problem. We have a lot of work to do."

"And you are . . . ?" Debbie Sue asked the pompous young man.

His spine stiffened. His nose lifted and he cleared his throat. "My name is Rooster Perdue, ma'am. I am Mrs. Denman's attorney."

The guy looked more like a college student than a hotshot defense lawyer qualified to defend a murder suspect. Debbie Sue glanced at Edwina, whose dark brows had shot all the way to her hairline, a sure look of panic.

"Listen, Darla," Edwina said, looking around. Satisfied no one was listening, she continued in a low tone, "Me and Debbie Sue and our husbands are going to Nashville tomorrow. We'll be gone two or three days. My place will be empty. I want you to stay there."

"Oh, Edwina, I couldn't—"

"Well you can't stay at Debbie Sue and Buddy's house with Bob. Think of how that will look. Salt Lick's a small town, you know, and Koweba Sanders might be blind as a bat and deaf as a post, but she knows everything that goes on up and down that street. Bob can continue to stay there and you'll stay at my place and that's final. There's plenty of food. We get all the good TV channels. If you want to use the Internet we've got that too. Short of room service and a maid, you'll be as comfortable as staying at a resort."

"I'll probably be on the flight back to Nashville with you," Bob said, also keeping his voice low. "I'm going out tomorrow as well."

Darla's eyes moistened and she laid her hand on Debbie Sue's forearm. "I wish I could go with you to show you the sights."

"Don't worry about it," Debbie Sue said. "You will one day. This really isn't a pleasure trip anyway."

"Right," Edwina added.

"I'll be coming back here after Roxie's service," Bob said. "Darla won't be alone for long."

"Well then, everything's set," Debbie Sue said. "Darla, we'll meet you back in Salt Lick at the house so you can pick up your stuff. Listen, keep your chin up. Everything's gonna be fine."

"That's exactly what I told her," the attorney said. "As long as I'm on the case, there's nothing to worry about." His briefcase popped open and all of his papers, including two Spider Man comic books, fluttered down to the courthouse steps. He dropped to his knees and began gathering everything into a wad.

Everyone exchanged worried glances. "My God," Edwina mumbled. "He looks like a chicken with his head cut off."

Debbie Sue gave her a glower.

Edwina lifted a shoulder. "Or maybe more like a Rooster."

Put a sock in it, Ed, Debbie Sue wanted to say. "Look, let's help him," she said instead, also sinking to her knees and gathering loose papers. Darla left the courthouse with Bob in Vic's pickup.

On the drive back to Salt Lick, Edwina said, "What do you think of the lawyer?"

"Nothing," Debbie Sue answered, not willing to voice her concerns aloud.

"Hah," Edwina said. "You're lying to me. If I know you, your opinion is worse than mine."

"Look, he got her out of jail, which I didn't believe anyone could do on a murder charge. So he can't be as inept as he looks."

"But she pled not guilty."

"Everyone pleads not guilty."

Edwina drew a great breath. "I'll never understand the legal system. First she confesses, then she pleads not guilty and they let her out of jail."

"I know," Debbie Sue said. "It is confusing. I'm going to talk to Buddy about it."

They rode a few more miles in silence. Debbie Sue hadn't even turned on the radio.

"We need to get to the airport a couple of hours early tomorrow, you know," Edwina said.

"Not the Midland Airport, Ed," Debbie Sue replied. "We've got an early flight. If we planned to be there two hours early, we'd have to get there before daylight."

"They say to arrive at the airport two hours early when you're going somewhere. Anything you read about flying safety advises you to arrive early."

"At DFW or LaGuardia, Ed," Debbie Sue said. "But not the Midland Airport. My God, there won't be seven people getting on board our flight."

"And it only takes one terrorist to bring us down, Miss Smarty Pants."

"If we went that early, we'd be there long enough before boarding for you to really get to know everyone on our flight. Maybe you could talk a terrorist out of his plan. Besides, we'll have Vic and Buddy with us. That's like traveling with our own private sky marshals. Of course they won't be armed, but—"

"Oh, hell, that doesn't matter. Vic can do more damage with his bare hands than most people can do with a gun."

"Right," Debbie Sue said.

"I still want to go early."

"Fine. You and Vic go two hours early. Buddy and I'll meet you there."

chapter twenty-four

The next morning, Debbie Sue and Buddy met Edwina and Vic and Bob at the Midland Airport. Bob had returned Vic's pickup and the three of them had ridden together. Sure enough, they had arrived before daylight.

Now, as all of them waited, a boarding announcement was called. They gathered their belongings and found a place in line. As they passed into the Jetway, Debbie Sue turned to Vic and said out of Edwina's hearing, "I gave Edwina her two pills about an hour ago. She should be fine."

Vic's eyes narrowed. "What? I thought *I* was supposed to give her the pills. I gave her two just before you got here."

"Shit," Debbie Sue said, staring at Edwina's back.

"That little scoundrel," Vic muttered.

"Maybe it'll be all right. She seems okay so far."

Just then Edwina whirled, threw an arm in the air in a signal of triumph. "Whoa-ho!" she said in a loud voice. "Let's light this candle, baby!"

Debbie Sue, Buddy and Vic exchanged looks. "Oh, crap," they chorused.

The flight went well. Edwina slept the entire time, snoring loudly enough to draw tittering and scowls from fellow travelers. Bob sat four rows ahead of them. Debbie Sue found herself studying his profile. Her heart went out to him. He was going home, carrying the remains of his murdered wife in a sealed urn, leaving behind his ex-wife, whom he still loved. Debbie Sue couldn't imagine all of the emotions he must be processing—grief, guilt, worry, fear, regrets, you name it. She didn't envy the drama that surrounded him.

After a smooth landing, they disembarked and gathered in the Nashville Airport. "How do we want to do this?" Bob asked. "Do we want to go in cabs?"

Buddy stepped forward. "Bob, we'll rent a minivan or an SUV for the time we're here. There's more than enough room for you to ride with us. After the service we'll give you a ride home or back here, or wherever you need to be."

"Thanks." Bob smiled self-consciously. "I need to wait for my bags. I put the urn in my suitcase. My car's at my home, so if y'all will take me there after the service, I'll be fine."

"Are you flying back or are you driving?" Edwina asked.

"I'll drive. No telling how long I might be there."

"I understand," Buddy said. "Vic, let's find the Enterprise desk and see what they've got."

After Buddy and Vic walked away, Debbie Sue inched closer to Bob. "Do you need any money, Bob? Buddy and I talked about it and if you need funds . . ."

"Oh, gracious, no. I've sold some stock I had almost forgotten about and I'm in good shape. In fact, I want to repay you for your kindness and I plan on getting a room in Midland when I get back. If you can suggest—"

"You'll not repay us for a thing," Edwina said. "If you do you'll ruin our act of kindness and turn it all into just a loan. I won't speak for Debbie Sue, but I need all the brownie points I can get with the man upstairs."

"And please do continue to stay in the house," Debbie Sue said. "I know it's a drive from Salt Lick up to Midland, but the house is free and I hate seeing it sitting empty. Besides, a trial might not even take place." She leaned closer. "Ed and I might just solve that problem while we're here," she whispered. "But don't say anything to Buddy and Vic. They think we're here only to go to Roxie's funeral, then do some sightseeing stuff."

"Oh, okay," Bob said. "My lips are sealed. I hope you can do what you think you can."

Buddy and Vic returned. "We're all set," Buddy said, folding a sheaf of papers and stuffing them into his breast pocket. "Let's get a move on."

Buddy drove, taking directions from Bob, who sat in the front passenger seat. Debbie Sue dug through her purse searching for her cell phone, pulling out items and placing them in her lap.

"Did your mom say where we're staying?" Edwina asked.

"Nope. She was planning on telling me where she made reservations when we got here. . . . Here it is!"

At the same time Buddy looked over his right shoulder and said, "Make it quick, Flash. We're at the funeral home."

Debbie Sue pressed in a number as Buddy drove to the rear entrance of the building. When her mother picked up she said, "Mom, we're here."

"Hi, sweetheart," her mother said. "I knew that had to be you. Did you have a good flight?"

"Very uneventful. We're just about to go into the funeral home now."

"Then you must be at the one on Donelson Pike. McAlister's is the name of it, I think, if it's the one close to the airport."

Debbie Sue looked around for a sign. "Um, yep, that's the name."

"What time is the service, dear?"

"Not for a couple of hours. We're dropping Bob Denman off. He's going to stay here to greet anyone who comes just for visitation. We're going to get checked in and come back for the service."

"I've got you booked at the Gaylord Opryland. You won't have any trouble getting back to the funeral home."

"Gaylord. Oh, Mom, that must be pretty expensive. I hope it's within our budget."

"It's very much in your budget. The manager owed me a favor. I helped him get some last-minute entertainment when a band didn't show for a big shindig they had, so he's comping the rooms. But, honey, don't expect much. They'll be the basic rooms. No frills."

"Are you serious? That doesn't matter to us. Just being there will be a treat."

"What? What's wrong? What did she say? Where are we staying?" Edwina carped like a parrot.

Debbie Sue covered the phone with her hand. "Criminy, Ed, would you let me get off the phone?" She returned her attention to her mother. "Okay, Mom. I'll call you later and we'll plan on meeting for dinner."

Debbie Sue snapped the phone shut and before she could

place it in her purse again, Edwina was pumping her for information. "What's too expensive? Let me guess! No, tell me."

"Mama Doll," Vic said, laughing, "give her a chance to answer. I can see right now I need to get you out of Salt Lick more often."

"She got us rooms at the Gaylord, for free."

"How?" Vic asked.

"The manager owed her a favor. She said not to get too excited because they're basic rooms. But I don't care. I'm excited."

Bob turned and added to the conversation. "Even a basic room at Gaylord Opryland is nice. Well, I need to get inside now. Thanks again for everything. See you in a while. Buddy, you think you can find your way back?"

Buddy's briefcase rested on the console. He popped it open and pulled out a GPS device. "These days, I never leave home without it," he said.

"Good, I won't worry. See you in an hour."

Bob entered the back entrance to the funeral home and was immediately greeted by a man who introduced himself as the director. The anteroom was dimly lit and fragrant with flowers. Soothing organ music, barely audible, came from somewhere and ultra-thick carpet muffled other sound.

"I'm so sorry for your loss," the director said in a smooth-as-silk voice.

"Thank you," Bob replied. "Have there been any calls, any messages?"

The director looked somewhat uncomfortable but regained his composure quickly. "Um, no. No, I'm sorry. There have been no inquiries, but it's early yet." He reached out with both hands. "Would you like me to take the departed for you?"

For a fraction of a second Bob didn't understand the question and then he reacted. "Oh, certainly, yes." He released his hold on the urn that held Roxie's ashes. "Should I, I mean is it all right if I go with you?"

"Why, of course, sir. We have a lovely room available and a registration book at the front entrance. A family member usually sits or stands there to greet visitors as they enter."

Bob smiled appreciatively but didn't have the heart to explain that it was unlikely there would be any visitors except for the people he had traveled with from Texas. He followed the gentleman into a chapel and stopped dead in his tracks when he saw Mike already present.

"Hey, boss. We thought you might appreciate some company."

"We didn't mean to run out on you, Bob," Eddie said.

"But we're here for you now," Mike added.

Valetta Rose stood near Mike, but said nothing. This didn't trouble Bob. She probably didn't know what to say. With the exception of himself, she was probably the closest to Roxie.

Moisture formed in Bob's eyes and a lump that had sprung to his throat prevented him from speaking for a few seconds. What more could be said anyway? He gathered all three in a bearlike hug.

With Buddy's expert driving and the help of the GPS, Debbie Sue and her group arrived at the Gaylord Opryland Hotel. Debbie Sue's mom had been right. The hotel was so close they probably could have found it on their own. They were all admiring its beauty when Debbie Sue said, "Let me out at the front door and I'll go in and register us."

"Great idea," Buddy said. "Since we'll be leaving so soon,

I'm not going to use valet parking. I'll find a spot in the parking lot."

"I'll go with you, Debbie Sue," Edwina volunteered.

They entered through the massive doors and headed for the registration desk. Edwina babbled on about the size and beauty of the lobby. "I feel just like Scarlett O'Hara arriving at Tara." She stopped at a directory near the registration desk. "Good Lord, Debbie Sue, come look at this map. This place has eight bars and seven restaurants, all under one roof! I'm moving here, right here to this spot."

Debbie Sue turned away from the desk with a set of key cards and a puzzled expression on her face. "Uh, Ed, they said we have a suite, the Presidential Suite."

"Cool. What does that mean?"

"I'm not altogether sure, but it doesn't sound *basic*."

Buddy and Vic came through the doorway with a young man behind them wheeling a cart loaded with bags and suitcases.

"Here she is," Buddy said to the bellhop. He approached Debbie Sue. "What are our room numbers, darlin'?"

"There's no number. It just says the Presidential Suite."

"Ah, yes," the bellhop said. "The elevator's to your left. We'll be going to the ninth floor."

They entered the elevator and the bellhop pressed the ninth floor button. When the doors glided open, he said, "It's to your left, at the end of the hallway."

Everyone turned left and trekked up the long hallway with the young man towing the baggage cart behind them. At the end of the hall Debbie Sue started to insert her key card in a door on the left, but she was halted by the bellhop. "Oh, no, not that door, ma'am. That's your kitchen. You'll want to use the door directly in front of you."

Debbie Sue and Edwina exchanged glances. "Would you look at that?" Edwina said. "There's a doorbell at the door in front of me. I didn't know hotel rooms had doorbells."

The bellhop stepped ahead of them, lifted the key card from Debbie Sue's hand and opened the door. "The Presidential Suite does."

Debbie Sue and her group entered the suite, one by one. "Good Lord," she said.

She could see an expansive room before them, with adjoining rooms. They strolled farther and found a dining room large enough to accommodate at least a dozen people, a modern kitchen, two oversized bedrooms and three bathrooms, all opulently furnished. No one said a word.

The bellhop's look swung to each of them. "Is everything all right?"

"Absolutely. Thank you," Buddy said and dug cash from his pocket for a tip.

As soon as the bellhop was out of sight, Debbie Sue pawed in her purse for her cell phone. "I'm calling Mom. We're not going out to supper tonight. I'm telling her to come over here. We're having supper in our suite."

"The Presidential Suite," Virginia Pratt Miller exclaimed, when she came on the phone with Debbie Sue. "My goodness, I didn't expect Harold to be that hospitable. That band I got for him must have been better than I thought."

Debbie Sue laughed. "We want to have dinner here tonight, Mom, in our suite."

"Are you going to use room service?"

"Seeing as how we're not paying for a room, maybe we can afford it."

"Who'll be there? Do I need to dress up?"

"I wouldn't recognize you in anything other than jeans, Mom. There'll be the four of us, plus you and Doc and Bob Denman. Hopefully, he'll have Darla's backup musicians and a young girl who did their makeup."

"What time should we be there?"

"You come whenever you want, Mom. I can't wait to see you. We're going to the funeral service soon, but we should be back in a couple of hours. Can you come early? We've got a lot to catch up on."

"I've been ready to see you since you called. Give me a ring when you get back to the hotel and we'll come right over."

Debbie Sue hung up and wrapped herself in a body hug. "I can't wait! It'll be nice having a bunch of people here this evening. Better than going out to a restaurant."

"Edwina!" Vic's voice boomed from one of the bedrooms. "C'mere. You need to see this."

"Well that sounds inviting," Edwina said, then called out to Vic, "I'm on my way, Puddin'."

Buddy walked up, finishing the last button on a fresh shirt, "Did you talk to Virginia?"

Debbie Sue smoothed Buddy's collar. "She and Doc are coming. They'll be here when we get back. I want to ask Bob to come back with us and if Mike, Eddie and Valetta Rose are there, they should come, too."

"For dinner?"

"If they want to."

"Isn't that time you'll want to spend with Virginia and Doc Miller? Why would you want to bring in strangers?"

Debbie Sue hesitated. Buddy's question made perfect sense, but she couldn't let him know her real intention was interrogation.

"I think it would be a decent thing to do is all. We're going to a funeral and whether we liked her or not, Roxie was Bob's wife. Someone needs to extend a hand of kindness."

Buddy moseyed to the wing chair that flanked the massive velvet couch and took a seat. "We've flown all the way up here from West Texas. I think that's showing quite a bit of kindness."

Debbie Sue could feel her scalp crawling, as it always did when she feared Buddy was on to her true motives. Dammit, where was Edwina? She could use that woman's ability to change the subject and stick her foot in her mouth about now. What could Vic have found that was so enticing that she would be tied up this long?

"Don't forget that Mom's in the music business too. She has some things in common with these people. Besides, we can't invite Bob and not the others."

"*If* they even come to the service."

Damn, that trio just *had* to be at Roxie's service. "You're right," Debbie Sue acknowledged reluctantly. "If they come."

Just then, Vic and Edwina strolled in the room, arm in arm. Debbie Sue was afraid to ask what they had been up to.

"Man, this place is really something. Mama Doll, what say we stay here for a couple of months?"

"My God, I wouldn't be worth a plugged nickel if I stayed here that long. Being waited on hand and foot, maid service, room service? Holey moley."

"I thought you'd gotten lost," Debbie Sue said.

"I decided to touch up my makeup and hair. And then Vic and I tried that big tub out. We didn't fill it with water, of course, but we did get inside to see if we're gonna fit later on."

Buddy laughed.

"That's more information than I was counting on, Ed," Debbie Sue groused.

Buddy glanced at his watch. "Let's head out. We don't want to be late."

chapter twenty-five

The mood in the SUV became somber as they neared the funeral home. Everyone seemed to be lost in his own thoughts. "I still can't believe all of this," Debbie Sue said to Buddy in a hushed voice. "I wish you and Vic could've heard her sing."

"If only songs had been all that came out of her mouth," Edwina said from the backseat.

"Ed, that's a terrible thing to say," Debbie Sue said.

"Let's don't be hypocrites, Debbie Sue. As far as I could see, she was a first-class bitch to everybody who knew her, even her husband. You wanted to knock the fillings out of her teeth yourself. You said so."

"It sounds like there could be more than one person who might like to see her dead," Buddy said.

"I wouldn't go as far as to say anyone wanted her dead,"

Debbie Sue said, "but Ed's right. We never saw her treat anyone very nice."

"She pissed off more people than Bernie Madoff," Edwina quipped.

"Buddy, what if someone kills a person accidentally?" Debbie Sue asked. "What's the penalty for that?"

"That's manslaughter if the DA wants to go in that direction. Depends on a hundred things. Killing someone accidentally or in self-defense isn't a capital crime. It doesn't call for the penalty that premeditated murder does, but there's still been a death and somebody has to pay."

Everyone became quiet again and soon Buddy turned into the funeral home parking lot and parked in front. They exited the SUV and walked through the massive oak entrance. Buddy lifted off his hat.

A gentleman dressed impeccably in a dark suit with a dark tie and a red carnation on his lapel appeared from out of nowhere. "May I be of assistance?"

"We're here for the Denman service."

"Yes, sir, please follow me."

Debbie Sue deliberately looked for his footprints in the deep pile carpet because he appeared to be gliding instead of walking. After passing several open entrances to rooms of various sizes, he stopped and gestured toward a small parlor with the sweep of his left arm.

Bob was sitting there with two men and a woman. It took a few seconds for Debbie Sue to realize his companions were Mike, Eddie and Valetta Rose. They'd shown up.

Debbie Sue's heartbeat quickened. She immediately glanced at Mike's hand. The bandage was still there. Now it was a large Band-Aid that blended so well with the color of his skin, she could see how it could be missed. She was still positive that she hadn't seen it before Roxie was killed. She wondered if Detective Finley had seen it and questioned Mike about it.

Bob looked across his shoulder, rose immediately and came to them. "Thanks for coming," he said, touching cheeks with both Debbie Sue and Edwina.

Buddy and Vic voiced their condolences then. Bob introduced them to the three members of Darla's entourage. Debbie Sue watched closely for any undue nervousness or uneasy reaction when Bob mentioned that Buddy was a sergeant in the Texas Rangers. That information usually got people's attention. Debbie Sue had seen people drop things and stammer in Buddy's presence. She thought she saw a flicker of something in Mike's face, but in the darkened room it was hard to read anything.

Everyone took a seat and within minutes music began to filter through the speaker system. It was Roxie's rendition of "Amazing Grace." A shiver crept up Debbie Sue's spine. The deceased Roxie's beautiful, pure-as-crystal voice singing the haunting words of the old hymn soon had moisture threatening Debbie Sue's eyes.

The gentleman who had met them stepped to a small podium and read a poem and a scripture from the Bible, and just as quickly as it started, it was over. No one had shed a tear.

The small group met again in the lobby for good-byes and Debbie Sue invited them for dinner in their suite at the Gaylord, trying to sound cordial and not as desperate as she felt.

Bob accepted graciously, but Eddie, Mike and Valetta Rose exchanged glances. Finally Valetta Rose said, "Sure, we'll come. I've always wanted to see a suite at the Gaylord."

"You won't be disappointed," Debbie Sue said much too gaily.

"Yeah," Edwina said, "it's not often you get to stay in a mansion in the sky."

"Except when you die," Eddie mumbled. "That hotel might be my only chance."

They delivered Bob to his address, a loft downtown he said Roxie had insisted on buying. "Roxie believed that anyone who's anyone lives downtown," he said dully, as if he was thinking of something else altogether. Debbie Sue still didn't have a read on his true feelings, but she suspected his mind and heart were back in Texas.

"Are you having food served from the hotel restaurant?" he asked before leaving the SUV.

"We haven't made a plan about that yet," Debbie Sue answered.

"The best barbeque pork ribs you'll ever eat are right here in Nashville at Maggie Mae's," he said. "You might hear the best is somewhere in Memphis, but take my word for it, Maggie Mae's is the best."

"Sounds good to me," Edwina said. "I've never had Southern-style barbecue."

"If you decide on that, don't forget to get the apple pecan cobbler for dessert," Bob added. "That's their signature dish."

"Oh, yum," Edwina said. "Bring on the pecans. I swear, I just put on ten pounds."

"That sounds like a winner, Bob," Debbie Sue told him. "We'd better go. We'll see you this evening."

Buddy keyed in the Gaylord address and the GPS voice gave him the directions.

"Too bad they don't have one of those gadgets for life," Edwina said. "You know, marry him, don't marry him. Run like hell, this one is a wacko, that one already has a wife in El Paso."

"I think there is one, Ed," Buddy said. "It's called common sense."

"Well, I'll be damned," Edwina replied. "I've never had that in my whole life. Guess that's why I need a GPS for living."

They pulled into the hotel's port cochere and an unmistakable voice could be heard through the closed windows. "Debbie Suuue! Honey! Buddeee!"

Debbie Sue turned toward the voice and saw her mom, an older, shorter, slightly heavier version of herself. She was waving her purse in the air and fast-walking toward her, leaving Doc Miller behind. Debbie Sue made an exit from the SUV and matched her pace and the two met in the middle in a warm embrace topped off with kisses.

"Mom, I've missed you so much."

"I know, but isn't it wonderful seeing you in Nashville?" She looked around. "Oh, my gosh. Where's Doc?"

Debbie Sue had to grin. Her mother had worked years for Salt Lick's only veterinarian at the time and after all these years and a marriage to boot, she still called him Doc, just as she had when she drew a paycheck from him.

Dr. Miller joined the group. The atmosphere became festive and Debbie Sue momentarily forgot why they were here. "Mom, you won't believe the suite they've given us. Our house in Salt Lick could fit in it twice."

"But that wouldn't make it a home would it?"

"No ma'am," Debbie Sue said with pure affection. "It sure wouldn't."

After another hug, she continued, "We're ordering dinner

tonight from a place called Maggie Mae's. Have you heard of it?"

"Oh, heavens, no one in Nashville can say they haven't. Have you called in the order yet? Be sure to get the apple pecan cobbler."

"That's twice we've been told that," Edwina said. "Vic, when you call the order in, get plenty of that."

"Let's go upstairs," Debbie Sue said. "We've got lots to catch up on."

They made their way through the lobby to the elevator and up to their suite. While Buddy, Vic and Doc enjoyed ice-cold beers from the kitchen refrigerator, the women toured the suite, oohing and aahing and gasping.

"So this is where rich people stay when they need a hotel room," Virginia said with a laugh.

"It's a far cry from the way my life has always been," Edwina said. "I'm trained to go the low-on-funds route. You know, everybody pile into one room in the cheapest place you could find, which is usually the most flea-bitten dive in town."

Debbie Sue's mom laughed warmly. "I'm glad to see you haven't changed, Edwina."

Buddy came into the room. "Y'all are having too much fun in here. We've called the order in for ribs. It won't be ready for another thirty minutes, but we're going to pick it up now."

"Why now?" Debbie Sue asked.

"I'm guessing Doc wants to show them the Tennessee Titans stadium," Virginia said.

Phooey! Debbie Sue had been counting on having the time to do a little snooping while they toured the Titans stadium. If they did it now, it would throw everything off and now, even more than before, she needed to focus on Mike. "You're not taking the tour now, are you?"

"Naw, we're just going to drive past it. We'll be back in less than an hour."

"How much beer's in that fridge?" Edwina asked as soon as the men had left. She marched to it, opened the door and found three bottles. They had no sooner sat down to relax in the living room before the doorbell buzzed.

"Lord, I might never get accustomed to having a doorbell in a hotel room," Debbie Sue said. "I don't even have a doorbell at home."

She left her comfortable spot on the sofa. Looking through the peephole, she saw Bob Denman in the hallway. She opened the door and he stepped into the foyer. "I know I'm early," he said, "but I called and no one answered."

"Oh, hell, I turned off my phone during the funeral and forgot to turn in back on."

"I was going to call everyone and tell them I'd pick them up and we'd all come here together, but Mike's landlady told me he'd rushed in, packed most of his stuff and left."

Alarm shot through Debbie Sue. She hadn't thought of Mike running.

"What do you mean left?"

"Left. Scrammed. He's gone."

"Did he tell her where he was headed?"

"To pick up Valetta Rose at her job and from there, I have no idea."

"*Crap!* Dammit, Bob, this whole ball of twine is about to come unwound. Where does Valetta Rose work?"

"McAllister's Funeral Home. When she got back to Nashville, they hired her back to do makeup on the deceased."

"McAllister's? Isn't that the name of the place we just came from?"

"The very one."

"Well at least I know how to get there. Bob, follow me."

"Wait a minute. I came here so that Vic and Buddy could go stop them."

"Well, Vic and Buddy aren't here, Bob, so it looks like all there is between Darla and prison time, or worse, is Ed and me. Come on."

Walking back into the living room with Bob in tow, Debbie Sue said, "Mom, I can't go into all the details, but Ed and I have got to go."

"What?" Edwina asked. "Where are we going, I haven't finished my beer."

"What's going on, sweetheart?" Virginia asked.

"Mom, this is Bob Denman. Bob, my mom, Virginia. Bob can fill you in on the details, Mom. I don't have time. But you've got to trust me. Now both of you, when Buddy and Vic get back, tell them Ed and I are downstairs in the gift shop."

"But honey, I'm not going to lie—"

"I haven't told you where we're going. For all you know the gift shop is our destination. Bob, loan me your car keys."

"Of course." He pulled his keys out of his pants pocket. "And here's the valet ticket, but—"

"Come on, Ed," Debbie Sue ordered, grabbing her purse.

"Super. Let me get my purse, too. I spotted a purse in that shop just loaded with turquoise stones and beads. It practically called my name when I went past it!"

Before anyone had time to offer up more questions, Debbie Sue grabbed Edwina by the arm, ushered her out of the room and fast-walked her up the hallway toward the elevator. All the while the crazy woman continued to prattle on about the purse in the gift shop.

The elevator door opened and Debbie Sue pushed her inside. "Ed, forchristsake, we are not going to the gift shop."

"Then where are we going?"

"You have to trust me," Debbie Sue said, watching the floor numbers descend.

"Oh, no," Edwina said moving back to a corner. "Every time you start out with that *trust me* shit I end up praying like there's no tomorrow."

"We're going back to the funeral home."

"Give me one good reason for that?"

"I'll give you two. Mike and Valetta Rose are about to leave for God knows where. They're on the run and we're gonna stop them."

"Debbie Sue, we cannot do that. We cannot stop two people who are dead set on leaving. We can't—"

Debbie Sue grabbed Edwina by each shoulder and turned her to face her. "Repeat after me, Edwina Perkins-Martin. There is nothing the Domestic Equalizers cannot do, have not done before and would not do again given the chance."

Edwina looked at Debbie Sue's face, her brown eyes wide and unblinking. "We're going to die in Nashville and go back to Texas in a flower vase."

"Good enough," Debbie Sue declared.

chapter twenty-six

Debbie Sue broke at least a dozen laws racing back to McAllister's Funeral Home—speeding, cutting corners, going the wrong way on a one-way street and failing to make a complete stop at a red light, just to name a few. Once she even flew through a bay at a corner gas station to avoid a red light.

Bracing a hand against the dashboard to steady herself, Edwina asked, "Do you know if we're going in the right direction?"

"Look around us, Ed. Don't you remember seeing any of this?"

"We're going too fast for me to look around. Do you even know what we're gonna do when we get there? I doubt our saying, 'We'd really rather you not leave' is going to persuade them."

"Dammit, Ed, could you try to be more positive? Right now I'm going on adrenaline and working from pure gut instinct. A little reinforcement would go a long way."

"Trust me, Dippity-do, you *do not* want to hear what I'm positive of at this moment."

"There it is!" Debbie Sue suddenly shouted. "Right up there on the left. Oh, my God, I've got my own built-in GPS." She careened into the parking lot. "Great, there's only one car in front."

"Go to the back," Edwina said.

Debbie Sue wheeled around the corner of the building and saw another parked car. "With any luck, these two cars belong to Mike and Valetta Rose."

She rounded the building toward the front and screeched to a stop in the portico. "I'll stay here. You go around back," she told Edwina. "That way they can't get past us." She grabbed her cell phone from her purse.

"I've got a better idea," Edwina said, digging out her own phone. "Let's stay together and with any luck *they'll* get past *us*."

Debbie Sue gripped Edwina's forearm. "Dammit, Ed, don't say that. Just keep repeating, 'We're the Domestic Equalizers. We are professionals and we're on a mission to save Darla.' Got it?"

"I feel more like Lucy and Ethel," Edwina grumbled. "And I'm not sure we can even save ourselves."

"You're my partner, Ed. I have to know I can depend on you. Otherwise, we go back to the Gaylord and keep our fingers crossed for Darla and hope it all turns out okay."

"If it doesn't, we can always send her a Christmas fruitcake with a file inside."

"C'mon, Ed. We've been in worse situations," Debbie Sue said.

Chastened, Edwina bit her lip. "You're right, Debbie Sue. I'm sorry. Having Vic around makes me act all girly. I tend to want to step back and let him take care of everything. You know, kill the big bug, check under the bed for the bogeyman."

"That's okay, Ed. I do the same thing. But Vic and Buddy aren't here. You know what that means, don't you?"

"Lemme guess. We have to strap on our Wonder Woman bracelets and go fight the bogeyman?"

"You got it." Debbie Sue opened the driver's door. "You and I are the only ones available to fight the bogeyman."

"I was afraid you were gonna say that. Okay, I'm ready. Let me at that fucker." Edwina scooted out of the SUV and started for the rear of the building, her platform shoe soles clacking against the pavement.

Debbie Sue called after her, "Keep your phone handy, in case I need to contact you."

"Likewise," Ed yelled back and disappeared around the corner of the building.

Debbie Sue approached the front door and turned the knob, found it unlocked. She stepped back and studied the building, checking for other entrances or exits, but saw none. This door appeared to be the only way in on this side of the building.

As she approached the door again, before she even put her hand on the knob, it opened with a *whoosh* and there stood Valetta Rose. Both Debbie Sue and the younger woman froze, their eyes locked on each other. Then the door slammed and Debbie Sue heard the *snicks* and *clacks* of door locks.

Shit, shit, shit, shit, shit. "Hey! Open up!" Teeth gritted, Debbie Sue pounded the door with her fist, but to no avail.

How could she have just stood there? She and Valetta Rose both had been caught off guard, but the other woman had reacted, while she, Debbie Sue, super-detective, had just stood like a dunce.

She had to warn Edwina. She grabbed the cell phone from her pocket and punched in the single digit to call Edwina. *Pick up, pick up, pick up,* she prayed. The phone rang and rang. When Edwina didn't pick up, Debbie Sue broke into a dead run around the corner of the building.

Edwina's voice came through the phone. "This is Edwina Perkins-Martin. Leave a message and keep it clean."

A sense of relief washed over Debbie Sue, but it was quickly replaced by dread when she saw no Edwina at the back of the building, near the back door or otherwise. The only thing present was her cell phone lying on the ground, speaker function engaged.

Debbie Sue picked up the phone and a fear she had rarely felt burned through her system. Edwina had not disappeared on her own accord. That much was certain. Debbie Sue's thoughts tumbled like numbers in a Bingo cage. Should she call Buddy? God help her, should she call Vic? The reality was that at this moment, it was her, and only her, who could help her best friend.

And with that fact came a white hot anger. How dare some cute little number who knew tricks with makeup threaten Edwina? Yessir, Debbie Sue was going in. Going after her friend, and there had better not be a single dyed hair on her head lost or even out of place. Debbie Sue Overstreet, Domestic Equalizer, was a force to be reckoned with and she reckoned now was as good a time as any to prove it.

She drew a deep breath and eased the door open. Seeing

nothing but a dim hallway, the same one she had walked up just an hour before with her husband and friends, she stole through the doorway and pressed her back to the wall, allowing her eyes to adjust to the darkness. The place was quiet as a tomb. *Oooh, bad turn of phrase, Debbie Sue.*

The clovelike fragrance of carnations gave her the heebie-jeebies. She was trembling inside. She reminded herself that it wasn't the departed souls she needed to fear, but the very much alive living and breathing human beings who could cause her bodily harm.

She pried her body from the wall and began moving furtively from door to door, peeking cautiously inside each doorway before proceeding. She was almost all the way through the building and nearing the front door when she heard a noise. It had come from behind a door marked: NOT AN EXIT—EMPLOYEES ONLY BEYOND THIS POINT.

She gulped. Since she hadn't found a room she could define as the corpse preparation area, there was a good chance it was located behind this door. She had no idea what she might encounter in there—blood and other bodily fluids, embalming fluid, a gathering of corpses, coffins.

And possibly Edwina.

She reached for the doorknob as if it were a hot iron, couldn't believe it was unlocked. She pushed it open, cringed as the hinges creaked. She paused and waited for an alarm to go off announcing an intruder, but she heard no sound save two people, male and female, distinctly arguing.

She had no weapon, couldn't spot an object to use as one. If they were planning to run, how could she stop them? With a threat? A really nasty, harsh look? And at that moment, she faced that her pride wasn't worth Edwina's safety. She would utilize any means she could to save her best friend. Dammit, she was calling Buddy.

She dug her phone from her jacket pocket and cursed silently at the message: No Signal. She had to retreat, return possibly all the way outside until she got reception on her phone.

Reaching behind herself, she found the doorknob and opened the door slowly, inching back into the hallway from where she had just come. She checked her phone again for a signal. A slight noise made her look up, but all she saw was a white cloth approaching her face and then . . .

Blackness.

Debbie Sue awoke with a splitting headache. She attempted to move, but quickly realized she was flat on her back on a table with her arms strapped down and her legs tied together at the ankles. Good God, she had been unconscious, but she had no idea how long. "What the fuck?" she mumbled.

"Hey, kiddo, got a headache?"

Debbie Sue turned her head to her left, toward the voice she recognized. Lying within a foot of her was Edwina, similarly restrained, but alive and well and not a hair out of place. "Ed!"

"I feel like somebody used my head for a basketball," Edwina said.

Debbie Sue began to cry, relieved to find her best friend alive and well and for the mess they were now in and for the damned headache that felt like a bass drum pounding inside her skull.

"Don't cry," Edwina said. "It'll only make the headache worse."

Debbie Sue sniffled. "Are you all right, Ed?"

"I don't know. For sure, I know now how a turkey feels on Thanksgiving."

"How long have I been out?"

"I dunno. Maybe fifteen minutes."

"That's all? Where—"

"Debbie Sue, are you all right?" A female voice asked.

She turned her head to see Valetta Rose wringing her hands, her youthful face a picture of concern.

"Valetta Rose," Debbie Sue cried. "Are you the one who did this? Why? Let us go and—"

"And you'll have the cops here so fast it'll make your head spin faster than it already is," Mike said, walking up behind Valetta Rose.

"Mike! Mike, let us go," Edwina said. "We didn't come here to hurt you."

"Bullshit. There's no other reason for you to be here."

"No, no," Debbie Sue said. "We only came to talk, to find out what happened to Roxie."

A long silence. Debbie Sue waited for his explanation, but none came.

She pressed forward. "We know it was an accident, Mike."

"Of course it was an accident," Mike spat. "Who in their right mind premeditates murder with a fingernail file?"

Debbie Sue could see Valetta Rose pacing. "Valetta Rose, you're just a kid. You haven't done anything. Stay here. Let Mike run."

"Hon," Edwina chimed in, "take my old war horse's advice and don't tie yourself to a man in trouble. He'll only take you down with him."

The two hostage-takers exchanged looks Debbie Sue couldn't read, but before she could say more, the white cloth was coming toward her again.

Then there was blackness.

chapter twenty-seven

Debbie Sue came around again. She had been drugged for the second time with what she could only guess was ether. Her head was splitting down the middle, her arms and legs were still bound and this time she had a gag in her mouth. Though she was conscious, she was lying in pitch darkness. She turned her head and saw nothing. No Edwina, no Mike and no Valetta Rose.

Why was it so dark? Had she been out long enough for the entire day to have passed? Something smooth and cool surrounded her. Then it dawned on her where she was. She was in a coffin! She screamed, but no sound came out.

Some time later, Debbie Sue had thrashed herself into exhaustion, trying to make enough noise to get someone's attention. No one had come to her rescue and worse yet, she heard nothing but her own sounds. Where was Edwina?

Despite her confinement, Debbie Sue was breathing easily. If she were buried, that wouldn't be possible, would it? Maybe her mind was playing tricks on her to keep herself from losing it altogether.

As with every bad situation in which she found herself, she tried to think of something positive to offset the bad. All she could think of was that it was a plus in her favor that she wasn't claustrophobic.

Suddenly "The Eyes of Texas" blasted from her pocket. She still had her cell phone with her. She couldn't reach it, but when the music stopped, the sweetest sound she had ever heard warmed her heart. "Debbie Sue, where the hell are you? Call me back." It was Buddy. Her dear sweet Buddy.

Tears leaked from the corners of her eyes and pooled in her ears. Call me back. Such a simple request. If only she could comply.

Eventually she slept again. She was now dreaming, looking up into the face of her beloved husband. He was stroking her hair away from her face, kissing her lips. Edwina was there too. Her makeup was smudged and her beehive hair was hanging lopsided, but she was smiling. All at once Debbie Sue realized she was returning Edwina's smile. Her gag was gone. Her arms and legs were no longer restrained. "Am I dreaming?"

She reached up for Buddy.

"You're awake all right," Buddy said. "Jesus, Flash, let me get you out of there. I can't stand seeing you in a damned coffin." He scooped her up, lifted her and held her against his chest. She could feel his beating heart. *Oh, thank you, God.*

Debbie Sue's senses were coming alive. Her head was slowly clearing and with the awakening came a dread. She turned her gaze from her husband to her friend. "Ed? You okay?"

"Shit," Edwina said. "I'll never be able to sleep on satin sheets again."

Just then, she spotted Mike and Valetta Rose sitting in separate chairs, ankles cinched together with plastic flex-cuffs and hands behind their backs. Vic stood over them, his muscular legs slightly apart, in line with his wide shoulders, his brawny arms crossed over his chest.

"You two!" Debbie Sue screeched, pointing a finger. "Buddy, arrest them! No, wait, shoot them! Just shoot them!" She tried to scramble from Buddy's arms. He lost his grip on her and she fell back into the coffin. A stab of pain shot from temple to temple. She cradled her head with her hands. "Aarrgh, my head is killing me."

Buddy reached for her again and Debbie Sue allowed him to lift her out and sit her carefully down on a love seat positioned against the wall. "Where are we?" she asked, looking around the room that was decorated in heavy blue velvet draperies. "Ed, don't you have a headache?"

"No, it must be the perm solutions. I've been smelling them for a lot more years than you have. Guess I've worked up an immunity."

"This is the sales room," Valetta Rose said through sniffles. "Grieving family members come in here to pick out the coffins for the deceased. I wasn't going to let anything happen to you. I was going to call Mr. McAllister when we got out of town and—"

"Don't say anything else," Mike barked.

"What does it matter now, Mike? How much more trouble could we be in?"

"Best take your girlfriend's advice, Mike," Buddy said. "I'm hauling you two back to Texas. You're looking at a murder charge. Add assault and kidnapping and with any Texas jury, that'll get you the death penalty."

"Go ahead and let the law deal with the woman, Buddy." Vic's baritone voice echoed off the walls. "I'll take this dude outside and give him my own brand of justice."

"Yeah," Edwina said, squaring her shoulders.

Mike's eyes grew wide. "Whoa! Ho—hold on, man."

"Why did you do it, Mike?" Debbie Sue said. "Why did you kill Roxie? And what's with the bandage on your hand? Did she bite you or something?"

"Yeah," Edwina said again. "She was a pain in the ass, but to kill her?"

Mike struggled in his chair, pulled at his restraints. "Dammit, I didn't kill anybody. Here, look at my hand, see for yourself. She didn't bite me. See for yourself."

Buddy looked from the two women on the small couch to Vic and shrugged.

Vic approached Mike. He went behind him and with a single motion freed him. "You just try something, sucker. I wish you would."

"Hold your hand out," Buddy ordered.

Mike raised his arm and held his hand in front of him. "See?"

Debbie Sue rose unsteadily from her seat and went to where he sat. She grabbed the corner of the bandage and yanked it off in one clean movement. Mike yelped.

Debbie Sue peered down. Buddy moved in for a look and Edwina pressed her face between their shoulders. On Mike's hand, in bold black letters two inches wide, with a small heart dotting the letter *i*, was the name Roxie. "What the hell is that?"

"That's pretty gutsy," Edwina said, "getting a married

woman's name tattooed on your hand, right under her husband's nose. I'm surprised *you* weren't the one killed."

"You're not just a murderer, you're an asshole!" Debbie Sue punched Mike's shoulder with her fist. "Bob Denman was good to you. And to Roxie, too, for that matter."

"I didn't want to do this," Mike said. "It was her idea." He shook his head, a mournful frown on his face. "You don't know how she was, what it was like to be around her all the time. A person couldn't tell her no."

"That won't wash, friend," Vic said. "Sitting for a tattoo takes time and it can hurt like hell, especially on the back of the hand. You *could* have said no."

"You don't understand," Mike said, shaking his head. "It's temporary ink. You know that tattoo dude, Matt? We spent the afternoon at his place. You know, the tatt den out on the Interstate. He had some bodacious weed and we got stoned. When my head cleared I had this." He held up his hand for all to see. "I slapped a bandage on it so that Bob wouldn't see it at the show."

"You stabbed a woman to death because you got tatted up with her name?" Vic asked. "Sheesh. And I've been called barbaric."

Mike looked up at Vic and leaned away from him.

Valetta Rose sniffled. "Mike—"

"Shut up, Rosie! I told you'd I'd take care of this!"

"No," she yelled back. "This has gone on long enough." Sobbing now, she turned to Debbie Sue and Edwina. "I did it. I killed Roxie. But it was an accident."

Her shoulders began to shake and wails came from her mouth. A waterfall of tears spilled down her cheeks. "She promised me so much and then she started getting nervous. She didn't want anyone to find out she'd had an affair with a woman. That kind of news might not hurt her in the pop music culture, but it would never work in country."

"No, no. She's lying," Mike shouted.

"You were sleeping with Roxie *and* Mike?" Debbie Sue asked.

"Well, Jesus Christ," Edwina said, propping a fist on her hip. "And I thought I'd been around the block."

"I'm not lying," Valetta Rose said. "My blood's at the scene if it can be found with all of Roxie's. I—I touched her and she stabbed my hand with the nail file." She looked up at Buddy. "If you'll cut these bands, I'll show you."

Vic moved behind her and cut the plastic that bound her. She spat on the top of her hand and began rubbing off a heavy skin concealer that covered a reddened puncture wound.

"We had a fight after she stabbed me," Valetta Rose said between sobs. "I fell on top of her and somehow the file must have gotten stuck into her neck. When I saw what had happened, I panicked and ran."

Debbie Sue shook her head in disbelief. "Holy shit. This is even more bizarre than I imagined." She stared at Mike. "You're innocent, man. Why go down with her? You could face accessory to murder charges for aiding and abetting a murderer. Tell him, Buddy."

Now Mike's eyes showed a glimmer of wetness. "I'm only guilty of one thing," he said softly. "And that's of being a big brother protecting my little sister."

Edwina's face twisted into a frown and a scrunched-up nose. "What?"

Debbie Sue stepped back a couple of steps and dropped to the couch. "I don't remember hearing anything about y'all being brother and sister."

"We didn't tell anybody," Mike said. "Not even Bob. Family members traveling together on the road are generally frowned on."

"Mike thought it was a great opportunity for me," Valetta Rose said, taking her brother's hand in hers. "He didn't want to ruin any chance I might have to further my career as a makeup artist to the stars."

"Rosie and I even slept in the same bedroom one night to throw them off," Mike said, then laughed bitterly.

Valetta Rose looked at him with tenderness. "As I remember it, Mike, you did that to keep me from sleeping with Roxie again."

Mike hung his head. "I was only trying to protect you from that viper."

"I did go into her room," Valetta Rose said to her captors, "but it was to talk to her so she wouldn't be so mad at everyone. She threatened to ruin Mike and Eddie in Nashville in the music community."

"Could she do that?" Edwina asked.

"What's going to happen?" Valetta Rose asked Buddy. "Mike isn't guilty of anything. Couldn't you just let him go and take me back to Midland?"

"No. Hell, no," Mike said. "I'm not letting you go alone. Rosie. We're family. We're in this together." Bringing both of his arms up, he pressed his wrists together and turned to Buddy. "I'll need you to replace those cuffs."

Bob fell back into the plush cushion of the couch located in the town house living room, shaking his head in disbelief. "You mean to tell me that Valetta Rose and Mike weren't sleeping together after all?"

"Well, they were," Debbie Sue said leaning toward him, "but not in the biblical sense."

"The biblical sense?" Bob echoed.

"You know," Edwina piped in, "screwing. They weren't screwing."

"I know what it means. I guess I'm in shock. I didn't see that coming. She talked about her brother in Nashville . . ." he paused to run his fingers through his hair. "And it was Mike. I heard Roxie having sex with someone when I got home from your house the other night. I assumed it was Mike, I could see Eddie on the couch asleep," Bob said, still shaking his head.

"Bless your heart," Debbie Sue cried, "if I hadn't just heard Valetta Rose confess to the murder, I'd think you did it for sure."

"It might have insulted my manhood, but I was past caring what Roxie did," Bob said softly. "I thought I was past being surprised by her too, but I was wrong."

"You're surprised?" Edwina stammered. "The last person I'd think was a lesbian was Roxie."

"She wasn't lesbian, Ed, she was bi," Debbie Sue explained.

"Well I'm not buying that," Edwina said. "If you have sex with a woman, and you're a woman, you're a lesbian."

Debbie Sue sighed. "In this case you're neither one. You're dead."

"True enough," Edwina agreed.

"Where—where is everyone now?" Debbie Sue's mother asked tentatively.

"Buddy and Vic took Mike and Valetta Rose to the police station. He said they'd get things cleared to take them back to Texas."

"Do you think there'll be a problem doing that?" Bob asked.

"When you're a Texas Ranger you can do a lot of things," Debbie Sue answered with a measure of pride. "Valetta Rose being a minor should work in her—"

"A what?" Bob shrieked.

Debbie Sue looked around the room at the other faces. "She's a minor. She's only seventeen."

"Oh, my God!" Bob said. "That poor kid, I feel so responsible."

"None of it was your fault, Bob. Roxie's death was an accident. You have nothing to feel guilty about."

"Oh, my God," Bob said again, shaking his head and dropping his face into his palms.

"Don't be so hard on yourself, Bob," Debbie Sue said.

"I could tell she was young and she had this devoted, hero worship of Roxie going on, but I thought that's all it was. Just hero worship. I should have asked more questions, demanded some accountability. I didn't because I had stopped caring. And now look at this mess."

The room fell silent. Bob rose to his full height. "I'll see to it that she gets the best defense attorney I can find. That kid's never had a break. I'll be damned if this turns out to be a continuation of what she's had to endure in her past short lifetime."

Debbie Sue stood and put a hand on his shoulder. Bob looked at her. "Has anyone thought to get the news to Darla?"

Debbie Sue exchanged glances with Edwina. "We thought you'd like to be the one to tell her."

Bob smiled for the first time. "You were right. If y'all will excuse me, I'll try to get a call through to her now." He left the room.

Debbie Sue's mother said, "Good heavens, Debbie Sue. Do

you mean to tell me this is the kind of thing you two girls deal with in your detective agency?"

"Mom," Debbie Sue said, looping her arm around her mother's shoulder, "you don't want to know the things we've dealt with. Right, Ed?"

Edwina didn't answer. She was frowning and chewing on her bottom lip, obviously in deep thought.

"Ed? Did you hear what I said?"

"I heard. I'm just trying to figure out how we're getting on that airplane with all this food, especially this apple pecan cobbler."

"At least you've still got your priorities in order, Ed."

Edwina grinned. "Abso-fucking-lutely."

epilogue

Debbie Sue and Buddy and Edwina and Vic returned to Texas with Mike and Valetta Rose in custody. Detective Finley took control of the siblings at the airport and thanked everyone for his contribution in finding Roxie's killer.

By now all of them had learned that Valetta Rose had led a tough life that contributed to her early maturity.

Charges against Darla were dropped and she and Bob returned to Nashville, where they remarried. Later she resumed her comeback tour accompanied only by Bob. She played the best theater venues throughout the country to sold-out audiences and then she and Bob retired to their beloved Nashville.

No jury trial took place. Following the advice of the attorney that Bob had retained for her, Valetta Rose claimed self-defense and a judge believed her. He released her and declared the incident "an unfortunate accident."

Mike and Valetta Rose quickly left Midland, headed for Mexico, where Mike got a job entertaining rich Americans on vacation in Cabo San Lucas. He met and married a wealthy widow who had traveled to the resort area to forget the passing of the "great love of her life" and to spend some of the fifty million dollars he had left her.

With his new wife's money, Mike helped Valetta Rose open an exclusive spa near the finest American hotels in Cabo. She developed her own line of cosmetics, selling it to millions of women on Telemundo Las Compras en Casa, Mexico's answer to QVC, and earning a small fortune of her own.

Everyone lived happily ever after.

FROM

DIXIE CASH

AND

WILLIAM MORROW
An Imprint of *HarperCollins*Publishers

COUNTRY WESTERN MUSIC

A lot has been written, including several books, about the evolution of country western music as a cultural element of American life. These days, it and its artists are one of the more profitable parts of the music industry. This is obviously why many musicians from other genres have adopted "country" as their sound.

From what I can learn from reading about this important patch of the American quilt, basically, country western music began as folk music, somewhere in the Cumberland Mountains. As dirt-poor immigrants, the Scottish pioneers who settled that region brought their old-world folk songs and ballads from their native Scottish highlands. They also brought their musical instrument, the fiddle, a stringed instrument modified from the more elaborate English violin. Eventually, "new" folk songs and ballads emerged, telling stories of hard work, sorrow and real-world tragedies.

Just as music has been a form of expression within every society in human history, so has dancing. From its beginning, country music was "dancing music." The Scots and the Irish performed their reels and jigs to the accompaniment of the music from their fiddles and against a backdrop of the struggle to just survive. The dances we know as square dances are derived from the "cotillion," the "quadrille" and other pattern dances that kept bodily contact to a minimum. Without a doubt, the only forms of entertainment that *all* of the original rural Americans (men, women and children) could enjoy were music and dancing.

Things began to change on the music front with the Civil War, the incursion of the railroads into remote areas where they hadn't been before and traveling minstrel shows. The folk musicians of Scots-Irish origin met the outside world and some new musical instruments, namely the banjo. Of African origin, it was played by African slaves in the minstrel shows. Later came exposure to the Spanish guitar, the autoharp and the dulcimer. Somehow, it all became amalgamated into a "sound," and the sound and style that emerged was what we now call "bluegrass."

Country music became viral with the invention of the phonograph and the birth of radio. Radio stations in Georgia and Texas broadcast "folk music" and "old-time music" and launched the first "barn dance" show. "Old-time music" became "hillbilly music" as an effort on the part of radio stations to separate "race music," produced only by black people, from "white music," produced only by white people.

As the country expanded to the west, widely diverse people found commonality in music and dancing, including cowboys. Cowboys, many of them teenagers, were not necessarily schooled in formal manners or prone to appreciate the finesse of ballrooms. After spending long hours and days in the saddle, exposed to the worst nature could hand them, their goals were usually relaxation, liquor and lust, but that didn't mean they left behind the teachings of their respective immigrant cultures. With most of them being of Scottish or Irish heritage, they had seen a jig or two. Even today, cowboy line dancing is derived from the old reels.

We hope you think the titles to the Dixie Cash books are clever. You might have thought they have a country music connection. If so, you thought right. Here are, in Dixie's opinion, some of the best of the worst country western songs ever written. These are real, folks.

1. Saddle Up the Stove, Ma, I'm Riding the Range Tonight
2. If I Had Shot You When I Wanted To, I'd Be Out of Prison by Now
3. Four on the Floor and a Fifth Under the Seat
4. You're the Reason Our Kids Are So Ugly
5. I Got in at Two with a Ten, and Woke Up at Ten with a Two
6. I Went Back to My Fourth Wife for the Third Time and Gave Her a Second Chance To Make a First-Class Fool out of Me
7. I Gave Her My Heart and a Diamond, and She Clubbed Me with a Spade
8. How Can I Kiss the Lips Good Night That Have Chewed on My Ass All Day?
9. If I Say You Have a Beautiful Body Would You Hold It Against Me?

And our personal all-time favorite (drumroll):

10. Get Off the Table Mabel, the Two Dollars Is for the Beer!

You gotta love it.

Dixie

SOME OF THE BEST HONKY-TONKS IN TEXAS

The term *honky-tonk* was used as early as 1875 in reference to wild saloons in the Old West. No one really knows the origin of the label, but the story is undoubtedly a colorful one.

Anyone who claims to love country music has never really heard it until they've sat in a smoky honky-tonk amid a kaleidoscope of neon lights, and listened to every word of the heartbreaking lyrics. The stories in the tunes are all the same: misery, longing, love, marriage, happiness and ultimately, divorce. In dimly lit rooms housing a bandstand, tables and chairs, with dance floors of varying sizes, this world becomes a haven. It's a church for the beaten down, an escape from a house too quiet for too long or a place to become a hero.

Texas is full of honky-tonks and dance halls. Listed here are some of the best. If you've never visited one, don't hesitate. They're dying out quickly. Don't be timid or fearful. You'll find yourself in the company of what makes America the great nation it is: hardworking, tax-paying individuals just looking for a little, if momentary, slice of heaven in a troubled world. These are only a few of the dozens of honky tonk/dance halls in the vast state of Texas:

1. Anhalt Hall, established 1875, in Anhalt, Texas: The oldest farmers' cooperative society in Texas has met here since 1875. It boasts a 6,000-square-foot hardwood dance floor.

2. Arkey Blue's Silver Dollar Saloon, established in the 1930s, Bandera, Texas: This great old honky-tonk is the center of "the cowboy capital of Texas." Frequent visitors include Willie Nelson, Tommy Alverson and Charlie Robison.

3. Bandera Cabaret Dance Hall, established 1936, Bandera, Texas: Numerous country stars have played

this hall, including Bob Wills, Hank Thompson, Ray Price, Jim Reeves and Willie Nelson.

4. Billy Bob's Texas, World's Largest Honky-Tonk, Fort Worth, Texas: Covering 127,000 square feet, with forty bar stations, there is still plenty of room for dancing in this "all under one roof" party, which has a capacity of 6,000. Billy Bob's has been awarded the Best Country Music Nightclub by the Country Music Association and the Academy of Country Music seven times. But don't look for a mechanical bull here, folks. Only the real thing will do. A rodeo arena gives patrons a chance to view bull riding by either real cowboys or those longing to be.

5. Braun Hall, established 1893, San Antonio, Texas: "If you're dancin', you're not dying" is Braun's motto. It has a unique bandstand—a "cove" in one side of the wall—allowing more floor space for dancers.

6. Broken Spoke, established 1964, Austin, Texas: This is the real deal. The owner's creed is, "We ain't fancy, but we sure are country." The list of performers who have played "The Spoke" reads like a country western stars' *Who's Who*. Bob Wills, Ernest Tubb, Tex Ritter, Willie Nelson, George Strait, Asleep at the Wheel, Gary P. Nunn, just to name a few.

7. Cherry Springs Dance Hall, established 1889, Cherry Springs, Texas: This great dance hall has seen them all: Lefty Frizzell, Ernest Tubb, Buck Owens, Hank Williams, Faron Young, Patsy Cline, George Jones, and in 1956, a young Elvis Presley. Located on the old Pinta Trail, the hall, with old adobe bunk houses in the rear, was originally opened as a stop for cattle drives. Herman Lehmann, adopted son of Comanche chief Quanah Parker, ran the hall for several years.

8. Gruene Hall, established 1878, Gruene, Texas: The dance hall was built by Heinrich Gruene, along with a store and saloon for the local farmers. Every major country music star, old and new, has passed through this honky-tonk, either as a performer or a customer.

9. Luckenbach Dance Hall, established 1849, Luckenbach, Texas: In 1849, Minna Engle opened a post office-store-saloon on Snail Creek. It became a trading post for Indians and a source of supplies and entertainment for the locals. In 1970, a Texan traveling the countryside wanted a cold beer and stopped at the hall, but it was closed. He eventually not only bought his beer but the whole town, and has made Luckenbach Dance Hall a must-stop in Texas.

10. Schroeder Dance Hall, established 1890, Schroeder, Texas: German immigrants began settling the area in the 1840s. This establishment, which became a combination shoe, hardware, grocery store and saloon, still supplied these items up until 1986. Roy Clark played to his first live audience at Schroeder's. The town has a population of only 350 during the week, but on Saturday nights the population triples.

As you might have noticed, many of the dance halls have German names and are located in towns and cities with German names. The influence of the original German settlers in South Central Texas is alive and well.

We think we'll plan our next vacation as an odyssey. We're going to see how many honky-tonks we can visit and how many memories we can capture. Enough to fill several books, no doubt.

Edwina and Debbie Sue

THE NUDIE SUIT

In the very early days of country western music, anyone who was anyone wore apparel fashioned by the famous Nudie "Rodeo Tailors."

Nudie, known publicly by only his last name, was born in Kiev, Russia, in 1902. In the early thirties, Nudie knew he wanted to be a tailor. He was the first to sew rhinestones on clothing, though initially, it was the G-strings of burlesque house strippers. Still, he was on his way to becoming the "Rhinestone Cowboy."

Nudie's unorthodox fashions were only enhanced by his own eccentricity. He was often seen in public wearing one of his jewel-encrusted outfits, complete with an ornate cowboy hat, and wearing two different boots. The mismatched boots were meant to send the message that he was a man rich enough to own not just one pair of beautiful boots, but two. This practice was surely the result of his humble beginnings.

The first stars he approached about clothing design were Roy Rogers and Dale Evans. They agreed to purchase his designs and, as they say, the rest is history.

In 1957, Nudie made the infamous gold lame suit for Elvis Presley at a whopping price tag of $10,000.

To add to his flashy style, Nudie created a fleet of eighteen silver-studded, gun-toting, cattle-stampeding automobiles that were distributed throughout the nation. Nudie left one behind, the 1975 Cadillac El Dorado, for his bride, Bobbie, to ride off into the sunset.

Country music started the fashion, but I can't help but feel that these flashy, beautiful costumes set the precedent for other musical artists' style. Cher, Elton John, Pink, Beyoncé, even Lady Gaga would be right at home in designs of this gifted tailor.

Nudie passed away in 1984, at the age of 81. Anyone lucky enough to own an original Nudie suit is lucky indeed. It's a priceless article of art meant to be treasured and passed down from generation to generation.

A+ material wouldn't be complete without a sprinkling of Edwina Perkins-Martin's sage advice to the lovelorn. The Salt Lick newspaper still routinely publishes her column.

Dear Edwina,

More than anything in the world, I want to become a country western star. I've been told I'm beautiful. I have long blond hair and a body to die for. Unfortunately I don't sing very well. In fact, I'm totally tone deaf. Should I follow my heart or give up on my lifelong dream?

Singing to myself in the shower,
Vicki F.

Dear Keep-it-to-yourself,

Far be it for me to tell anybody to abandon her dreams. Everybody needs something to keep 'em going. Be it a dream, a new pair of really good-looking shoes or the next episode of *True Blood* on HBO. Where would country music be today if Willie Nelson had listened when they said he couldn't carry a tune? Or if George Jones had quit when he was told he was too nasal? I shudder to think.

You keep on, hon, and if you can't dazzle 'em with your vocals, maybe you'll bring out another reaction. PITY! Never underestimate the power of pity.

I'll look for you on iTunes,
Edwina

Dear Ms. Edwina,

I saw your performance at the telethon that aired recently. I hate to say this, but I do feel it my Christian duty to tell you that you were terrible. You weren't in time with the music, you looked like you were scared to death and those red shoes you were wearing looked like they came out of a catalog for women of "questionable means."

Please reconsider singing and appearing in public in the future.

A Christian only meaning to help,
Reverend Pat Miback

Dear Rev. Well-someone-should,

Aren't you just the most precious thing? Please take this helpful hint in the same manner your message was delivered.

Be careful when you step off that soapbox. It would be a cryin' shame to deprive the world of your insight. What you say about my showmanship doesn't bother me, but be careful when you slam my shoes. Not just me, but a certain Jimmy Choo might take offense.

Keep your thoughts in a safe place—to yourself.

Edwina "Red Shoes" Perkins-Martin

Dear Ms. Martin;

I hope you can help me with a problem that has me baffled.

My husband, Ernest, gets up every weekday morning at five A.M. *and drives twenty miles to work. This drive takes him about fifteen minutes. He gets off at four and follows the same route, but it takes him over ninety minutes to make the drive home.*

Should I be concerned?

Baffled Betsy

Dear Yes-you-should-be,

Let me just say one thing right off, I was told there would be no math when I agreed to take on this column. There are three things I don't do: 1) eat sushi 2) math, and the third is between me and God.

Now, back to your problem; seems to me it's time to do some *subtraction* in your household. Things don't *add* up. But remember; if it comes time to *divide* things up, follow my plan: one for you—two for me.

Good luck!
Ed "Don't ask me math" Perkins-Martin

© Rash Photography

DIXIE CASH is Pam Cumbie and her sister, Jeffery McClanahan. They grew up in rural West Texas among "real life fictional characters" and 100 percent real cowboys and cowgirls. Some were relatives and some weren't. Pam has always had a zany sense of humor and Jeffery has always had a dry wit. Surrounded by country western music, when they can stop laughing long enough, they work together creating hilarity on paper. Both live in Texas—Pam in the Fort Worth/Dallas Metroplex and Jeffery in a small town near Fort Worth.

BOOKS BY DIXIE CASH

SINCE YOU'RE LEAVING ANYWAY, TAKE OUT THE TRASH

ISBN 978-0-06-059536-4
(mass market paperback)

"A rollicking debut. Authentic dialogue and a strong Texas flavor. . . . Debbie Sue and her posse are sure to keep readers laughing all the way to the last page." —*Publishers Weekly*

MY HEART MAY BE BROKEN, BUT MY HAIR STILL LOOKS GREAT

A Novel

ISBN 978-0-06-113423-4 (paperback)

"This big-hearted, relaxing read is as much fun as watching a Tim McGraw video while drinking a margarita with your best friend—and without the calories!" —Nancy Thayer, best-selling author of *The Hot Flash Club*

I GAVE YOU MY HEART, BUT YOU SOLD IT ONLINE

A Novel

ISBN 978-0-06-082972-8 (paperback)

"Nobody beats Dixie Cash for humor and inventive situations." —Linda Lael Miller

DON'T MAKE ME CHOOSE BETWEEN YOU AND MY SHOES
A Novel

ISBN 978-0-06-082974-2 (paperback)

"Quick witted, fast paced, and plain old fun, Cash's madcap series just keeps getting better." —*Booklist*

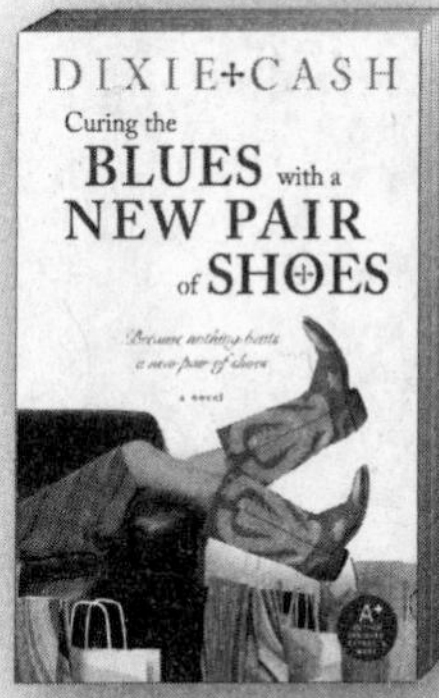

CURING THE BLUES WITH A NEW PAIR OF SHOES
A Novel

ISBN 978-0-06-143438-9 (paperback)

"The Equalizers must don their best big-hair thinking caps to find a way out of this cowpoke mess. Tangy and a little bit dirty—a mystery cooked up in the heart of BBQ country." —*Kirkus Reviews*

OUR RED HOT ROMANCE IS LEAVING ME BLUE
A Novel

ISBN 978-0-06-143439-6 (paperback)

"Belly-grabbing West Texas humor dished up with delightful relish . . . West Texas witty—smart and funny. Will keep you up late laughing!" —Joan Johnston

I CAN'T MAKE YOU LOVE ME, BUT I CAN MAKE YOU LEAVE
A Novel

ISBN 978-0-06-191014-2 (paperback)

"Cash's good ol' gals always get their man, and deliver big laughs in the process." —*Booklist*

Visit www.DixieCashAuthor.com for excerpts and fun author features!